Cross Your Fingers

K L Finalley

Published by Copper Penny Press

Copyright © 2015 K L Finalley

ISBN: 0692422684

ISBN-13: 978-0692422687

DEDICATION

To my wife, who has to share me with the long days and closed doors that come with trying to fulfill my dreams and who deals with the anxiety that occurs when I feel that I have failed, all my love and thanks for understanding my little projects

1

It was nearly two-thirty in the morning when Jacqueline Emerson's eyes blinked open. Staring out upon her dark and fuzzy world, she wasn't sure what time it was, but she was positive that it wasn't time to be awake. She rolled onto her back and reached her arm towards her nightstand. Fumbling in the dark, her fingers found the power cord to her cell phone. She tugged at it until the phone slid off the nightstand and crashed onto the floor. With a hard yank, she whipped the phone from the floor onto the bed next to her. Having successfully completed a trial in the cell phone Olympics, she brought it within inches of her face. Without her glasses on, she squinted to read the time. As her mind made sense of the blurred words, she thought, *Great. Three hours worth of sleep!*

Despite her obscured vision, she noticed that she had a message alert on her locked screen. Recognizing the depth of her visual impairment, Jacqueline reached for her glasses. Placing the cold frames on her warm skin, she shook her head and waited for the world to come into focus. Now, poised to read, she unplugged the phone and swiped it open to reveal her message.

Mallory had sent it after she'd fallen asleep. It read:

```
I hope that this doesn't wake you. I was lying here
thinking of you. I hope you're getting some sleep. I'll
go look for you in my dreams. Goodnight, Jax.
```

Jacqueline read over the message a few times. Analyzing it with Sherlock Holmes' precision, she reviewed each word, its placement in the sentence, and the juxtaposition of each sentence relative to the other sentences. Despite all of her efforts, she still wasn't certain what to think.

Jacqueline's mind recalled its first image of Mallory. Prior to their introduction, she knew of Mallory Cummings by reputation only. She had been a quickly rising star in the central Florida newspaper circuit. She had started her career writing articles regarding regional news, but she had found recent success revamping the Daytona Beach Star's Arts and Entertainment department. Hence, Jacqueline was excited to hear that she would be joining the Tampa Sun Tribune. Jacqueline thought her presence was certain to draw more talent from around the state; and those changes were the kind that would propel the Sun to national recognition.

Upon their initial meeting, Jacqueline approached her with professionalism. She was eager to make Mallory's acquaintance. However, when she saw Mallory, Jacqueline found herself taking more notice of her than she'd expected. She was a thin woman with piercing green eyes and long, red waves of curls that cascaded down her back. That first morning, she was wearing dark gray slacks and a gray and pink print blouse. Inside of her blouse laid a gold lariat necklace that captured Jacqueline's attention. As it dangled below the closed flap of her shirt, Jacqueline wanted to reach for it. She wanted to hold it in her hands and fully inspect it. She wondered if Mallory ever noticed how she had stared at it, or, worse, she feared that Mallory thought that she'd been trying to look down her shirt.

That was five years ago. Since that time, they had forged a close friendship. In recent months, they had been spending a lot of time alone together rather than in the company of their mutual friends, Alex and Paige. The times alone had given them an opportunity to get to know each other better and become closer than Jacqueline had ever experienced with another person. However, the closeness had caused her some uncertainty. The relationship had become more intimate, more flirtatious. Jacqueline had caught herself looking at Mallory in ways that brought caution to her mind. She had been trying very hard to maintain a level head and not to confuse their friendship as anything more.

It was nearly three in the morning when Jacqueline stopped re-reading the text conversation that they had shared from the day before. After work, the two had enjoyed at a Tampa Bay Rays game. They had eaten at the Trop and stayed through the eighth inning. Comfortable that the Rays would secure the victory, Jacqueline drove Mallory home. Sitting in her driveway talking, Jacqueline had thought that she might be invited inside. Now hours later the strangeness of that thought returned to her. She had been inside Mallory's house on plenty of prior occasions. It was well after ten o'clock on a weeknight. Moreover, she wasn't certain why she wanted to be invited inside or why she had given the fact that she wasn't any thought at all. After some time, Jacqueline realized that she was overanalyzing this and opted to discard the entire oddity.

With a heavy sigh, Jacqueline became aware that her chance to fall back to sleep had passed. Rather than belabor on Mallory or her insomnia, she returned her phone to her nightstand and swung her body upright. She stretched her brown arms into the air. Her jerky movements created a symphony of cracking joints and bones. Once her body fell silent, she lunged from her high bed to the floor.

Barefoot, she walked out of her bedroom into the darkness of her home, a penthouse condominium. It was empty. As the only inhabitant, the condo spent most evenings in darkness, coldly awaiting a visitor. In the absence of guest, it sat still as a museum.

Knowing her home, Jacqueline often walked from room to room in darkness. Without children, friends who visited often, a spouse, or roommates, everything remained exactly as Jacqueline had left it. She had mentally mapped all its contents and didn't need light to guide her way.

In darkness, Jacqueline entered the kitchen and turned on the lights. She placed a kettle of water onto the stove, retrieved her tea infuser, and selected a loose-leaf green tea from her pantry. Waiting on the water to boil, she withdrew a mug from the cabinet. As she rotated the mug in her hand, she remembered that it was the mug that Mallory had given her last Christmas.

The two had opened gifts at the condo alone before meeting Paige and Alex. Each had purchased gifts that they had deemed too special to open in front of other people. The gifts were without innuendo, but they were items that reflected the new depth that their relationship had reached. Jacqueline had given Mallory a diamond watch that had a mother of pearl face. Mallory had purchased clothing that she wanted to Jacqueline to wear. They had thanked each other with a long embrace that was both too long and not long enough.

Nearly an hour after their personal exchange, the two met Alex and Paige and opened other gifts. In that second exchange, they swapped candy, books, makeup, alcohol, tea, coffee, DVDs, Rays gear, scarves – all the innocuous gifts that friends share.

This morning, Jacqueline stood in her kitchen drinking from her Rays mug and tried to focus on the day ahead. She walked down the hall into her office, gathered her notes, her laptop, and her iPad. She had worked when she arrived home last night. She had been working many hours from home most nights these last few weeks. Placing all of her work into her messenger bag, Jacqueline carried it to the front door. Making certain not to forget it, she hung it on the doorknob. She returned the mug to the kitchen and decided to get dressed and head into work.

It was four a.m. when Jacqueline arrived at work. Of course, four was not her normal start time for a Tuesday, or any day for that matter. Unlike most companies that were barren in the early hours of the morning, a newspaper office was always buzzing with activity. Newspapers had to be proofread, previewed, prepared, printed, and bound for circulation at night. The creation of the newspaper was a nonstop project. Jacqueline loved that. The news was as active as she was.

Every morning, no matter what the time, she parked her black, 1985 Wrangler Laredo in the parking garage across from the office. Dragging her messenger bag behind her, she slipped out of the Laredo. Jacketless, she tucked her hands tightly into her pockets and strolled across the street in the cool, morning air. On mornings that started this early, she entered the building from its rear. She walked among the delivery trucks as they sat in the loading bays. As she passed them, she ran her outstretched fingers across the Sun Tribune logo. That sun radiating over the metropolitan backdrop always felt warm to her even on the side of a cold delivery truck.

If she entered from the front of the building, she would have had to take an elevator down to where she was now. From the building's main façade, she was in the basement. But, in reality, it wasn't underground at all. It wasn't some place to be hidden away. It was the heartbeat of the paper.

She passed the machinery and felt the hum it created in the room. The vibration radiated through her body. The paper felt alive. The work felt alive. It silenced her mind of all her anxieties and reminded her that this is why she did what she did.

After walking far enough inside the building, she was overcome with its smell. The smell of ink wafted around the floor as if it could be tasted. It engulfed all who came within its reach. The scent lingered in their hair and clothes even when they left this part of the building. Jacqueline loved it. To her, it was the smell of their labor of love.

Walking around amongst the production operators and distribution crew, Jacqueline admired the look of people moving about with purpose but without direct instruction. As Managing Editor, she rarely had a need to come to the production floor. In fact, it was out of her way. It was out of the way of everyone in the building who worked on a floor with a number, but Jacqueline thought of it as the most impressive part of the operation. It was the place that inspired her to proceed up the elevator with purpose and clarity.

At such an ungodly hour, very few people acknowledged her presence. There were no 'good mornings' or 'what're ya doing here so early.' She didn't think of the lack of conversation as cold or impolite. In truth, it was only in the employee's steady pace of independent work that the Sun had been what it was in the community. The nod a passer-by gave her or the hard shove of a door by the person ahead of her was enough of a 'good morning.'

After soaking it all in, Jacqueline took the elevator up to the first floor. Most of the other staff wouldn't be in for four more hours. On mornings, when she arrived closer to eight, Jacqueline would pass through the main aisle of the first floor amid people bustling ahead of and behind her. Slowly sauntering, even on busy mornings, she was never struck by anyone; often, she smiled to herself imagining how she must appear from a bird's eye view. She could imagine how her slow pace must have appeared in the midst of their frenzy. The idea of which made her snicker.

At the back of the first floor, there was the office of Paige Little, the Production Manager. Paige was a small woman with a sweet sounding voice, but a confidence and knowledge that demanded discipline and expected success. Jacqueline and Paige had known each other for a number of years. Paige was one of Jacqueline's first work friends. Paige was already working at the Sun when Jacqueline was hired.

On Jacqueline's third day, she was outside enjoying the sunshine during her lunch break when Paige introduced herself. Paige was naturally engaging. Without qualm or confrontation, she asked Jacqueline about herself and how she was enjoying working at the Sun. The two became friends immediately.

This Tuesday morning, Paige was already in her office. As Jacqueline approached, she knew that they'd only talk if Paige could spare time, which would be unlikely. She knocked on the glass window of Paige's office. Paige looked up from her drafting board, smiled, and lowered her head. Jacqueline smiled back and thought that she should just leave her to work. But, for a moment, she stood at the window staring into the well-decorated office. Her office was from the cover of a magazine. Her whitewashed desk was neatly appropriated. The walls were decorated with art pieces, both Paige's original creations and the art prints of local artists who she liked. When meetings were had in her office, Paige played soothing music and surrounded the visitor with the smell of cinnamon potpourri. Visitors were transported from a newspaper office to a visit to their favorite aunt's lanai. Jacqueline dallied there for only a short while staring at Paige in her natural habitat. When she became aware of how odd this would be if Paige were to look up, she moved quickly to the elevator.

Back in the elevator, Jacqueline skipped the rectangular L button that was placed in the middle of the panel. There was no reason to exit into the lobby at this hour of morning. By the elevator's strata, the lobby sat on the second floor. The building's façade lifted it into the air and held there by four sets of twelve steps. Upon entry into the building, a visitor or employee would hear the clickety clack of shoes on the marble floor. The lobby was home only to security guards, the mailroom, and the switchboard operators. Most of the room on this huge floor was used as a gathering place. Complete with conversation places, the lobby was used as an informal meeting area. It had been refurnished with modern pieces of furniture. There was a collection of black, leather chairs and couches with glass tables of varying sizes strewn about the lobby. At the back of the lobby, there sat the elevators that Jacqueline was riding.

She passed the third floor and headed on to the fourth floor. The third floor was a labyrinth of miscellaneous, albeit important departments. The entire left side was home to sales and advertising associates. Each was committed to how the paper interacted in the community. The right side of the floor was a mix of human resources associates and desk spaces for independent IT professionals who needed office space when servicing the office's machinery. Jacqueline wouldn't exit there so early in the morning. The floor would be empty. All of these employees would be in the office later in the morning. She'd wait to make an appearance until after lunch.

The fourth floor was the news floor. It was massive. It housed writers, reporters, fact checkers, and critics set up in sections based upon the area of the newspaper in which they worked. Daily, Jacqueline exited the elevator on the fourth floor to reach her office. As with every floor, she passed through the main aisle. On the fourth floor, more than any other floor, she was most certain to be stopped at least five times every time she was seen. From sycophants to new hires, from department heads to couriers, everyone wanted a chance to talk to her. And, she gave them that chance without trepidation or sarcasm.

At the end of that long aisle, there was a slim elevator that led to the highest floor in the building, the fifth floor. The elevator itself was a beautiful piece of art with gold filigree pictures that lined the inside of the car. In moments of stress, she would stand for her few moments of travel and reflect upon the tales told in those golden pictures.

When the elevator doors opened, the occupant stepped out into a foyer and was greeted by two desks, one on the right, and one on the left. Behind each desk was a door that led into an office. If the visitor turned left, she would face Grant Kincaid, Jacqueline's assistant. Behind him sat the door to Jacqueline's office. If the visitor turned right, she would face Mrs. Katherine Pennington, the Editor-in-Chief's secretary. Behind her, there was a door that led to Jack Boyd's office, the Editor-in-Chief.

Directly in front of the elevator door was the Conference room. A room filled with a beautiful mahogany table, high back leather chairs, and mahogany woodwork. Natural light flowed into the room from the floor to ceiling glass windows that overlooked Tampa Bay. It was stunning. It was so stunning that in Board meetings Jacqueline often found herself staring into the Bay dreaming of more leisurely activities. Use of the Conference room rather than other conference rooms around the building was an indication of bad tidings to most of the employees. Jacqueline always regarded that as a shame. It was immaculate, but she understood the stigma attached to being called into the Conference room. It was where the Board met; it was where department restructures were announced; it was where layoffs were performed; and, it was where Mr. Boyd, the illusive Editor, announced to the staff just three weeks ago that the paper was planning to focus more on its online presence than on the physical paper's production in the coming months.

Jacqueline thought that Jack was too flippant when he shared this news. Jack Boyd had inherited his position in the Sun Tribune. He has been less of a journalist and more of a businessman. His father, Big Jack Boyd, had managed the paper with the proper balance between ferocity and decency in the forty-two years that he served as Editor-in-Chief. Big Jack was never formal and riding the elevator up to him was never as foreboding as it had recently become. But, Big Jack was no longer steering the ship. After years of excess, whether it be smoking cigars, drinking whiskey and sodas in mid-morning meetings, or the enjoying of hearty meals full of salt, cream, gravy, and beef before drifting off into a pleasant slumber on the couch in his office, Big Jack had suffered a stroke and a heart attack in the same year. The Board, which consisted of small shareowners, ushered Jack from heading the sales and marketing area to Editor-in-Chief. Jack had a sharp eye for business. He was friendly and engaging in meetings between him and Jacqueline; but in the presence of all the staff, he withdrew and appeared, as Jacqueline had feared that he might, as aloof and hollow.

Not helping his lack of positive interaction with the staff, he had discovered recently that his office contained an elevator that allowed him passage from the back corner of the building to the security guard station. It was a secret passage installed in the building years ago when employees were still taking flights of stairs. This discovery gave him a path to exit and enter the building unseen. Jack was elated with this discovery. He called from his office to Jacqueline's office almost immediately after it was discovered. Despite her hesitance, Jack declared, "I've finally found something great about this job." He saw this as a path that he could take in and out of the building without having to engage in grueling interviews with staff that had been trained to do so. However, the presence of elevator repair people and construction workers made the employees ask even more questions. Consequently, it was not long until it was discovered that there was a path that was only for Mr. Boyd's travel. The discovery gave the employees space to make conjecture about Mr. Boyd's intentions; in turn, they deduced incorrectly that he wanted to spy on them. This was one of the many falsehoods at the Sun that only Jacqueline knew.

Sitting on the corner of her glass desk, Jacqueline was deep in thought. She was replaying the last meeting with the staff in the Conference room. As a businessperson, Jack recognized that the second most circulated newspaper in a metropolitan area would need foresight in order to continue to compete. Through his many connections, Jack had found out that the Florida Times Journal, the number one newspaper of southwest Florida, had a small online presence and no immediate intention to increase that. Using that information, Jack discerned that this was the best way for the Sun Tribune to overtake the Journal, or, at the very least, maintain its position in second, for years to come. Jack's plan was promising, but Jacqueline had thought that it was Jack's delivery that left something to be desired.

Using the same PowerPoint presentation and cardboard charts used in his presentation to the Board, Jack gave a forty-minute presentation to the staff on the future of the newspaper business, Internet activity, environmental consciousness, and the increase in production costs and worker's compensation claims. At the end of which, Jack mumbled through the part that all of the staff were most concerned with - job eliminations. He failed to communicate that new jobs would also be created, provide a timeline for job eliminations, or discuss separation packages. To make matters worse, Jack referred to the paper as the Tribune, instead of the Sun as Big Jack always had. It was bad icing on top of undone cake. Jack delivered his entire presentation and, then without asking for feedback from the staff, he packed up the presentation and left the room. Mouths dropped; employees sat in shock. Jacqueline was shocked herself. She let the employees leave before she rushed to Jack's office. Crossing from the Conference room, into Jack's office, she heard the elevator doors close as she opened his door. Knowing that she couldn't reach the lobby before he would, she picked up her phone and texted him. The message was simple:

```
Got a minute to talk about next steps?
```

Sitting on the couch in his office, awaiting his reply, she noticed how he had removed all of the old world woodwork and redone the entire office with more modern furniture just as he had had ordered around the building. It was a weird mix of old and new. Remembering the giant wood desk Big Jack sat behind, she could smell his cigar smoke that used to permeate into the hall. When her phone rang, it shocked her back from her memories. It was Jack.

"I wanted to brainstorm some next steps. Do you have few minutes to talk?" she asked cautiously. She and Jack had been thrown together like roommates in a reality show. She was uncertain of Jack's habits or outlook, but she was learning quickly how to deal with him.

He responded as if he hadn't heard her, "Things didn't go as well as I hoped." Jacqueline thought *you don't say*, but said, "It was a lot to absorb and I'm sure that they still have plenty of questions."

"That came to me at the end. I realized that I hadn't told them what I was planning. Then, I realized that I hadn't planned much." Stunned, she sat still. In that moment, she realized how much there was to fear and wished for a comforting waft of cigar smoke to fill her nostrils.

She said, "I have some ideas. Maybe, we can hash them out tomorrow. Do you have any meetings at, say, eight tomorrow morning?"

"Why don't you come out to the house and we can talk about them tonight? I'm not going to show my face around there for a few days." He said softly as though he as staring out the window.

She buried her face in her hands and responded, "Of course. What time?"

"Good. Mrs. Pennington can tell you when dinner is. I don't know myself. My wife calls her with the details. Even, poor Misty has to add things to my calendar."

"Should I check with Misty and see if there's room for company?"

"Nonsense. Come on out. It's fine." She thought that was the end of conversation. She was prepared to hang up and work on some ideas of her own, but before she could say good-bye he added, "Will you be bringing anyone?"

With a wrinkled brow, she said, "Just me, myself, and I." With an okay, he was gone. For a second, she wasn't sure what that meant. He knew that she wasn't dating anyone. She didn't really have time to think on it, so she pushed it from her mind. *Today has been weird enough without wondering what the hell Jack means,* she thought. She stood, straightened her clothes, and closed the door to his office.

Before she could ask Mrs. Pennington about dinnertime, she said, "Dinner is at six-thirty and veal will be served." Jacqueline smiled and thanked her for the information. She walked into her office, chewing on her thumbnail. As she closed the door behind her, Grant opened it. She hadn't made it to her chair when he spoke.

"I keep telling myself that this won't affect me. Surely, I'm fine as long as you're fine and it looks like you're gonna be just fine." Grant pressed his thin fingers down on the glass. His fingertips were red from the pressure he was applying.

"We're fine, Grant. If something were to change with me, you'd be the first to know," she said to him assuredly and sat in her chair.

"I know it's selfish. I know that plenty of people are gonna lose their jobs, but in moments like these, it's so hard not to just think of yourself." He was looking from side to side nervously.

Off in space, thinking of how to make these changes needed with the least amount of impact, she responded with a simple "Don't I know it?" With that said, Grant lifted his hands from her desk and rolled them around one another. She noticed the dampness his fingers had left on her desk.

That was three weeks ago today. In that time, she has implemented a number of changes with many, more changes ahead. She was the Managing Editor of the Sun Tribune, but she was acting as its Editor-in-Chief. But, sitting on her desk at almost five on a Tuesday morning, staring off over her empty universe, she couldn't say that she was fulfilled, or better yet, happy.

2

When Alexandra Stevens' phone rattled to life, she fumbled through the lilac silk sheets searching for it. Without cracking open her eyes, she silenced the jubilant sounds of the newest female pop star before she could finish the chorus. Sighing heavily, Alex rolled onto her stomach. She was awake, but not quite functioning. She laid there hoping that she had a few more moments of rest before it was time to start her day.

She dozed back off only to be awakened again by the bellows of the young diva. This time, she rolled from her belly to her side, found the phone, and stared into young woman's face. Beguiled with the girl's bright smile, Alex peered at her picture. Alex could feel the ridicule of this child. With her excitement-filled life, complete with interviews, parties, borrowed designer clothes, gala openings, and international flights, Alex knew that this girl had no Tuesdays. Every day was a Friday or a Saturday or a Sunday for her. This girl would never know what it was like to be a weekday warrior. This young darling was an eternal weekend princess.

Angry, Alex pulled her legs to her chest and rolled towards the floor. She had mastered this move and executed it flawlessly since she was a child. She thought of herself as a gymnast dismounting from the balance beam. However, she was still wrapped in her comforter and didn't land safely on her feet this Tuesday morning; instead, her lilac-flowered comforter caused an impressive slide. Off balance, she flailed her arms to search for balance, but there was none to be found. Rather than sticking her landing upright on her cool, tile floors, Alex started her Tuesday morning wrapped in her comforter like an enchilada flat on her back.

"Fuck!" she screamed and stamped her feet. And, as she did, the youngster gleefully chanted on and on. After a few moments of stomping her feet and swearing, Alex unraveled and silenced the phone. She balled up the comforter and threw it violently towards her bed; however, the force created from anger and frustration coupled with polyblend material prevented an accurate throw. Instead of landing gently on the bed, the comforter glided across the bed and splashed on the floor.

"Fuck!" she screamed again and waved her hand dismissively in the direction of this mayhem and limped into her bathroom.

While sitting on the toilet, she heard a sound. She knew that the sound hadn't come from her bedroom. She leaned toward the slow, hissing sound and strained to hear. Then, she knew exactly what it was. It was the sound of running late. It was the sound of trying to slip in both unnoticed and the object of everyone's attention.

"Dammit!" she yelled and ran out of the bathroom. She darted into the bedroom, down her hall, through the living room, and into the kitchen. Immediately, her eyes fixated upon the countertop of Cuisinart appliances. Her eyes zoned in on the coffee pot. It was programmed to turn itself off at eight every morning. Normally, by then, she would be walking into work. However, today, it was already eight in the morning. Rather than sauntering into the office, she was standing in her kitchen listening to the machine turn itself off and cool itself down until its routine restarted tomorrow at six. Alex glanced from side to side. She was amazed how any of this could have happened. She felt the cold glares of disappointed stainless steel appliances.

Dazed, she ran to her clothes dryer to see what was inside. She found nothing. It was empty. Her laundry had been put away - not by her, of course. However, she gave that little thought. Disappointed by her temporary closet's lack of help during this most serious predicament, she scurried back to her bedroom. Moving too fast in sock-covered feet, she slid in the hall and failed to make the gradual turn that would be crucial to launch herself into her bedroom. Instead, she slid into the doorframe of her bedroom. BAM!

"Fuck!" she screamed, again. In her haze of pain, she planned a quick outfit. It was one of Alex's favorites. She walked to the closet and removed her navy blue dress that had a white trim that ruffled down the front. It was complete with a wide, shiny, white belt and white heart buttons. She knew that it wouldn't need ironing; and, even better, it would guarantee her plenty of attention. She pulled the dress from its hanger and flung it onto her bed. Bending down, she dug through the mound of shoes that lay at her feet. After some tears and more adult words, Alex was able to locate two simple nude heels. As she forced the doors closed, she thought, *I need to purge some of those.*

After twenty minutes of pinning, buttoning, and wiggling, Alex was ready to go. She had finger-combed her natural hair back against her head and used a navy and white paisley, silk scarf to hold the coif in place. What little makeup that she was going to wear today, she decided could be applied from what was in her purse. Furthermore, she knew that she could apply that makeup between red lights while driving to work.

As she locked the front door of her apartment behind her, she looked up in the sky and took a deep breath. She was confident that she'd trapped the worst of the day in her apartment. She ran down the three flights of stairs. Looking around, she was amazed that no one was out. Then, she remembered, *Shit, they're probably already at work.* As she hit the concrete landing, she was smiling and confident that all would be well.

When she arrived at her car, she opened the door and tossed her purse inside. The engine roared to life. She cranked on the radio and squealed towards work.

Racing through the traffic, Alex was rushing despite already being nearly two hours late. When she arrived down the street from work, she checked the time. She was proud of how far she'd come in such a short time.

It was nine forty-five a.m. She had been awake for less than two hours, but she sat at the red light around the corner from the company's parking garage. She had applied her entire face waiting on the light to change. Before she could apply her lip stain, electronica roared into the car's cabin. She knew exactly who it was. After all, it was his song. She turned off the radio and answered the phone through the stereo.

"Hey, baby," she said enthusiastically.

"Hey, babe. How's your day going?" Elet said.

She could hear the smile in his voice. Coyly, she said, "Same ole same ole. What're you doing today?"

"Right now, I'm working on formatting some pieces at the studio. I thought about inviting you to lunch, but I think dinner would be so much nicer. Whadya think? Is there a place within fifty miles that you haven't been to or reviewed?"

"Well, of course, I don't review the old places. The classics. People already know that they are great. They don't need me to drum up business."

"Well. Then. Hmm." He thought as she applied lip stain. Excitedly, he said, "I've got just the place. I'll pick you up at seven."

"Let's take my car."

"If we take your car, then I'm not picking you up."

"Semantics, baby. Besides, you can carry me down the stairs to my car."

"It's a good truck, you know."

"Oh, it's a great truck. Ford tough."

"That's Ram Tough," he corrected her.

"Whatever. Rams are tough, but, a convertible Mustang is cool. And cool says date night."

"Yes, it does. Alright, I love you."

"You too," she replied and hung up. As she tossed the phone into the passenger's seat, she was smiling. She was late to work. Very late. The morning had started in dishevel and she thought it best not to tell a soul. Not even Elet.

She had arrived at the parking garage. She brushed her natural hair back and retied the scarf around it, making sure to corral her mane. She checked her make-up. Pleased with herself, she got out of the car. Walking around to the passenger's side, she opened that door and picked up her purse and her phone. Sunglasses still on her face, she strutted out of the garage, across the street, and into the Sun Tribune building.

The click of her shoes sounded like a mini-marching band. It was rhythmically entrancing. Alex commanded attention everywhere she went. She knew it and everyone that saw her knew that she knew it. Women looked and asked about the dress, the shoes, the scarf, and the purse. The men she knew spoke. The men she didn't know just looked at her and smiled hoping to catch her gaze. When the elevator door opened, she walked in and stood in the very center of the car. As she stopped on the third floor, two men from sales joined her. She never stepped aside. They made room for themselves to either side of her at the back of the car. The younger sales clerk asked, "Excuse me, but I love the smell of that perfume. What're you wearing?"

She smiled to herself. As the doors opened, she said, back over her shoulder to him, "Charisma." She wouldn't know it, but he leaned forward into the closing doors. She snickered as she walked down the main aisle of fourth floor. This was exactly the kind of morning she wanted to pretend to be having.

Alex spoke to every person she passed on her way to her desk. She remembered their stories. She asked how they were, how their parents were, how the dogs were, how the weight loss regimen was going. When she hit her row off the main aisle, she turned with such force that the back of her dress sashayed around the corner grabbing the file cabinet as if leaving an arrow for those who might have missed her.

Entering her desk area, she greeted her desk neighbor, Evelyn Hall, with a bright "Good morning."

In turn, Evelyn responded. "Nice of you to join us."

Alex thought, *old bitch*. Alex had failed to win over Evelyn no matter how many times she applauded her or told her how honored she was to sit next to someone with the legacy of Evelyn Hall, the advice columnist of the Sun for the last four decades. Alex had brought her foods and desserts from restaurants and bakeries all over the city. She had given her gifts on all her birthdays and holidays. One Mother's Day, Alex bought her a Like A Mother card. None of it had worked.

Evelyn worked twelve hours per week for forty-eight weeks per year for the last twenty years, an arrangement that Big Jack had made with her. She cared very little for the changes happening around the office, for Alex, or whatever it was that everyone saw in Alex. Alex had heard all of it before, but she was never depressed by Evelyn's caustic personality. She had discovered the joy of sitting near the oldest staff member in the building. Evelyn knew everything that was going on at the Sun and had no one but Alex to tell. And, she was delighted by her access to Evelyn's plethora of gossip.

Nonchalantly, Evelyn said, "Mallory was looking for you."

"When?"

"Around eight, when you were supposed to be here."

"I'm sure that she just wanted to chitchat about last night's opening of *Les Mis*."

Unaffected by Alex's declaration of where she had gone and what she had seen, Evelyn said, "Maybe. Or, it could be that she's gonna be boss and you're gonna get fired for being late." Alex whipped around to face Evelyn. But, of course, Evelyn was not facing her.

Alex asked, "Have you heard something? I haven't heard anything. You know that I applied for the job too?"

Evelyn said, "Of course, I know. You told everyone who would listen. I think everyone whose staying applied for the job. And, no, I haven't heard anything. "

Alex felt better hearing that Evelyn hadn't heard anything. If anyone would know, Evelyn would know. She knew everything. She was the first person to know that voluntary retirement was being offered to anyone either over fifty-five or with more than twenty years of service. Evelyn knew and volunteered that she had already agreed. The company promised everyone who volunteered for early retirement the ability to cash in any unused vacation and sick time, continual insurance coverage for a year, immediate access to pension plans, and a severance package based upon length of service. It was a wonderful package. Evelyn said that she and the other 'old-timers,' as she called them, would be fools not to take it. It was Jacqueline's first initiative. It reduced the payroll and employee base without much disruption to the stock price and prevented a great wave of layoffs.

A week after that initiative was introduced, Mr. Boyd with Jacqueline, at his side, in the conference room announced that every department would need to have an official editor. All persons in good standing within the company were free to apply, but the company would be allowing outside candidates to apply as well. This was a welcoming sign. For most people, who may or may not have considered management as their next step, management seemed to be a place of safety amidst the new changes.

While Alex was the most recognized writer for the paper, she was young and had only a few years with the Sun. None of this stopped her from applying for the Lifestyles department Editor. She had had two interviews. The first interview was done with a tag team of other department editors. Her interview was with Paige, the Production Manager, and Bob, the Politics Editor. It was professional and quick. She thought Paige looked uncomfortable interviewing a friend. It was a small, close-knit operation. People knew that they were friends. Most people were being interviewed by their friends or their relatives as well. The second interview was with Jacqueline. Grant was present as the note taker, but it seemed obvious that Jacqueline also had him there to be a witness of her professionalism. Alex felt that she handled herself well. There were some questions that Jacqueline posed that Alex wasn't sure how to answer, but she gave the best evasive answers she could. Alex, nor Evelyn, had heard of anyone having a third interview with Mr. Boyd or Jacqueline and Mr. Boyd.

Still wondering why Mallory had come to her desk, she asked Evelyn, "Did you get any idea what Mallory might have wanted?"

Evelyn said, "Tickets to the next show of *Les Mis*?" and looked smug doing it.

Alex decided not to search for Mallory. She would look more suspicious if she did. Alex decided to stay in her area and work on her review. She reached into her purse and pulled out her phone. She had stopped making physical notes while at a show, restaurant, nightclub, or other area event. She had started using a note-taking app. Typing away on her phone let her blend into the rest of the world better than making notes in a moleskin. This way, she looked less like a reviewer and more like a patron.

As usual, the idea was great, but her application of the idea sometimes left something to be desired. The notes weren't always as direct and descriptive as they could've been. Last night's note said:

```
•   before  dinner,  French-American  fusion;  after
dinner, actor-writer fusion?
•   tall,  blond,  6'2"  25-28 Marius  is  cute  enough  to
die for
•   Jean Valjean is ripped. Definite distraction
•   Jax would love Fantine. I wonder if I can get her
number.
•   Buy opera glasses before next show. eBay? Amazon?
Antique-shop
```

But, these notes never failed to jog her memory and let her write a review that the Sun and the community would love. It was eleven a.m. and her Tuesday had finally started.

She was well into the first draft when she received an IM. She hadn't read it before it faded away. Flashing in orange on Alex's taskbar was Mallory's name. Alex sat back in her chair and tapped a pen on her desk. Mallory was Alex's friend. Jacqueline had introduced them when Alex joined the company. However, they were currently rivals for the same job. She shook her head trying to overcome her paranoia and retrieved Mallory's conversation from her taskbar.

Mallory Cummings: Morning. How was the show?
Alexandra Stevens: Good morning. It was beautiful. I'm still swooning!!
Mallory Cummings: It's Tuesday. Are we having lunch today or are you going to lunch with Elet?
Alexandra Stevens: Elet for dinner. Y'all for lunch.
Mallory Cummings: Don't say it like that.
Alexandra Stevens: Like what?
Mallory Cummings: Read the above.
Alexandra Stevens: You know what I meant, nasty. I'll be downstairs to join you and the crew for lunch. We got plans to talk about!!
Mallory Cummings: :) Yea, we do!!!!!!!

Alex felt relieved. She thought for certain that Mallory was ready to tell her that she had had a third interview, or worse that she had been offered the job. Mallory had worked for Sun for three years longer than Alex had. She was well known, well respected, and well feared. She produced amazing, insightful work reviewing cultural events in the area. She had even contributed pieces to other sections of the paper. Her work was candid and never tempered. As far as Alex was concerned, her friend was her only competition.

With almost an hour left before lunch, Alex pressed hard to finish the first draft. She ignored her sister's repeated calls to her desk phone, cell phone, and text messages. She read them on preview to know that no one was dying. Realizing that there was no real emergency, she stopped reading Josephine's rant. When Josephine called her desk the second time, Evelyn groaned aloud.

Alex responded, "You know how sisters can be."

Without inflection, Evelyn said, "No, my sister died from polio when I was seven."

3

Sitting on the edge of her desk sipping hot tea, Jacqueline stared out over the newsroom floor as employees began to trickle into work. She watched as the overhead lights came on and the floor came to life. It was obvious the Managing Editor's office was designed on an ill-conceived panoptic design. From her vantage point, she could surveil the employees. The idea had disturbed her so much that she had blinds installed. This morning, as the office came to life, she rose to her feet and walked to the edge of her office. Facing the glass, she ran her hand over a six inch panel. As she did, blinds began to lower. They blocked her view of the news floor. She felt that her surveillance was as much of a distraction to her as it was to them. That was the move that signified the official start of the work day.

Returning to her desk, she removed a pad of paper filled with pages of notes from her well-worn leather messenger bag. She flipped through the pad and reread several pages of garbled words. Unbeknownst to those around her, she was in charge of executing Jack's plans. Jack had the vision of what the company needed to become to achieve its rightful place in the news market, but he had limited experience and no knowledge of what it would take in order to bring the dream to fruition. He admitted all of this to Jacqueline when they met at his house three weeks ago.

After enjoying a master chef dinner in a sprawling eat-in kitchen, Jacqueline followed Jack to the pool house. Out there, Jack said, "I never thought I'd be Editor-in-Chief. I was content to run Sales and Marketing." Slowly, drinking his bourbon sour, he continued, "I never wanted to be a journalist. I don't even watch the news. When Dad got sick, I always thought that he would be back to work. I never saw me in his office sitting behind his desk." The reflection of the pool lights danced on his face. Jacqueline didn't say anything. She never foresaw Jack as Editor-in-Chief either. He turned to her and said, "I bet you were surprised that it was me, and not you."

Sighing, she replied, "I never thought about it. I was happy being Managing Editor. I never saw Big Jack not being in the office across the hall." It was true. Despite how many people had asked or been upset on her behalf, she never thought, even in the wake of Big Jack's illness, that she would become Editor-in-Chief.

Jack went on, "He loves you, you know. He thinks that you have a great head on your shoulders. He compliments you and your rise through the company whenever he talks about the 'old paper biz'." He said that poking his stomach out and rubbing it, imitating his father. "He calls you the face of the company's future. And, you know what," he said, turning towards her, "I believed it, too. The Board made me Editor-in-Chief, because the family still owns fifty-two percent of the stock. Effectively, we are our own largest shareholder. Big Jack was brilliant when he did that." He was sucking on the ice from his bourbon sour. "They picked me out of respect for Big Jack, but I don't have any fuckin' idea what I'm doing. Misty says that I should just ask for a place on the Board. I don't think it's time, but I think that it will be one day. Until then, I guess I'm stuck...stuck as Editor-in-fuckin-Chief."

Jacqueline said nothing. Though, her face must have seemed perplexed, because Jack began to speak again. He said, "I called you out here, because we have to be partners, you and I." He pointed at her with his drink. "Just like you and Big Jack were. I know that you knew his secrets. Now, you know mine. The difference is I don't plan to run the business. Not the day-to-day shit. I think we agree that I've a good idea, but no clue how to get there. I need you," now he was walking towards her, "to get us there. And, I know you can. Hell, everyone knows you can. The funny thing is, I'm gonna pay you more money, but I bet you don't even need it offered to you to do what needs to be done. Hell, I know what you make now and you're still driving around in that piece of shit Laredo." He laughed. Jacqueline sneered; she thought *don't talk shit about my YJ*. He came and stood next to her. He turned his head so that his eyes would meet hers and said, "When we pull this off, I will get a seat on the Board and you will be Editor-in-Chief. I promise you that. Hell, I'll put it in writing."

Jacqueline wasn't sure that that was what she wanted. Editor-in-Chief is so far removed from the parts of the job that she enjoyed so much, but tonight wasn't the time to split hairs. She asked Jack, "How do you think that this is going to all work? The staff will notice that you aren't in the office. Mrs. Pennington will notice that you aren't around to make the changes that are being implemented. Hell, Jack, what about HR?" Now, she was screaming. She felt anxious as though they were plotting a crime.

Gently, he said, "There is no rule that says that I can't let the second-in-command lead the platoon. Just come by and bounce ideas off me. You have better ones than I do anyhow. We will flesh them out and tell people who need to know. Then, when you are ready to announce it to the staff, I will come into the meeting with the staff. I'm just the muscle. Just the figurehead. You won't be doing anything I don't know about, so even if old Mrs. P., HR, or anyone else says or asks anything, of course, I will agree. See? It's perfect." And, it really was.

As Jacqueline told him about her ideas, Jack clanked the ice against the side of his highball. She mentioned voluntary retirement, streamlining job titles, hiring department editors for all departments, centralizing more control within the departments that funneled up to her, and having an onsite IT department. Jack agreed to her every idea. In addition, he made suggestions about a rating system for the employees that would allow more accountability and documentable plans to allow employees to be involuntary separated from the Tribune.

She stopped him and said, "Stop calling it the Tribune." Confused, he cocked his head. She repeated, "Stop calling it the Tribune. Remember your audience. These people spend hours choosing the right word for the purpose of connotation. A tribune is a defender of the people. It is a wonderful idea, but it's very...oh, I don't know...aggressive." With shrugged shoulders, she went on, "Big Jack said we were more like the Sun, shining through the dark."

Throwing his ice, into the pool, he said, "He's such a bullshitter."

Moving towards him, she said, "But we love the bullshit."

"Alright, alright, alright...I will try to remember to call it the fucking Sun. Anything else?" he said dismissively.

"Well, while we're on it, if you get nervous or run out of things to say in a meeting, look at me. Ask if I have anything to add. Lemme bail you out. Don't just walk out."

He saluted. "Aye, Aye, Capt'n."

She chuckled. "Okay, this has been fun, but I got shit to do. I'm going to head home." She was cleaning up after herself.

She noticed that he had started to fumble. He suddenly seemed uncomfortable. "Misty says that you should bring someone if you've got someone that you want to bring to dinner or whatever. I mean, it's okay. We didn't want you to think that it wasn't okay."

She smiled. "Thank her for me, but there's no one to bring." Jack cocked his head as if he was in on a secret. In response, Jacqueline shrugged her shoulders like she didn't know the secret. Then, she thanked him for a lovely evening and excused herself.

Now, she sat her desk writing the job descriptions and determining pay scales. She had finished assignment editor, contribution writer, copy editor, fact checker, feature writer, and critic when she heard someone outside her office door. At first, she thought it was Grant settling in, but there was a faint tapping on her door.

Leaning forward towards the door, she said, "Hello?"

The door opened slowly. It was Mallory. She knew it was her before she ever saw her. She smelled her perfume. It was some perfume whose name she had been told on many occasions but could never remember. But, it was a scent that she couldn't forget. It was like standing in a valley of flowers with the sun beaming overhead. It was the kind of valley that always appeared in commercials. It was a sunflower-filled valley. There was a woman walking through it with her fingers outstretched gently touching the tops of the flowers as she graced them with her presence.

Mallory peeked her head around the door, smiled, and squinted her eyes as if she would have to do if she was standing in the sun of a crisp, spring day. With a sweet, simple voice, she said, "There you are."

"Here I are," responded Jacqueline.

"You know, Jax," a nickname that Mallory had given Jacqueline, "when I come into the office I look up here to see you. Even when you aren't looking back, I'm happy that I can see you." Mallory had entered Jacqueline's office and closed the door behind her. She was in classic black heels, black trousers, and a green, silk, button-up shirt. There was nothing flashy or overdone, but in it, Mallory looked amazing. Jacqueline thought about how she looked for so long that she was forgetting to listen. Her mind had recorded all of what Mallory said and replayed it for her without too much of a recognizable delay.

"You don't think it's creepy?" Jacqueline pushed back from the desk and walked to the other side of the room where Mallory was. "Sometimes, I feel like the warden keeping a lookout on the inmates," Jacqueline said with her arms folded.

"Now that you say it that way. I guess that could be true." Walking to the glass, she placed her head against it. "I wonder if you could push someone out of it." She giggled, like a child who had said the wrong thing but was looking forward to the scolding.

"I'm glad that you brought that up. It's the next phase of Tampa Sun Tribune to Infinity and Beyond." They both chuckled. Jacqueline sat down in one of the chairs on the other side of her desk and watched Mallory walk along the edge of the glass as though it was a tightrope. Jacqueline asked, "What time did you get here?"

Mallory stopped, put her hands on her hips, and said, "When did you get here? You looked awfully settled in. Could you not sleep again? Did you try the melatonin I got you?"

Like a scolded child, "The melatonin doesn't keep me asleep all night. It just helps me fall asleep."

"I bet you didn't read the directions." She was back on the tight rope. "It's almost eight. I didn't come in early. You've just lost track of time sitting in here executing Jack's master plans."

"Almost eight? Crap. I have to head down to HR and get some final approvals." Jacqueline said as she walked back to her side of her desk.

Off the window's edge, Mallory darted to Jacqueline's desk and leaned over it to ask, "About the editor jobs?" She batted her eyes demurely.

Smiling a sly smile, she said, "Wouldn't you like to know?"

Pouting, Mallory said, "Fine" and headed for the door. As she left, she said, "I'll come pick you up for lunch." Before Jacqueline could agree or disagree, Mallory was outside the door speaking to Mrs. Pennington and Grant.

4

Jacqueline's days had become mind-boggling. She was trying to be strong and reassuring to staff who were uncertain about their future, maintain the illusion that Jack could guide the Sun towards a promising future, and make all of these promises a reality. In what felt like a constant vacuum of time, Jacqueline found herself increasingly overwhelmed. In these moments, Jacqueline started to notice that Mallory's presence had become her saving grace. This Tuesday was no different.

As she had declared, Mallory returned promptly at twelve-thirty to go to lunch. Jacqueline was sitting behind her desk reviewing editorials for tomorrow's edition, but she could hear Mallory talking to Grant. She was asking him about his lunch. Jacqueline stopped reviewing, leaned back in her chair, and listened.

Excited that someone had asked about his lunch, Grant took Mallory on a chef's journey. He went to great extremes to explain how he seasoned and prepared his grilled tofu. Jacqueline giggled when she realized that Grant had no idea that Mallory was being sarcastic as she asked questions about his marinades. Instead of rescuing Grant, Jacqueline sat in her chair facing the closed door and smirked. She couldn't see Mallory's face, but she knew the face that she must be making. Her lips were pursed. Her eyes were lowered like a hawk searching for its prey. Mallory was certainly not listening, but she was waiting for a pause in the explanation of his recipe, so that she could say 'uh huh' and walk past him. These were the moments when people complained that she was churlish. Jacqueline would entertain all of their concerns and promise to address the issue with her. Rarely did she. Although Jacqueline recognized how things might have appeared, somewhere deep inside, Jacqueline was intrigued by how Mallory had this impact on people.

Having listened long enough to be in good spirits and fearing an afternoon of consoling Grant, Jacqueline called, "Oh, Mallory." In response, she heard Mallory say, "Gotta go," and her office door creak open.

Jacqueline said, "Close the door behind you."

"Ooh, should I close the blinds, too?"

"Very funny. Why are you tormenting Grant? He's smart, talented, and very efficient. He likes everyone. The man probably doesn't have a mean bone in his body."

Pretending to be innocent, Mallory said, "What? I was just talking to him. You told me to stop just walking by him like he didn't exist."

With an heavy exhale, Jacqueline stood up and said, "What's for lunch?"

"It's Tuesday."

"Is it? I guess that I forgot. Is Alex in the office? I thought that she might have lunch plans with Elet."

"Nope. She's here. Wait til you see her outfit," Mallory rolled her eyes.

"I'm sure everyone loves it...but, you, of course."

"Don't let me prejudice your decision. Judge for yourself."

"Okay. May we go?" Jacqueline asked pointing towards the door with an upwards pointed palm. As they left, Jacqueline closed the blinds to the office and turned off the lights. She stopped at Grant's desk to say that she was headed to lunch.

He spoke first, "Heading to lunch? Be back in an hour or so?"

She said, "Yes. How'd you know?" She hadn't overheard Mallory tell him and she didn't recall mentioning it to him this morning.

He said, "It's Tuesday" with shoulders and hands raised as if there was meaning that everyone knew about Tuesday.

"Am I that predictable?" she wondered as she waited on the elevator door to open.

As she and Mallory entered, he replied, "No, Mallory has me block an hour and a half out of your schedule every Tuesday for lunch." She looked at Mallory who turned and faced the back of the elevator but Jacqueline could see the corner of her lips lift up into a smile.

When the doors opened on the fourth floor, Jacqueline headed to the main aisle. Mallory pulled her arm and said, "Don't! If you go over there, we'll never make it to lunch."

Jacqueline said, "I was going to go get Alex."

"Don't! I'll text her." With that, Malory walked behind Jacqueline and pushed her in the direction of the elevator. When it arrived, Jacqueline selected the first floor. She was planning to go get Paige. Quickly, Mallory pressed L for lobby. She told Jacqueline that she had already spoken with Paige and reminded her about lunch as well.

Jacqueline retorted, "Well, I guess you've thought of everything."

The doors opened and Jacqueline and Mallory stepped out into the lobby. Plenty of passersby spoke to Jacqueline. As she tried to greet them all, Mallory put on her sunglasses and escorted Jacqueline outside into the sun. Having come into work at four in the morning, Jacqueline had felt tired in her office, but she was rejuvenated the instant that she walked out into the midday Florida sun. She stood there for a second soaking it all in.

Standing beside her, Mallory said, "See, this is better." And, it was. Jacqueline just wanted to stop and sit on the concrete flowerbeds. She was neither hungry nor thirsty. She just wanted to sit outside in the sun and share a few laughs with Mallory. She didn't dare say any of this. She just kept in step with Mallory's lead. It was Tuesday, after all, and lunch was to be shared with friends.

After a pleasant stroll across the street and down to the corner, the two entered a small Greek cafe, Spartan Times. Paige was seated in a large booth in the section dedicated to the Parthenon. The table was surrounded with food and she sat regally with a far-reaching smile.

Paige was a pleasant woman. She was full of compassion in all matters. She was petite and curvy without being short and fat. In fact, her maiden name was Smalls. Having completely embraced the crafting world, Paige painted and made jewelry in her spare time. She sold sell these items at craft and art shows in the area. Four years ago, while she was having pieces judged, the stage she stood on gave way. The stage assemblyman, Brett Little, recognized what was occurring and ran towards her. As she fell through the stage, he dashed to catch her...and missed. The two found themselves on the ground side-by-side.

They were married ten months later. Changing her name, she became Paige Smalls Little. Mallory joked about it often. Paige never saw the humor but never reprimanded her or complained about the constant teasing.

As Jacqueline approached the table, she realized immediately that Paige went to great lengths to arrive early enough at the café to order, not only her own lunch, but also foods for everyone. Mallory scooted into the booth, opposite of Paige, across from her salad, and said, "Why are you the only one with a drink?"

Jacqueline hung her head and said to Paige, "But, thanks for doing all this. This is great."

Ignoring Jacqueline, Paige responded to Mallory, "So, your ice wouldn't dilute your drink. I already ordered your drinks but I told the waitress to wait until you arrived to bring it."

Jacqueline pinched Mallory and said, "Paige, you're the best."

Known for quoting phrases that no one had ever heard of, she replied, "First one in the tub heats it up for everyone" and smiled. Then, she looked at Mallory and said, "Where's Alex?"

"Uh, I'm not her keeper." Mallory snapped back.

Cowering a bit, Paige said, "I only asked since she sits two rows from you."

Ever the peacemaker, Jacqueline diffused the moment, "Rumor has it that Alex had a late start. Mallory sent her a text to remind her about lunch. I'm sure that she's coming."

"You knew that she got to the office late?" Mallory questioned.

The server showed up with the drinks. While Jacqueline helped direct the waitress on where to place each drink, she said, "Of course. I have eyes everywhere. Nothing goes on that I don't know about." Actually, Evelyn and Mrs. Pennington were old friends. She heard them talking about Alex when Grant forgot to close her door.

When Jacqueline started to eat her gyro, Paige said, "Aren't we waiting on Alex?" *Crap*, Jacqueline thought. Quickly, she told Mallory, "Call her and see where she is." Mallory began dialing her number, but before she could finish,

Alex appeared. Paige flagged her to the table. Alex approached with her phone to her ear.

Jacqueline said, "Hi, Elet." Alex slapped Jacqueline on the arm and shushed her. Immediately, Alex ended the conversation. Before she sat down, Alex twirled around in her dress. Paige clapped as though Alex had just performed a dance routine. Mallory rolled her eyes at the exhibition and all Jacqueline asked, "Can I eat now?"

The four were good friends. Over lunch, they laughed and joked about clothes, work, dates, family, and children. They tasted each other dishes as though they hadn't tried them all before. Despite being stuffed with rice, lamb, feta, salad, and pita, Alex ordered loukoumades and coffee for the table. It was as if Alex had ordered a round of shots. When they arrived, there was much movement on the table as coffee was being creamed and sugared and the little golden-brown, doughy puffs placed on saucers.

In the midst of this, Alex, who had slipped off her shoes and was sitting on her right foot, said, "Let's talk business, bitches." She had their attention. Holding up three fingers, she said, "We leave for vacation in three days."

Paige let out a "Woot Woot."

With a spoon, Alex pointed to Paige and asked, "Are you ready? Is your mom going to help with the kids? Have you done everything that you need to do to be ready to go?"

Unenthusiastically, Paige said, "Yes."

"Paige!" Alex said firmly. She bounced on the booth seat so hard that she raised Paige up and watched her come back down again.

"Okay. I'm ready. I've done it all. Brett says not to worry, but I do. Bryce and Kelsey are so young. I haven't left them alone with him for a whole week before."

Looking up from her phone, Mallory said, "Those kids are four, almost five. They are fine at home with their father. Besides, your mom is down the street. And, the place that Jax rented is heaven."

Jacqueline could see the gears begin to churn inside Alex's mind. Jacqueline waited for Alex's question as it was sure to come. Alex now pointed to Mallory with the spoon and said, "Um, Mallory, how do you know it's a great place? I thought *Jax* found it."

"Yeah, she did, but I rode with her to check it out."

"Well, no one asked me if I wanted to go." Alex lifted her sculpted eyebrows and stared at Jacqueline and Mallory.

Jacqueline could feel Alex's glare. She tried to explain quickly, "It was a last minute deal. It seemed too good to be true. Mallory walked in while I was on the phone with the realtor who offered to let me tour the place. Mallory volunteered to ride down there with me to scope it out. Besides, I'm sure everyone was busy with something else."

"Oh, yeah. It was a great time. Since Zoe is at her dad's for the summer, I didn't have anything going on. So, I packed a bag and we headed down. The weather was incredible. We made a weekend of it." Mallory continued. She shared far more than Jacqueline had planned to admit.

"Yeah, we just checked the house out. I did the paperwork and we left. Rather than get a hotel by the interstate and drive back in the morning, Mallory thought it would be nice to go to Key West for the weekend since we were so close," explained a nervous Jacqueline.

Paige was nodding in agreement. Mallory had passed her phone to Paige who was scrolling through pictures of her and Jacqueline in the Keys. Jacqueline was seated across from Alex. She wasn't looking up at Alex, though. Instead, Jacqueline was swirling the residual honey, syrup, cinnamon mixture left on her saucer from the loukoumades. Alex spoke finally and said, "You two" still pointing with her spoon "went to Key West for the weekend and left Paige and I here?"

Drinking her tea, Jacqueline was staring outside the pane glass window wondering how long they had been here. Under her breath, she said, "It wasn't really planned."

Adding fuel to the fire, Mallory said, "Except the car rental and suite at the resort...."

Alex slapped her hand on the table and said, "No more vacations between you two. It's all of us or none of us. Capiche?"

Mallory giggled and continued trying to explain to Paige where the pictures were taken. Jacqueline held her head down. When the waitress appeared with the check, Jacqueline was rescued. She jumped up and followed her to the register to pay.

Noticing that Jacqueline had fled, Alex inquired, "How much of a raise do you think she got from Jack? Evelyn said it was life-changing money. Her words, not mine."

"Well, whatever it is, she deserves it. She is amazing and has done great things for the company. I'm excited to work for her and, even more proud that we are friends," Paige said.

Alex and Mallory both rolled their eyes at Paige. Paige said, "What?" As Jacqueline completed her transaction at the counter, the women stood up and walked towards the door.

Jacqueline joined them at the door and held it open as they walked out. Mallory waited on her while Alex and Paige sauntered ahead. Mallory said, "You know, you don't have to always pay for everything."

"I don't," said Jacqueline.

"Yeah, you do, but we'll work on that," said Mallory, walking beside her. Jacqueline chuckled and kept pace. The sun felt nice on her face and she had a full belly. It was a nice day to laugh and have a good time with friends. Jacqueline thought, *I love Tuesdays.*

5

When Alex arrived back to her desk after lunch, her voicemail light was on. For a moment, she thought of not listening to the messages. She knew who it was. Psychically, she knew that it wasn't work-related or a call from Elet or a call from an old friend or, even, a call she wanted to return. Instead of continuing to dodge her fate, she exhaled and pushed the voicemail button. Cradling the phone to her ear, she heard, "You have three new messages.

```
    Message one - I know you're avoiding me. I'm going to
keep calling.
    Message two - You're such a bitch. You think it's all
about you. I don't know why I even bother.
    Message three - Don't worry. I won't bother you
again.
```

Alex leaned back in her chair and tapped herself in the forehead repeatedly with the receiver. Every voicemail was from Josephine, her older sister. None of the messages said what she wanted, but Alex knew. Josephine would say that she wanted Alex's help with her parent's anniversary party on Friday. Alex knew that Jo didn't want or need Alex's help. Jo didn't need anyone's help. She only wanted people around to prove to them how little she really needed them. As her head started to pound, Alex stopped tapping her forehead and decided to return her sister's calls.

"In Touch Salon, this is Mimi. How can I help you?"

"Hey, Mimi," Alex said rubbing her head, "It's Alex. Is Jo available?"

"Hey, big-time! Girl, I read your piece on that club out in Clearwater. Girl, me and Erika rode out there and it was as good as you said it was. We got free drinks all night when I told them that we grew up together and still hang out."

Alex thought, *Great, glad I could help y'all get your drink on*, but said, "I'm glad I could help. Let Jo know that I called her back and that I'll try to catch her later on tonight."

"Wait. Don't hang up! She's here. She can talk. Alex, you there?"

Rubbing wrinkles into her face, Alex replied, "Yep." Then, just like that, her stomach hurt, the way it always had when she knew that Jo was going to be upset with her. The pain reminded her exactly why she didn't visit, why she went to college instead of working in the salon with her sister, and why she didn't feel bad for the person she had become.

And, then, there was Jo, "Well, hello there, baby sister." It was the passive-aggressiveness that felt like home.

"Hi, Jo. How's it going? Is it slow in the shop?"

"Nah, it's pretty steady, but I had a minute and we need to talk. Are you coming to the party?"

Now, with her hand on her face, she said, "Of course, I am. They're my parents, too. Who asks that?"

"Well, I'm just asking. You said you were gonna help but you didn't do that. So, I just don't know with you. I call. You don't answer. And I think, she's working. She'll call me back. But, you don't. So, I just don't know anymore."

She thought she might vomit but decided that it was equally as possible that her pain could erupt from a lower orifice. Alex didn't say anything. She just sat there thinking about the pain in her belly. She didn't know if Jo was still talking or had stopped. She didn't know if the topic had changed or if they were still talking about how horrible of a person, sister, and daughter she was. Finally, she thought of something to say and just started talking, "Yeah, so, what do you need me to do?"

Jo had been talking, but she didn't mind the interruption in her diatribe. She responded, "Well, I have done almost everything."

Quickly, Alex responded, "Oh, okay, then, I will see you on Friday. Don't forget..."

Jo cut her off. Alex rolled her eyes. Jo said, "Wouldn't you like it if there was nothing for you to do? Well, baby sister, it would be great if you could come early and help decorate and you can pick up the cake."

"Consider it done. What time do you need us there?"

"Us?" questioned Jo.

"Jo, you knew that Elet and Jacqueline were coming. And, I'm bringing Mallory and Paige. You've met them before."

"Oh, yeah, I remember. I'm glad they're coming. They will make sure that you get here on time and Jacqueline will make sure you pull your weight." And, with that, Jo hung up.

Alex slammed the phone into the cradle. It was a good thing that Evelyn had left for the day. She certainly would have told Alex to simmer down. Now, with a headache and stomach pains, Alex stood up and headed to the bathroom.

Rather than saunter, Alex walked down the aisle with purpose. She passed Mallory who was talking to another staff writer, Hannah. They both looked up at Alex. It was obvious something was wrong. Mallory called after her, "You okay?"

Over her shoulder, Alex said, "I hate my sister."

Mallory responded, "I hate my brother."

And, Hannah joined in, "I can't stand my father."

When she got to the bathroom, her stomach was starting to settle. She was careful not to wash her face for fear that she would wash off all her makeup. Instead, she stood there running cold water over her hands. She even cupped some of it and drank. Griping the sides of the sink, she looked at herself in the mirror. She stayed there staring until she heard someone else enter the restroom. She gathered herself together, walked to the door, and shut off the light. Then, she heard, "Hey" from whomever she left in the bathroom. She replied, "Sorry," but she didn't turn the light back on.

She walked back down the aisle. Luckily, it was unusually empty. She walked past her row and headed to the back elevator. When it opened, Grant and Mrs. Pennington smiled at her. She didn't smile back. Mrs. Pennington rose and spoke first, "Honey, are you okay?"

Grant said, "Are you sick?," covering his mouth with his shirt and pushing back from his desk.

She waved them both off as if she was shooing away an insect. She explained, "Just a long day." She pointed to Jacqueline's closed door, and asked, "Does she have a moment?"

Grant said, "She just got off a conference call, but, if you just want to tell her that you need to leave for the day, I can tell her for you."

Angry now, she lashed out, "No, Grant. I don't need you to talk for me. I'm a grown ass woman."

Unabashedly, Grant responded, "Spicy! Go, right in then."

Alex opened the door without knocking. She said nothing as she walked across the office to the chair in front of Jacqueline's desk. Jacqueline watched her the entire time but stayed quiet. Slumped in the black leather chair, Alex said, "When I was little, I thought me and my sister were going to be close. Best friends. You know how some kids are best friends with their siblings. I thought that was going to be Jo and me. But, she can't stand me and I can't stand her."

Now, playing therapist, Jacqueline said, "I'm pretty sure that neither of you hates the other."

"Oh, it's true. You've seen us together. We fight and scream."

"Yeah, it gets crazy. But, I think that you are probably both disappointed in one another."

"Disappointed? I'm not disappointed in her. I just wish, I just wish...she was different!" Alex finally expressed.

"I'm sure that she wishes the same about you. Come on, we all think that you're great," Jacqueline said, "but, Jo leads a different life than you do. Your idea of greatness and her idea of greatness are two different things. That's all." Now, cleaning her glasses, she went on, "Look, my family wanted something different than who they got in me. I'm sure that deep down they are a little disappointed. They may never admit it, but they have to be. We've learned through the years to make the most of it. And, I'm not sure that you and Jo ever have."

"Ugh. This is why she likes you better than me," Alex admitted. "Hey, don't forget that we're going to the party at my parents on Friday night."

"I know. I already got their gift."

"Their gift? You bought my parents a gift?" Alex sounded stunned. Moreover, she realized that she hadn't gotten them a gift.

"Well, yeah. Of course, I've known them for years and it's their anniversary. I think guests are expected to bring gifts. And, yes, I remember that we're all going to the party," said Jacqueline, placing her glasses back on her face.

"How are we gonna work out the cars?" asked Alex.

"Well, I think your fabulous boss gave you the day off. Paige is also off. Do you remember any of this?" Alex didn't and Jacqueline could tell. "Paige volunteered to help you with last minute party stuff. Then, the two of you are going to drive to the rental house. I'll be here waiting on Mallory. She is working for part of the morning. When she's done, we'll head out and meet you and Paige at the house. If we get everything done on some kind of decent timetable, we should have a few minutes to clean up before we leave for the party," Jacqueline said, proud of herself for having a master plan.

"Mallory is working part of Friday? And, you," pointing to Jacqueline, "are waiting for her?" asked Alex.

Jacqueline raised he left shoulder and squinted her left eye, and responded, "Of course."

"Of course?"

"Of course."

"Jacqueline, what the hell's going on?"

Confused, Jacqueline looked around. "What're you talking about?"

"Me? What am *I* talking about? You two are taking trips to Key West together. You two saw the vacation house together. You two didn't even wait on me for lunch. You two sat by each other at lunch, and now, you're waiting on her on Friday. What the fuck?"

Again, Jacqueline shrugged.

"Listen, we've been friends a long time. We used to hang out all the time. I know you. And, I'm friends with Mallory, but I want you to tell me if something is going on."

"Oh my God! Nothing is going on. We're just hanging out." Pointing at Alex and then herself, "Like we used to before you fell in love."

"Mmmhmm. You know that I know what you do. I just don't want you to do it in our circle. Mallory is a pain in the ass, but I love her. That's my girl. Okay? Can we just agree that you won't do your seek and conquer routine?"

"We're just friends. We are the only two people who aren't with someone. That's all!" reaffirmed Jacqueline.

"And, have you thought about that? Is she talking to anyone? Why isn't she dating anymore?"

Starting to become angry, Jacqueline said, "I don't know if she is talking to anyone. She could be. She could be out there on the phone with some dude right now."

"Wouldn't she have told us? We're friends, remember? And, what about you? Why aren't you out there trying to date someone? You told me that you were tired of just being casual, but I don't see you trying to meet anyone. Is that because you think you already have?" Alex lifted her eyebrows and folded her arms.

"I don't even want to know what you think is going on. We hang out. Have dinners. See movies. It's no big deal. Drop it." Jacqueline was mad now.

"Anything you say, *Jax.*" Alex pursed her lips and left Jacqueline's office abruptly. When she left, Jacqueline walked from behind her desk to the glass wall. She looked out over the floor. Off to the right, she saw the top of Mallory's head. It was always easy to find her red locks in the sea of black, brown, gray, bald, and blond. Jacqueline repeated aloud, "We're just friends." As she said it, Mallory looked up at the glass, saw Jacqueline standing there, smiled, and waved. Jacqueline smiled back.

At four, Alex packed up to leave for the day. She had been at work for six solid, unproductive hours. She gathered up the makeup and notes that lay about her desk. All of it was shoved into her purse. As she stood up, she was pleased to discover that her saunter had returned. Men stopped to look. Women said, "Good night." But, in Alex's mind, there were all saying the same thing - *Good night, Alexandra Stevens, most recognized writer of the Sun Tribune. Thanks for making our pathetic lives just a little bit brighter.*

As she reached the end of the aisle, Alex could see Mallory at the copy machine. As she sauntered towards the door, Mallory quipped, "Night, bitch," and hit her in the butt with her newly made photocopies. It ruined the entire praising dialogue Alex had been imagining. She hung her head and left the floor.

As she exited the building, Elet called, "Hey, baby. You didn't forget about me, did you?"

Smiling at construction workers and twirling in a semi-circle for their attention, she said, "How could I? I'm leaving now to go get pretty. Where are we going?"

"It's a surprise. I'm not telling you."

Seriousness crossed her face and her pace slowed. She said, "No, honey, don't you remember the last surprise? You took me to the Rocky Point off the Causeway and made me s'mores."

"You know that I love it down there. It's great."

"Yes, baby, it's great, but you told me to dress for a romantic night out. I was in a strapless Michael Kors dress and Jimmy Choo's sitting on the tailgate while you made s'mores."

"On the beach. S'mores on the beach. S'mores on the beach at night."

Rolling her eyes, she gave up. Most women would have loved that. All women love Elet. Hell, some guys love Elet. That's why they were perfect together. She thought how they were a power couple. Successful. Attractive. Big personality. They had the world at their fingertips.

Feeling bad when Alex did not respond, he said, "I promise that tonight won't be like that."

In turn, she promised to go to the causeway one night next week for s'mores. She knew how happy that would make him. Ever thoughtful, he told her to drive safely and he would be at her house by six thirty. She made kissing sounds in the phone until he hung up.

6

The natural decline of energy hit Jacqueline about two. She had been in the office since the very early hours of the morning. She had worked hard, had countless meetings, and enjoyed the company of her closest friends. Since lunch, she had yawned fifty or more times. She had made four cups of tea and chewed a pack of gum. She was sitting behind her desk gazing outwards - through the glass over the newsroom floor - when her mind began to wonder.

In her daydream, the sun was shining bright overhead. She could feel its warmth on her back. She was riding a motorcycle, more cruiser than crotch rocket. She had dark, wrap-around sunglasses on her face. She felt the mesh of a motorcycle jacket adhered to her skin, yet she could feel a breeze flowing through it. She was cruising along an oceanfront road enjoying the fresh air. As she drew close to an intersection, she noticed a red, convertible sports car approaching from the opposite direction. The car was a make she could not place, but she was more interested in the driver than she was in the car itself. She lowered her sunglasses to peer in the car's direction. As she did, she noticed the other driver staring back her. Jacqueline was too far away to make out the details of the woman's face. She could see that the woman was wearing sunglasses. She noticed the thin straps of a tank top and loose, unconfined hair flowing in the wind. Running the light, Jacqueline aimed to move her bike closer to the woman. But, before Jacqueline pulled alongside the car, she was awoken from her daydream.

"Uh, are you in there?" Mallory said. Jacqueline heard her, but she couldn't respond. Trying to hold onto the dream as it began to fade away, Jacqueline leaned forward to talk to the woman in her dream. But, the woman was disappearing. As Mallory spoke again, the woman dissipated completely, "I think you should go home and get some sleep."

"Huh, what? Me? Oh, I'm fine," Jacqueline, responded finally. "It was just a little daydream."

"Yes, I noticed you sitting there peering out over our heads. I looked at you so long that other people started to look as well." Mallory pointed to the staff. She stood from behind her desk and looked down at the news floor. Pockets of the staff giggled and waved at an embarrassed Jacqueline. Mallory began to laugh.

"Well, that's embarrassing."

"Yea, that's why I came up here. I thought someone should put you out of your misery. You really should go home and get some rest."

Jacqueline rubbed her face. As she started to stretch she said, "I can't. I have to meet Jack at his house in an hour. And, if I go to sleep now, then I will sleep until the middle of the night and wake up at the witching hour. I'll be right back here tomorrow at four in the morning." Jacqueline sat behind her desk and put her cheek against the cool glass.

Mallory sat in the chair on the other side. "That's true. How long is the meeting with Jack?"

"Not long, it's just to touch base. It'll be an hour at most." Jacqueline yawned again.

"Okay. Are you going straight home after the meeting?"

"Sure am."

"Okay. Text me when you get home and get settled. I will let you sleep until six, and then I will wake you up."

"Why six?" Jacqueline was calculating in her mind. *An hour meeting with Jack would end about three-thirty or so. It'll take about a half hour to get home and another thirty minutes to settle in. I will fall asleep at four thirty, and then she's gonna call at six? What the hell?*

"For dinner," Mallory said.

Jacqueline was tired and confused. She worried that she had forgotten something. She tried quickly to run through all the conversations, emails, and IMs that she had received. She remembered no standing plans for this evening. Finally, she had to admit, "Do I have plans that I have forgotten?"

"None that I know of, but I'm trying to get you to make some," she smiled and bit the tip of her tongue.

Jacqueline had a burst of energy. Her mind cleared and she thought, *an hour and a half is long enough.* "Should I make reservations?"

"Nah, you're too tired for that. We can just stay in."

Surprised, Jacqueline said, "You're gonna cook for me?"

"Hell no! You know, I don't cook. I'm gonna get off from work, go home and change clothes, go pick up a few things from the store, bring them to your house, and entertain you while you cook. Then, we're gonna eat, watch a movie, and you're gonna drift off to sleep again."

"Well, I guess that's a plan. What am I cooking?" Jacqueline said as she started to gather her notes, folio, laptop, and other belongings.

"I don't know. I'll let the store guide me." Mallory stood up and walked to the office door.

"Won't you be upset if you come to my place and I fall asleep?"

"No way. Who wouldn't want a giant penthouse all to herself?" Mallory giggled. She and Jacqueline walked out of the office. Jacqueline said good night to Grant as Mallory pressed the button for the elevator. When the door opened and the two were inside, Mallory said, "Besides, this might be the only way that I make sure that you finally get some sleep." Jacqueline didn't say anything, but she peered at Mallory who was looking at the gold filigree. She smirked. Mallory whirled around and smiled.

As they exited into the lobby, the light was so intense that Jacqueline could barely see her way out. The light shining through the windows reflected off the marble was so strong that Jacqueline thought she'd walked through the pearly gates of heaven.

Head down, snaking through the people doing their business in the lobby, Jacqueline was anxious to make it outdoors. Before she could reach them, she heard her name. She couldn't place the voice, but a woman was approaching her calling her name. The stranger stepped in the path of the sun and gave Jacqueline a glimpse of her. Desperately, Jacqueline was thinking of names – Susan, Carmen, Stephanie, Jessica. She hated these moments when people remembered her far better than she had remembered them.

The woman was in beige wedge heels and a flowered sundress. Jacqueline thought that she looked like she was out of a catalog. With a bright smile on her face, this woman with straight, straw-colored hair was stalking her with confidence. Obviously, she knew Jacqueline, but Jacqueline had very little idea of who she was. Jacqueline had decided that the smile on her face and the speed with which she was walking confirmed that she and the woman had had a personal relationship, not a business one. This discovery made Jacqueline feel all the more uncomfortable. Jacqueline searched for a way out of the lobby. She looked for someone with whom she could hurriedly go and speak. As Jacqueline glanced from right to left, all the faces around her were a blur – all the faces, except for Mallory. Mallory had been walking Jacqueline out of the office. They had just been making plans for the evening. Now, Jacqueline felt the mounting pressure of a past she liked to forget coming straight for her.

As the woman drew nearer, her arms were outstretched. Jacqueline grabbed the straps of her messenger bag as if she thought to run, but the time for avoidance had passed. With another utterance of Jacqueline's name, the woman pulled Jacqueline close. At the time of embrace, Jacqueline wrapped her left arm around the stranger's back. Inside the woman's embrace, Jacqueline's anxiety faded. She knew from the stranger's scent that she was, Tania Singer.

Wiggling free, Jacqueline addressed her, "Hi, Tania. How's it been?" Jacqueline was beaming, not at seeing the woman, but proud that she remembered who she was.

"My God, it feels like forever. It's been…years." The woman replied, quickly. "You look amazing. I'm so glad that we ran into each other. I wonder about you from time to time." Jacqueline wasn't quite sure how to responded to that. She hadn't thought of her. With nothing to add, Jacqueline opted not to answer. She was certain that Tania would continue without prodding.

As she stood still waiting on Tania to continue, Jacqueline could see Mallory, standing beside her with her weight shifted to her right leg and her left leg fully extended. Mallory's arms were crossed and she appeared to be sizing up Tania very, very slowly. She was looking her over from top to bottom. Tania continued, "I was down here dropping off my neighbor's spare key. She locked herself out of her apartment." Instantly, Tania became excited, "Do you know Sydney? Sydney Cullins? She's one of the phone operators. She's short. Dark eyes. Dark hair. Real thick, country accent?" Jacqueline thought that it was ironic that Tania made that comment with her own thick country accent.

"Sorry, I don't know her. I don't get to know the operators as much as I should. I'm the Managing Editor, now." Jacqueline replied.

"Oh, well. Congratulations. Things have worked out great for you, haven't they?" Jacqueline thanked Tania and noticed that Tania was standing still, not saying a word, but she was obviously thinking. She repeated Jacqueline's name. "Jacqueline Emerson. Jacqueline Emerson." She was rubbing her indexed finger over her lips. Jacqueline fixated on her lipstick. It was an orangish-red and appeared to last forever. Despite the firm sweeping motions on her lips, the color remained perfect.. Jacqueline thought that she would like very much to talk to Mallory about this, but as quickly as she thought of Mallory, she knew that the later conversation with Mallory would not be about lipstick.

Tania made her pitch. "You know, I would love for you and me to get together sometime." Tania's eyes appeared to be dancing more than they had a few moments ago.

Jacqueline felt relieved. She had discovered her way out of this wildly, uncomfortable moment. "That sounds great. I was on my way out of the office or we could've just stood here and made plans to get together. But, I tell you what," Jacqueline reached into her bag for her card case. She retrieved one and handed it to Tania. "Here's my card. Call my assistant and he will help you set up a date for us to get together. It was so good to see you." She leaned in and gave Tania a nice one-armed hug. This was her classic finishing move. Jacqueline felt that things had gone well and was preparing to run away when Mallory spoke.

"By the way, I'm Mallory. It was very nice to meet you. Tania, isn't it?" Mallory said, as she shook Tania's delicate hand.

"Oh, I'm sorry. I'm Tania Singer. Yes, it was nice to meet you, too."

Hoping to prevent any further interaction, Jacqueline said, "I really must be going, but we will get together soon." She nudged Mallory in the directions of the doors. They walked outside without speaking. Mallory's silence left Jacqueline to wonder what she was thinking. Once Jacqueline felt like they had escaped the building, she stopped at a cement planter, dropped her bag, and sat down.

"Let's have it."

Arms folded, Mallory said, "Who's Tania?"

"Well, to be honest, I'm not completely sure."

"What?"

"Well, I spent a lot of those last few minutes trying to figure out who she was. I didn't even know her name until she hugged me."

Rolling her eyes, Mallory said, "Don't tell me. When you felt her in your arms, you knew."

"No, but that's a good line. I knew who she was when I smelled her. The suntan lotion jogged my memory." Mallory laughed. Jacqueline smiled. "It has to have been years ago. Many years ago. Back in those years when girls all run together in your mind because, you weren't really investing a lot in them. I couldn't tell you much of anything else about her except that I hate the smell of a girl who sunbathes. And the dislike started with that girl." Jacqueline was pointing in Tania's direction who had long since walked down the street.

"Um, you gave her your card. She has your cell number, now."

"No, she doesn't. Some cards have my cell. Some don't." She tossed her card case to Mallory who opened it and saw a deck of cards on one side with all of Jacqueline's information and another set of cards on the other side with only business information. Beaming with pride, Jacqueline said, "Come on. I'm smarter than that. Now, just remind me to tell Grant that I will never be available when she calls." Jacqueline stood up and smiled.

Mallory shook her head. "Oh, don't worry. I'll stop by and tell Grant myself when I get back upstairs."

"I bet you will." Jacqueline placed her bag back on her shoulder. "Here," she removed a key from her key ring and handed it to Mallory. "I'll see you at six."

"How are you gonna get inside? You just gave me your key." Mallory said holding it up in the air as Jacqueline walked away.

Jacqueline answered without looking back at her. "That's the spare." She walked into the sunshine of the afternoon replaying the last few moments in her head and laughing aloud.

7

Alex had planned to be ready at six thirty, but it didn't happen. In fact, Elet was so accustomed to her tardiness that he had lied about when they needed to leave. He expected to arrive to a girlfriend, singing and dancing, with a towel wrapped around her body and only half a face of makeup. When he arrived, he wasn't disappointed. He had knocked on her door a few times, but Alex was in the back of the apartment. When she didn't answer, he used his key and let himself in. He was carrying a dozen roses, so he called out for her. Again, there was no answer. However, he could hear her bad karaoke rendition of some song he'd heard her try to sing before. He walked straight to the sound of her wailing. Upon entering the door, there she was dancing and singing, wrapped in a towel as he had expected. She was so enthralled in her routine that she jumped when she realized that he was standing there with roses tucked under his arm filming her on his cell phone.

"Stop it, Elet, or I swear I will post the one of you on the toilet," she croaked.

He stopped and laughed. "Fine," he said and handed her the flowers.

She thanked him for the flowers and said, "You look very nice wearing all those wonderful clothes your girlfriend bought you." He twirled around for her inspection. When she leaned in to kiss him, she was struck by his smell. "Well, well, well, Mr. Elet Walden, are you trying to impress a girl by wearing cologne and being clean shaven?"

If she had asked, he would say that he didn't like or need this praise, but, in truth, she knew that he loved it. As he headed out of the room, he noticed that there was a pair of jeans, an undershirt, and a button-up plaid shirt hanging on the back of her bedroom door.

Looking at it and pointing, he said, "Is your other boyfriend here?"

She laughed and said, "No, silly, that was your back-up outfit." Shooing him out of the room, she went back to singing and putting on her makeup. He went to the kitchen and put the flowers in water. He sat down to watch TV for what he assumed would be an hour long wait.

He hadn't been waiting more than thirty minutes when Alex paused the music to listen for movement in the living room. She could hear the television, but she didn't hear him. She wondered if he had fallen asleep. She walked into the living room to find it empty. She looked around the apartment and didn't see him. She called his name, but there was no response. She had returned to her room to get her cell phone to call him when she heard the door open.

"Where'd you go?" she asked.

"To my truck." he replied. "Is that okay?"

"I just didn't hear you."

"I was outside." He said pointing towards the door. "Are you planning to get dressed anytime soon?"

"As a matter of fact, I'm about to get dressed. Now, sit down and get ready for the big moment."

Rolling his eyes, he sat down. She returned wearing a blue cap-sleeved dress with lace panels on the side and on the top. She had twisted her hair, so that it had long, ringlet like curls. He was stunned. She pranced around in front of the television in her strappy, silver heels wanting his attention. And she, very obviously, had it.

He stood up and walked toward her. Placing his hand behind her head, he pulled her closer for a kiss. After kissing for a few minutes, she rested her head on his shoulder. He said, "You look amazing."

"You ain't half bad yourself," she teased. "Now, let's go before my ankles start to hurt."

As they drove along the interstate, she leaned his way and held his hand. She asked, "Are we close?"

"It's not too far." He smiled as he replied. She knew that he had something up his sleeve, but she didn't dare ask. She was looking forward to this surprise. He asked about her day. She still hadn't told him about running late or having words with her sister. It wasn't that he wouldn't understand. It was more that he would have some positive outlook. Elet was great for that. He wouldn't just slum in your anger or insanity with you. He would stand tall and try to pull you out. She wasn't sure that she wanted to be pulled up, but she did have something to tell him.

"Get this. Jacqueline and Mallory went to Key West together."

"What? Really? Without you guys?" She knew that she had peaked his interest. She enjoyed that he was a gossipy girl.

"I know, right. I asked Jacqueline about it and she said it was no big deal. That, she was going down to take a look at the house we're staying in for vacation and Mallory offered to tag along, so they thought they'd make a weekend of it and go to the Keys."

"You don't just go to Key West. That's a long ride no matter where you live. And, you can't tell me that Jacqueline did that on the spur of the moment. She doesn't do anything on the spur of the moment."

"There's something going on," Alex said biting her lip. "But, Jacqueline wouldn't tell me."

"Do you think that there's something going on," he was making air quote, "or, do you think that Jacqueline would like for something to be going on?"

"I don't know, but I told her to calm down. That would totally ruin everything. In just a few days, we are spending a week together in a house on the beach. I don't want shit to get weird."

"Maybe, I'll try to get it out of her at the party on Friday night. You'll be busy entertaining and being with your family. I'll talk to her." Elet pointed at himself with his thumbs.

"You'll talk to her?"

"Yes, remember? She and I go way back." He smiled with one side of this mouth and nodded as if to celebrate this fact.

"Uh huh. Well, don't go too far. Besides, I may need you to run defense between me and Jo."

"Oh, I almost forgot. Jo called me today. She wanted to know what you were doing to help."

Forgetting that the cabin of a sports car did not require loud voices, she screamed, "WHAT THE FUCK IS WRONG WITH HER?" Alex was rocking back and forth in the passenger's seat and stomping her heels on the floorboard. "She drives me fucking crazy."

He looked shocked. "Calm down, babe. I told her that I didn't know. That you had a lot going on, but I told her that I would help. I'm going to head to your parent's house on Friday about lunchtime and help Dom set up tents and pick up chairs. Ya know, just run errands to help out." He was stroking her hand.

This calmed her. She settled back into the seat and placed her hand over his. She knew that he had good intentions. But, she also knew that Jo knew exactly who to call to get what she wanted. She was boiling inside, but told Elet, "That was so sweet. I told her that I would come before the party and help as well. I gotta remember to get that damn cake, too."

Placing her hand on his chest, he said, "After the party, I won't see you for a week." He began to cry a fake cry.

Alex pulled her hand back and said, "Eight days. It'll go by in a flash." In the midst of their conversation, she had forgotten that they were heading to dinner. Noticing her surroundings, she said, "Uh, isn't this the way to the Clearwater Marina?"

"Yep" he said with a big smile.

She tried to think of a seafood restaurant that would be in the area. She could not think of anywhere the two of them could go where they were not overdressed. Racking her brain, she looked around as he parked the car. As he turned off the engine and turned to get out, she sat still convinced they were eating at the lunch counter inside. He walked to her side of the car, opened the door, and reached for her hand. As they walked, she noticed they were not angling towards the door of the marina but to the eastern side of the building.

With the marina behind them, there stood a 100-foot yacht adorned with lights from forward to aft. It was gorgeous. Her eagerness gave way and she was holding his arm as well as his hand. Intertwined, they smiled from ear to ear. As they walked aboard, a steward met them. "Good evening, folks. Please enjoy the ship. We sail in 20 minutes. Dinner will be served in 40 minutes. Feel free to explore and partake of drinks at either bar." He pointed upwards.

Alex was a writer for the Lifestyles department of the Sun. Her career was going to all of the happening events in the Bay area. She had been to gourmet restaurants, food truck competitions, art gallery openings, plays, operas, and concerts. Rarely was she stunned. Unfortunately for Elet, rarely was she impressed. But, tonight she was impressed. She looked around the room staring at the bright orange and red swirls in the carpet. She glanced upward at the giant glass chandeliers overhead. He leaned in and whispered, "There's a party upstairs and one on the main desk. Do you wanna go check it out?"

She didn't respond, but she allowed him to lead her up the winding stairs to the bar. Once they reached the top, the bar area was full of other guests. He said, "Why don't you get us that table? I'm going to run to the bathroom. Then I'll get us some drinks and meet you." He kissed her gently and watched her make her way head towards the empty tables.

When he exited the men's room, he scanned the area for her. He found her sitting at a table by the window. There was a man standing at the table holding onto the back of the empty chair. Elet wondered if the man may have known her from one of her many events or if the man may have seen her face in the paper. Then, he realized that it could very well be the case that this man saw a beautiful woman sitting at a table alone and went to talk to her. Without angst, anger, or fear, Elet thought, *hahaha, man, she's mine.* Confidently, he turned and went to the bar to order their drinks.

While Alex was sitting at the table by herself, men had complimented her, offered to buy her drinks, and most asked if they could join her. She had enjoyed the attention. And, if Elet weren't with her, she would have entertained their offers. She would have enjoyed the drinks and more of the conversations. She would have laughed and joked and, even, flirted. Chances are likely that she might have even given one of them her phone number. Although she loved Elet, she never thought of enjoying the company of other people, men included, as something that she should stop doing. When the last man, John, came to talk, she listened intently. He was a tall, dark-skinned lawyer with a shiny bald head from Sarasota. He was in Clearwater with his brother celebrating his brother's recent divorce. Alex had teased that a romantic dinner cruise was an odd place to celebrate divorce. She hadn't liked John's response that he and his brother were 'getting back in the game.' She had disliked even more how he constantly flexed his forearm muscles as he held onto the empty chair across from her. She had dismissed John from her mind.

With John still standing at the table trying to talk to her, she scanned the room for Elet. Eventually, she spotted his lanky six foot two inch frame at the bar. She thought of how great he looked tonight. She was proud of how well he had matched his printed, button-up shirt with the his new dark jeans, and the wonderful pair of wingtips that she gave him as a Christmas present. He looked incredible.

When John finally left her, she was able to focus on Elet. She saw a blonde talking to him. The Bottle Blonde was holding onto Elet's right arm pretending to be friendly, but certainly flirting. Bottle blondes were everything that Alex hated. She was a woman who looked like all the other women. To Alex, she was one of those women who saw Christie Brinkley as the model to whom they should all aim. There was nothing unique about her. This bottle blonde sat at the bar in her white chinos and striped, sailor shirt wearing black heels. Her legs were crossed, but they revealed nothing about her. They were certainly not her chief asset. And, Alex thought there was no point to crossing your legs on a barstool unless they were the epitome of your package.

However, this Bottle Blonde had captured Elet's attention. He was looking at her with his big, blue, ocean eyes. He was smiling, Alex was certain of it. She started to fume. Arm muscles tried to come back and talk with her again, but she couldn't pay attention to him. She needed to monitor the bar. She wished Mallory were here. Mallory would have walked over and said something to that whore.

Alex sat and stared, hoping she could read Elet's lips and figure out what was causing this girl to laugh so hard that she lost control of her neck muscles so easily. In that moment, she thought of going to meet him at the bar and pretend to have been looking for him. Elet would never ignore her and that Bottle Blonde would see that he had an attractive, engaging, well-dressed girlfriend. Just as she made up her mind to go over there, she saw Elet pick up two glasses from the bar, nod his close-cropped sandy-blonde locks at Bottle Blonde, and head towards her. Carrying an Appletini, in one hand, and a craft beer, in the other, he was careful not to spill anything. As he strode across the floor, the Blonde looked to see where he was going. Alex made sure to make eye contact with her and smile the smile that says *yeah, bitch, he's mine.* When he placed her drink on the table in front of her, she looked up at him, smiled, and said, "Thanks, baby."

He said, "Sorry about the wait. The bar is crowded."

Alex looked around him at Bottle Blonde and said, "Yeah, I see."

They sat there at the table waiting to head into the dining room. She asked how the house was going. Elet had bought a beautiful, old bungalow in Seminole Heights, a historic neighborhood on the rebound. He had decided that it was time to leave behind his loft and buy a beautiful place in which he could both live and work. Seminole Heights, he reasoned would be perfect. Admittedly, the area had a lot of personality with historic buildings and bungalows rather than master planned communities. Parts of the area still had the old streetcar lines intact. Elet had done well as a photographer and commercial designer. Even, the paintings and photography that he enjoyed doing as a hobby were going to be in their own gallery exhibit next month. He had hinted many times that he wanted Alex to move in. She had dodged every conversation. She planned to dodge it, again, if he mentioned it tonight.

"Oh, I forgot to tell you." He always said that. It didn't matter what it was. He always said he forgot to tell you. Actually, he never really forgot, but it seemed his days were so full of interesting discoveries that there were too many worthwhile conversations to have. "I was pulling out sheet rock to make the kitchen more open when I smelled something amazing. I knew it wasn't me." He laughed and touched her thigh. Alex thought, *eat your heart out, Blondie.* "So, I was walking around the house sniffing and sniffing, but I couldn't figure it out. After ten minutes, I gave up and focused on finishing the sheet rock. When I was done, I went outside to sit down and I smelled it again. I walked all along the house and when I came to the kitchen window, the smell was amazing. I dug around in the grass there and found ginger growing. There's ginger growing wild right there in the yard."

He was excited. Alex could care less about the ginger. Nevertheless, his smile made her smile. He held her hand on the table and said, "Ginger." She was going to make a joke, but nothing came to her. When the horn sounded, Alex was startled. She thought it might be a fire alarm. She was reassured when crew members announced it was time for dinner. All of the guests lined up to be seated in the dining area. Elet had arranged for them a window seat. It was a wonderful table with a great view of the water. Their waiter, David, introduced himself and mentioned the specials of the day. Alex was busy staring at the sun lighting the bay on fire. She hadn't heard a thing the waiter said. All she knew is that Elet ordered bread, two salads, and another rounds of drinks for them. He always knew how to get rid of the waiter when she wasn't ready to order.

She was still staring out the window when the waiter returned. She did not look up at David, but she did move her arms so that he could place the salad in front of her. She mumbled 'thank you' as he lowered the breadbasket onto the table. It was such a beautiful ship and such a wonderful night that she never noticed that Elet had gotten out of his seat. As she reached for bread from the basket, she felt something hard. She picked up the basket and pulled it to her to investigate. She had her face in the basket when everyone in the room, except for her, noticed Elet was on one knee beside her. Searching for what she thought to be a plastic container of butter, Alex discovered a very sizable, square cut diamond ring. When she removed it from the basket, Elet's face reflected into the stone.

In the blink of her false eyelashes, he said, "You're everything that I've ever wanted in a friend. I couldn't imagine a life without you by my side. I love you and I want you to be my wife. Will you?"

Stunned, Alex sat there staring at his face and at the ring. At his face. At the ring. The fifteen seconds of silence felt like an hour to both of them. Then, she said, "I love you" and kissed him. The room erupted in applause.

The waiter said, "She said yes." However, she hadn't really. She slipped the ring on her finger and stared at it. She rolled her hand from side to side. She held it close. She held it far away. Then, she noticed that Elet looked concerned.

She said, "Sorry."

"No, no, if those stares mean you love it, then stare at it all you want. If they mean that you don't love it, we can go exchange it for a ring you do love. I wasn't too sure about buying you a ring." His face looked disappointed.

"Elet, it's beautiful. I was just...I don't know...admiring it."

Looking relieved, he said, "Admire away." David brought a bottle of champagne, a gift from the ship's captain. Alex stared at the ring. She thought of how big it was and how heavy it made her hand feel, how heavy it made her feel. She loved Elet more than she loved any other man that she had ever dated, but marriage had felt like something other people did. But, how could she turn him down? How could she ruin the best thing that ever happened to her? Then, again, wasn't she just enjoying talking to and flirting with other men?

She turned from Elet's gaze. She looked around the room. Arm Muscles made eye contact, smiled, and nodded. Now, she wasn't sure, if that was flirtatious or if it was congratulatory. Bottle Blonde had her back turned. She had joined a collection of other screeching, giggling, mid-twenties, blondes.

She looked at Elet. His hand was resting on his palm. She said, "Whatcha thinking?"

"Wondering if I should update Facebook or tell my family?"

Alex felt hot and sweaty instantly. She was panicked, "Uh, let's wait."

"Wait?" She saw confusion cross Elet's face.

"Yeah. We shouldn't let our family and friends find out on Facebook."

"Yeah, you're right. I'm just so happy. I was so scared you'd say no or tell me that you needed to think about it."

Actually, she had wanted to say all of that. She didn't want to admit that she never said yes, but she was thinking it. Instead, she just smiled. He stroked her hand. Alex lost her appetite. They sat in silence. There was no more talking of the house or work or Jacqueline and Mallory. There was just silent stroking.

Finally, dinner was served. Many portions of food came and went. The entire time, Alex stared at the ring. The presence of the food started to suspend did not suspend the fact that they had just become engaged as Alex had hoped. Rather than discuss the elephant in the room, Alex got Elet to start talking about all kinds of things: his next project, her possible promotion. But, when the conversation turned to Alex's parent's anniversary party, Elet looked inspired. He said, with great excitement, "Let's tell your parents at their party."

"No."

"It's a great idea. Everyone you know and love will be there."

"But, that night's not about us. It's about them. Besides, Jo would never let me live it down."

"C'mon. What better news on your anniversary than your youngest child is getting married?"

"To a white boy," she said under her breath. She hadn't really meant it. In truth, her parents had never mentioned Elet's race to her. Sure, some of Jo's friends and cousins and distant relatives had teased her, but she could handle that. She didn't even know why she'd said it.

Elet sat back in his chair as though he didn't know that they were of two racial groups. "Do you think it's a problem? They never said anything. I never felt any different. Everyone's always treated me like a member of the family. Do you remember last year when your dad told all the boys to help with the yard work after Christmas dinner? Remember when I didn't move and he said, 'Son, I meant you, too.' Shit, I was happy he called me son. So happy, I didn't think about me weed-eating on Christmas."

"Yeah, I remember. Let's just tell them on our own terms, so if it's not welcomed, then we can talk to them without a crowd, okay?"

"Okay." He was deep in thought now.

She could see it on his face. *Dammit, I shouldn't have planted that seed*, she thought. She reached out and grabbed his hand. "It's gonna be fine. Don't worry."

He smiled. They finished eating before the cruise was over, so they decide to wander outside onto the deck. While out there, they discovered a bar and a band on the upper deck. They danced and laughed until the boat pulled into the shore. The night sky was full of stars. In Elet's arms, Alex felt safe and happy. She had forgotten about the ring and the proposal. They were happily absorbed in one another. Those were the moments that she loved the most. The moments when she wasn't trying to be cute or trying to get anyone's attention, but she knew that she had Elet's complete attention. In those moments, his attention was all that she needed. The entire world was right until the horn sounded again. It was time to disembark. As they passed the other passengers, Alex and Elet were showered with congratulations and well wishes. With each congrats, Elet pulled her closer and closer. Alex felt as though they had gotten engaged and married all aboard the ship in a matter of hours. The entire ordeal had left her feeling queasy.

When they got to the car, he asked her what she was thinking. Immediately, she said, "Jacqueline."

"Huh?"

"Oh, my friends, I was thinking that I want to tell them"

He smiled. She could see how that made him happy.

She went on. "Yea, I want to tell them altogether, you know. I can't tell one without the other. It just wouldn't be right. Hmm, what time is it?" She looked at the car radio. "Almost nine... Yeah, I bet everyone is still up."

"You're gonna try to conference call them?"

"No, I need to see them."

"Tonight?"

"Yeah, tonight. Right now! Aren't you spending the night with me?"

"Well, yeah, I thought we would stay together tonight. You know..." he raised his eyebrows up and down.

"It won't take long. I'm gonna send them a text and tell them to meet me at Jacqueline's at nine-thirty. I will drop you off, race over there, and be back soon for..." she raised her eyebrows.

"Why don't you just tell them at work?"

"Honey," she said, pouting.

"Okay, okay, you can go and play with your friends, but just for a little while. It's a school night, after all."

"Okay, Dad." With that, she picked up her phone and sent a text that said:

```
I need you. All of you! I'm calling an emergency
meeting at Jacqueline's house at nine-thirty tonight.
Paige, this means you, too, biotch.
```

CROSS YOUR FINGERS

8

Mallory had been to Jacqueline's place plenty of times. However, this time felt different. Jacqueline would not be in the lobby waiting to escort her upstairs. This time, Mallory was holding a key. For once, she was not a peasant visitor coming to call upon nobility in their far away castle. This time, she felt as though she belonged.

As she exited Interstate 275N, the route settled her with its familiarity. Snaking through historic northeast St. Petersburg, she rolled down her window and let in the evening breeze. She admired the manicured street corners and man-made lakes. There were more parks and outdoor markets in this area than in all of the rest of the county. Coming here felt like being in a neighborhood, it was rich with life and activity; and, yet, the area was bordered by downtown St. Petersburg's commercial district. As she drove along Bayshore Drive, Mallory daydreamed of being on one of many yachts docked in the marina. Sitting on the stern of the boat, she was absorbing the sunshine on her face and the wind in her hair. As she looked back from her seat on the stern, she saw Jacqueline in the boat's cockpit masterfully steering. Before she could get too engrossed in the daydream, Jacqueline's building appeared before her. It was a behemoth.

Mallory parked her car and gathered all the grocery bags. As she walked past the parking lot security guard patrolling in his golf cart, he offered to help. She declined, but smiled. Usually, entering Jacqueline's building made her tense, but, today, she strode inside with her head up. She glided to the glass front of the high-rise. She didn't hesitate when the doorman addressed her. She had seen him on many occasions.

"Good evening, Ms. Cummings. Ms. Emerson told me to expect you. Do you need any assistance?"

"Hi, Eduardo. No, I'm fine. Just a few groceries." Eduardo smiled and pressed the button for Jacqueline's penthouse. Jacqueline's building was not only beautiful, but both aesthetically and architecturally marvelous. It was a round, glass high-rise that sat on the St. Petersburg side of Tampa Bay. The lobby floor was covered in Venetian tile. In contrast to its luxurious look, it was also a state-of-the art building that provided each resident with her own private elevator entry.

As Mallory stepped inside of Jacqueline's elevator, she placed the bags on the floor. It was a journey to the eighteenth floor. Rubbing the fold of her arms where the bags had left indentions, she wondered why she hadn't allowed the security guard to give her a ride or allowed Eduardo to help with bags. She abandoned the thought and checked her makeup in the reflection of the well-polished stainless steel elevator walls.

When the elevator doors opened, Mallory was inside of Jacqueline's anteroom. It was a small receiving area that was outside of Jacqueline's door. If a person had emerged from the stairwell, then she would have had to open a door from the stairwell into the anteroom. The stairwell access, much like the elevator access, contained camera surveillance. The security guards would monitor the stairwell, all anterooms, and elevators, but residents had access to view their own elevators and anterooms as well. Jacqueline could view the occupant in the anteroom and grant or deny them access to the penthouse.

Once inside Jacqueline's anteroom, the visitor faced two massive hand-carved koa doors that Jacqueline had had custom carved by Hawaiian artisans, shipped to Florida, and installed. The doors were colossal. When closed, there was a koa tree carved, in relief form, on the outside. Once opened, the visitor could see only thick, relief carved branches. Her doors demanded to be touched. Mallory ran her fingers across them on each visit. To the right of the right door sat a security panel that required a pass code to enter. Mallory stood there. She rested her head against the mighty door. She realized Jacqueline had not given her the pass code.

She was deflated. She was suddenly anxious about being in the building. She replayed the afternoon in her mind wondering if maybe Jacqueline had told her the code and she had forgotten. With no memory of any code being given, Mallory began to think of what the code might be. She thought of Jacqueline's date of birth but reasoned that that might be too simple. She thought of Rays' player's numbers that the code could be or perhaps the address to the Trop. Any of these were possibilities, but if she failed, security would swarm her. They would be on walkie-talkies to one another. The ambient light of the anteroom would suddenly flash to LED lighting and a voice would question her via intercom. As she stood there trying to determine if she should just call Jacqueline's phone and have her wake up and open the door, Mallory remembered that she was being monitored by the security team.

After a few moments of anxiety-induced nausea, Mallory decided it was better to try to unlock the door and sound the alarm than to touch the alarm pad and look as though she was breaking in. Without hesitance, Mallory unlocked both the door lock and bolt lock. Each mechanism worked without any alarm. Collecting all of her belongings, she said, "Here goes nothing," and pushed open one of the giant doors.

There was no noise, no sound. Mallory closed the door behind her and locked it. The panel to her left had a sticky note on it. In Jacqueline's handwriting, the note read REARM and had an arrow pointing down. Mallory depressed the button to which the arrow pointed. When she did, she heard three quick beeps and one long beep. Mallory let out a deep breath. Happy to be inside, she turned to the right and delivered the bags to the kitchen. The silence of the condo was comforting. She glanced around and wondered how Jacqueline was having such trouble sleeping in a place as magnificent as this. It was a few minutes after six. Mallory thought about letting Jacqueline sleep a bit longer but decided against it. She feared that a long nap might ruin Jacqueline's chance to rest again that night.

Mallory walked across the condo in the reddish hue cast by the dusk stained evening. She stood outside the doors of Jacqueline's bedroom. On the many occasions that she had been to the apartment, she had never entered Jacqueline's bedroom. While she didn't think that the room was off-limits, it felt like uncharted territory. Mallory placed her ear to the door just to make sure that Jacqueline was not already awake. Hearing nothing, Mallory gently knocked on the door. There was no reply. Quietly, she turned the knob and entered the bedroom.

The bedroom floor had cork floors as did the rest of the penthouse. Jacqueline lay in her bed against the back wall of a huge room. Her wood canopy bed was also made of koa. It was hand carved as well. In the dark, Mallory could not determine the details on its carving. As she stepped closer to the bed, she felt the floor change. The bed was sitting atop a circular rug. It was less dense than the other rugs in the condo, but in the darkness, she could not tell how it looked. Standing over a sleeping Jacqueline, Mallory thought of not waking her. She appeared to be resting too well to be disturbed.

Mallory smiled down at her and quietly said her name. Jacqueline didn't move. Mallory's smile widened. Hovering over Jacqueline, Mallory slowly lowered herself on the edge of the bed. Jacqueline moved towards her but didn't awaken. To steady herself, Mallory placed her arm around Jacqueline's body. Her fist anchored in the covers near Jacqueline's stomach. Mallory could feel the rise and fall of her chest. Mallory leaned closer towards Jacqueline's face and said, "It's about quarter after six. Maybe you should get up for a bit."

Batting her eyes, Jacqueline said, "Hi, there."

"Hi." Mallory smiled wide. "How was your nap? You looked so peaceful I thought of not waking you."

"I'm glad you did." Jacqueline turned over and faced Mallory. "Have you been home long?" Jacqueline was unaware of what she'd said. But, Mallory knew and smiled to herself.

"Only long enough to put down the bags."

Jacqueline sighed. Talking in a whisper, she said, "I'm glad you're home," and started to doze back off.

Again, Mallory thought that it would be best if she let Jacqueline sleep a bit longer, so she removed her arm and was preparing to leave when Jacqueline awoke.

"I guess I should get up."

Mallory stopped. "That's up to you."

"Yeah, I should. I have dinner to cook, right?" Jacqueline said as she swung her legs underneath her and sat up on the side of her bed. "Well, welcome to the master suite." Picking up the remote that lay on the nightstand, Jacqueline aimed overhead and pressed several buttons. As she did, the curtains opened and recessed lighting illuminated the dark areas of the room. Mallory walked to the window and gazed out over the Bay. She had been on the balcony many times. It was huge, but Mallory never noticed that Jacqueline could exit to it from her bedroom. "Nice view, eh?"

"Yeah, I'll say." Mallory walked around to the other side of the bed and sat down. "I see you got the doors, a bed, and a bench."

Jacqueline had laid back down. She had rolled on her side and faced Mallory's back. "Yeah. I just love it. The wood. The workmanship. All of it. I can never figure out if I want to be buried with this bed or with the Laredo."

Mallory retorted, "You'll be buried with that old Laredo. I'm keeping the bed." Mallory leaned forward and grabbed the wooden post. Like the doors, the bed was carved in the same tree relief.

Noticing that Mallory was admiring the bed, Jacqueline said, "Lie beside me." Mallory whirled around and looked at her, but complied. When she did, Jacqueline turned on the lamps that sat on the nightstands on both sides of the bed. Unsure what they were doing, Mallory looked at Jacqueline with confusion. Jacqueline said, "Look up." Overhead in the wooden canopy, there was a relief carving of a sun rising in a Hawaiian valley. It was complete with a mountain range and canopies of trees. She said, "I just wanted you know what you were getting." Jacqueline stood up and walked around the bed towards the bathroom. When she got to the bathroom door, she looked back at Mallory curled up in her bed. She wasn't sure why she felt as happy as she did. She was tired and knew that there was a meal to prepare, but for a second, she stood at the doorframe to the bathroom and just stared at Mallory.

Walking into her bathroom, she wondered what was for dinner. "What'd you get from the store?"

"Huh?"

"What's for dinner?" Jacqueline repeated. This time, there was no answer. Jacqueline had planned to gargle and return to the bedroom and ask. However, before she could spit out the mouthwash, Mallory was standing in the doorway of her bathroom.

"Holy shit. This is a big ass bathroom."

"Well, I'm sure it was designed for a couple." Jacqueline felt awkward.

"A couple of giants." Mallory entered the bathroom with Jacqueline. She walked inside the glass shower. She sat inside the Jacuzzi tub. "Why do you have a chaise lounge in here?"

"The middle of the room looked bare without something there. I never sit on it, but at least it takes up some of the space." Jacqueline wiped her face and left the room.

"Do you use both sinks and both mirrors?" Mallory followed her.

"No, I buy the same stuff to decorate both but if you look underneath the sink or in the other medicine cabinet, it's all empty." Jacqueline left her room and Mallory followed her.

Jacqueline turned the light on in the kitchen, but left the room to go check the front door. Confident that the system was armed, she returned to the kitchen to find Mallory unbagging dinner.

"So, what are we having?"

"Steaks, potatoes, salad, and wine," Mallory said with a smile. "My favorite meal."

Jacqueline poured Mallory a glass of wine and began preparing the meal. She placed the steaks on the grill and the potatoes in the oven. Mallory joined her outside on the balcony. The two chatted as they waited on dinner.

Once the meal was complete, Jacqueline convinced Mallory that it would be better to eat inside. Jacqueline warned her that sitting on the balcony with food only gave a person a few minutes before the food was cold. Instead, the two gathered at the dining room table.

"When I was driving in, I was daydreaming about being out on a boat. You should buy one," Mallory suggested.

"Oh, I've thought about it. I mean, the building has its own marina. But, it seems odd to have a boat and no one to share it with."

"If you buy a boat, I guarantee that you will never be alone on it."

"You know, I rented the boat at the beach house. We will have to take it out."

"Is that a promise?" Mallory teased.

"Of course, it is." With that, Jacqueline stood up and started to clear the table. Mallory followed her lead. After they cleaned up from dinner, Jacqueline grabbed an ice bucket and the rest of Mallory's wine and headed for the couch. "You don't mind if we catch some of the game, do you?"

Mallory slipped off her shoes and said, "Not at all. Besides, you'll be asleep by the fifth inning and I'll have full control of the TV and access to the house."

Snuggling under a blanket, Jacqueline said, "You can have that now if you want. Mi casa es su casa." It was the top of the second.

Jacqueline's phone was charging in her bedroom when the chime awoke her. At was at the exact same time, Mallory's phone vibrated inside her purse. Without looking, Jacqueline said, "It's either Paige or Alex."

For a second, Mallory looked confused. Laughing to herself, Jacqueline responded, "They share a text tone."

Still confused, Mallory said, "Why don't I share this super-special text tone?"

"You have your own," Jacqueline said, as she got up off the couch and began to clear away the glasses from the coffee table. Mallory grabbed her purse from the chair.

"It's Alex. She's calling an emergency meeting. Here! In twenty minutes! What the fuck?"

Drying her hands on a dishtowel, Jacqueline said, "I wonder what's up."

"That's all you have to say. She's inviting herself and Paige over on a work night. That's a big imposition on you."

"She's inviting you, too." Jacqueline reminded her as she began putting away the dinner dishes. "I don't mind. We're all friends. If she's coming all the way over here at nine thirty on a Tuesday night, then it's something big."

The text tones sounded, again. Mallory read it to Jacqueline. "Paige wants to know if everything is okay."

Text tones again. "Alex says fuck no in all caps. Get your ass to Jacqueline's."

Text tones again. "It's Paige." Mallory read, "J's not answering. Maybe, she doesn't want us to come over." Text tone. "She's cleaning up. She always cleans up if you announce that you're coming over. She doesn't care. Besides, I know

Eduardo and have the spare key. I'm going. Get there now, Paige. Mallory, are you on the way yet?"

Mallory responded "already here." Jacqueline's text tone for Mallory went off. It was the sound of wind chimes blowing gently. Mallory smiled and said, "Aww, I like that."

"See, I told you that you had your own."

"But, not my own key." Jacqueline stood up from the cabinets under the sink expecting Mallory to be laughing or smirking. She was not. Jacqueline thought of telling her to keep the key she used to get into today, and then thought against it, at least, for right now.

Text tones went off. Mallory said, "Alex wants to know if I live with you now."

Mallory responded, "Not yet. Working on it." Jacqueline blankly stared at Mallory.

Text tones continued. This time, Jacqueline heard the intercom announce that her elevator had been engaged. "Dear, the guests have arrived." Jacqueline disarmed the alarm and opened the door to find Paige in the anteroom texting.

"Are you serious?" Paige said as she texted the same thing. She was so enthralled in her texting that she didn't realize the door had opened. Jacqueline bent down and tried to look in that space between Paige's face and her cell phone. Paige said, "Oh, I'm sorry, Jacqueline. I was busy responding to Mallory."

"Well, why don't you come in and tell her yourself?"

"Oh, yeah, okay." Paige said as she entered. "I didn't realize that your building had a doorman. I don't think I've ever even been to a place with a doorman. Who knew that Florida had places with doormen?" She stopped at the entrance and looked around. This was her first time in Jacqueline's place. In her rush over, she had overlooked that she had taken an elevator up to the highest floor of a bayfront, luxury building.

Standing in the foyer, she noticed that the condo was decorated in classic mahogany with leather furniture and thick, Persian rugs. Only then did she realize that the condo was on the highest floor of the building and that there a phenomenal, corner balcony. Paige walked around in awe, "This is amazing. I never would have thought that you'd have had a place like this." Realizing how that may have sounded, she hit herself in the head. "I'm sorry. I didn't mean it like that. I'm so sorry, Jacqueline."

Laughing, Jacqueline replied. "It's okay. I've heard that before." Heading to the well-stocked bar, she held up a bottle of wine and shook it at Paige. Paige showed an inch between her forefinger and thumb. Paige walked to Mallory who was curled up on the couch under a blanket.

"When did you get here?" Paige whispered.

"Around five-thirty or six," Mallory said, batting her eyes.

"What have you two been doing?" Paige asked as she looked from Jacqueline to Mallory.

"Well, the orgy ended at eight and I was just too tired to leave yet," Mallory teased.

Paige stared at her. Whispering, she leaned forward and said, "Orgy of men or orgy of women?"

Mallory thumped her with the pillow. "Paige, you idiot. Jax cooked dinner. We ate and watched some of the Rays game. She fell asleep and I became queen of the castle. So, I snooped around for a while. Once I had checked every closet and every drawer, I turned on a movie and watched it as she slept."

"Oh." Paige didn't appear to believe the story. However, she didn't appear to want to know anything more.

Jacqueline was placing a glass of wine for Paige and Mallory on the table when she heard a key in the door. Everyone turned and looked towards the door to see Alex entering.

Mallory moaned, "She really does have a key." Jacqueline pretended that she'd been shot in the heart.

Looking like she ran right over, Alex spoke all of her thoughts at once. "I'm so glad that you all came right over. I mean, I know some of you were already here, but we can talk about that later. Right now, I need to talk about me. I mean, not in the usual way, that I need to talk about me, but in that way that when you really mean that you need to talk about yourself that you really need to talk about yourself."

Getting irritated, Mallory said, "Well, talk and stop babbling."

Unfazed Alex went on, "I love Elet. We all know that, right? Right. I mean, I have grown a lot with him, but I never thought that. I don't know what I thought. I mean, I don't want to break up. But, who knew that we were there. I mean, I've been saying for years that I didn't want to do this. Everyone knew that, didn't they? Sure, they did. I'm not like other women. I mean, I'm not Jacqueline." Jacqueline looked perturbed by this. "But I don't need a man. I mean, I like men, but I don't need one like Paige." Paige looked offended. "And, there's so much I want to do. There's so much that I want to see and jobs to have. Why does this have to happen now? I'm on the cusp of a big, new job." Mallory looked deflated.

Jacqueline interrupted, "You may want to bring this home before we all kick your ass."

Alex said, "He fucking proposed tonight," and held up her hand. Her chest was heaving. She was sweating.

Paige grabbed her hand and said, "OMG, that's wonderful. Congratulations."

Alex snatched her hand from Paige, "Don't say that."

Paige said, "Say what?"

"Congratu-fucking-lations!!!"

"Oh," shooing into the air, Paige said, "Don't worry. Most women are nervous when the man they love proposes. It's normal to feel crazy and out of sorts for a while."

Mallory said, "Um, I'm not sure that that's what this is." She was circling Alex who was now sitting on the couch.

Jacqueline came over, sat down next to Alex, and said, "Tell us what happened." Alex told them the entire story.

At the end of which, Mallory yelped, "You left him at your apartment and came over here?!? Who does that?!?"

Jacqueline interrupted, "Well, we will get to that, but, first, I'm going to ask you honestly and I want an honest answer. You can tell us anything. We are your friends. Do you love Elet?"

"Yes"

"Do you want to marry Elet?"

"I don't know."

"Okay. Do you want Elet to be with someone else?"

"No, absolutely not."

"Okay. Is it the rest of your life with Elet that you fear?"

"No, I don't think so."

"Then, what's the problem?"

"I don't want to be a wife or a mother." Then, Alex began to cry. Jacqueline put her arm around her. Paige walked over, slid in the other side, and rubbed her back.

Mallory said, "This isn't about Elet. This is about Alex. She doesn't want to be committed."

"Fuck you, Mallory. I'm committed, now." Alex roared back.

"Really, you hang on more men than a tie does. You flirt. You give out your number and meet up with other men for lunches and dinners. Does any of this sound like a committed person?"

Jacqueline looked at Mallory disapprovingly. Mallory threw up her hands in surrender, "I'm just sayin'."

Ever the therapist, Jacqueline said, "Alex, are you scared of the way your life will change?"

"Yes," Alex said through the tears.

"Well, that's natural, but the good news is, Elet is probably not looking for things to change in any amazing way. I doubt he is going to many club openings. I doubt he is suddenly going to stop going away for days at a time on shoots. I doubt he is asking you to quit work and bake more often. I think he just loves you, probably wants to be with you, and wants to make it legal. That's not so bad, right?"

Paige was nodding that it wasn't so bad; and, after a long pause, Alex agreed. So, Jacqueline went on. "You know, it's all going to be okay. No one is suddenly going to change. We will still be friends and we will still hang out. You will just wear a ring all the time. That's it."

Mallory added, "And move to Seminole Heights." Alex cried, again. This time, it was louder. Jacqueline lowered her head in defeat.

Paige came to the rescue. "When Brett moved in, it took us a long time to get used to each other. You guys remember my shabby chic place. It was bright and airy like a picnic. Brett came in and wiped his oily hands on the decorative dish clothes, put his feet up on the wicker coffee table, and broke the glass. Oh, don't forget that his mongrel chewed the noses off all my gnomes. It takes time, but you'll figure it out. You'll come to love it and love coming home after a long day to a man who loves you, even if the coffee table never got a new piece of glass." Paige finished her wine.

Looking at Paige but talking to Alex, Jacqueline said, "Well, that's a different issue. But, living with someone is always hard in the beginning. You get used to it."

Starting to relax, Alex said, "You haven't lived with anyone, Jax."

"I have to."

Alex denied, "uh, no. No, you haven't. You've just been fucking around for the last twelve years." Mallory stared at Jacqueline with squinted eyes.

Jacqueline stood up from the couch and went to the sink to rinse out her glass. From there, she said, "Well, I've had roommates."

"That you fucked."

"How'd this become about me?" Jacqueline became defensive.

Paige righted the course. "Oh, honey, dry your face. There's nothing wrong with being scared. It's a big step, but no bigger than other steps, you've taken." Paige began to count off accomplishments on her fingers. "Leaving home to go to college. Moving to a city with no friends or family. Meeting a man that you love. Opening your heart, your home, and your life to him. You did all of that.

You'll be fine. And, we will be there with you." Paige did it. She always did. She was good at mother-henning. She pulled together their frayed ends better than any other person could.

Alex said, whipping her face, "You're right, Paige. It's just nerves. I love him. He loves me. It's gonna be fine." She got up from the couch and walked to the kitchen. She rubbed Jacqueline's arm and said, "Sorry for being a bitch."

"That's okay. Wanna move in? Looks like I need the experience."

"Not me but someone else might." Alex turned from the sink and faced Mallory who turned from Alex's gaze.

"Guess what?" Paige said, "Now, next week is a last hooray. Just like I had before I got married. Now, we have to go out and have a blast and celebrate every night. It's probably our last time together before Alex is a married woman."

Mallory said, "Hell yeah. Let's do it." For a moment, they stood there celebrating and smiling. With the crisis averted, Alex was sent home to celebrate with Elet. Paige left immediately after to go check on Brett and the twins. The apartment was back to just Mallory and Jacqueline.

Mallory sat on the couch and put her shoes on. "Thanks for dinner.....and the entertainment."

Rubbing the back of her neck, Jacqueline said, "Yeah, I didn't see that coming. Well, at least not tonight." She sat on the couch next to Mallory.

"Why didn't you tell me that you'd never been serious?"

"I'm not sure that you ever asked me."

"You know what I mean. I've talked about my divorce, past boyfriends, old loves. You never mentioned any of that. I think that I always thought you just weren't ready to tell me about relationships with women. But, you haven't had any."

"I've known Alex for a very long time. She knows my worst years as well as my best. I've done a lot of things that I'm not proud of. She likes the stories. It was a lot of fun back then, but now it's embarrassing. Sure, there were women who wanted more. I just wasn't in a place to give it."

"And, now?"

"Now. Now." Jacqueline was thinking. No one had asked the question before. "I could give it. I could have it. I have mature friendships and a more mature, more stable life. But, now, a girlfriend is probably hard to find. I guess now I've turned in on myself. I've gotten out of the habit of meeting people other than for business purposes."

Standing up and gathering her purse and her keys, Mallory said, "Happens to the best of us."

Fearing there was an elephant in the room, she said, "I hope you don't think less of me."

Looking back over her shoulder as she headed out the door, Mallory said, "I couldn't think any more of you."

9

As Alex and Paige drove down her parents' street, they saw a shirtless Elet dripping in sweat with metal poles hoisted onto his shoulder. In unison, they rolled down the windows, screamed his name, and catcalled him. Immediately, he turned a wonderful shade of red. All the commotion brought Alex's nephews to the street. They were also shirtless. The boys ran to Alex's car with the exuberance young boys have. She parked the car in her parent's driveway. As tried to push past them, Alex exclaimed, "No stinky boys." And, she ran from them, much to their delight. As the chase ensued, Paige cheered them on from the car.

This continued around the yard and into the street until Josephine appeared. Her relaxed hair was in a ponytail. She was wearing white capri pants and a stripped tank top. She yelled to her sons, "Boys, leave your Auntie Alex alone and get back to work."

Reluctantly, the boys sulked away. Alex said, "Thanks for the save, Jo. I don't think I can keep outrunning them. They are getting too fast." She walked back to her car and opened the door for Paige. Looking at her sister, she said, "This is my friend, Paige. Do you remember her? I think you've met a few times."

Friendlier now, Josephine left the entrance to the house and hugged Paige. "Of course, I remember Paige. It was great of you to come and help."

"Oh, it's my pleasure. My parents live in Pensacola and my husband's mother passed away in childbirth. I just love being a part of a family. I'm so happy you all let me be a part all of this."

Josephine responded, "Aren't you sweet?"

Bending into the back of her car, Alex yelled, "Not as sweet as this cake."

Josephine said, "Oh, lemme see it."

Alex raised a corner of the box lid and the women stood in the yard ogling the cake. Then, the boys reappeared. "Let us see, mama. We wanna see."

Jo quickly returned to motherly form and barked, "No! Didn't I tell you no? Now, go find your father!" For the second time, the boys slinked off.

The women entered the house. Looking around, Alex asked, "Where are Mama and Daddy?" It was unusual that neither of them were at home.

Josephine yelled from the kitchen, "Uncle Will is keeping them entertained until it's time for the party. The last thing that I needed was Daddy trying to help the guys put up the tents or, worse, run electricity. Or, Mama walking behind me telling me how to do everything."

Paige looked around the living room of the large house. It was filled with pictures of the girls when they were small. She could tell which pictures were school pictures. They were the only ones of the girls individually. When they were younger, they looked almost identical. Paige wondered what happened that caused them to look and act so completely different. Walking through the house admiring its furnishings and feeling a sense of family, Paige said, "The house is beautiful. I can almost hear you two as kids."

Josephine laughed, "This old house? Beautiful? Hmm, I don't know if that's the word that I'd use. Hell, there's not much in Brandon is beautiful."

Alex agreed, "Ain't that the truth."

Paige was taken aback. She wasn't accustomed to this Alex. Looking around the room, Paige wondered if that was a glimpse of the Alex that her family knew. She looked into the backyard and saw Josephine's sons, Elet, and another man. She asked, "Josephine, is that your husband?"

Josephine came to look as if a strange man may have possibly been in the backyard. But, it was her husband. All the women were looking out of the curtains in the dining room when Josephine finally responded, "Yep, that's my Dom. Special Vehicle Maintenance Airman Dominic Knight. And, our boys, the tall one over there with no shirt on is Isaac, who now wants to be called Izzy. The small one with a shirt sticking to his sweaty body and another on his head is our youngest, Levi. At least, he was still Levi as of this morning."

"What a wonderful family. Do you live close to by?"

"Oh, yeah. I live in our grandmother's house. She passed away right before Isaac was born. Dom and I didn't have a place to stay and larger base quarters for a family weren't available, so Daddy told us to stay there. We still live there. It's small, but it's home." Pointing out the side window, she said, "It's only around the corner. I guess life wasn't meant for us all to get out of Brandon. Someone had to stay behind and check on Mama and Daddy every day."

Growing frustrated, Alex said, "Shouldn't we be getting the guys to hurry up with the chairs? The food will be here soon. We need to get it setup, so Paige and I can leave, go get pretty, and be back for the party."

Stretching her back, Josephine yelled from the window, "Let's get a move on." The women exited the house into the backyard.

Mallory had promised that she would be ready to leave the office by ten, so Jacqueline planned for an early day. She had packed her stuff into the Laredo early on Friday morning and left to pick up Mallory. After loading the Jeep, they drove to work together, so they could leave from the office and start their vacation. The plan was for Paige and Alex to meet them at the rental house by late afternoon. Once together, they would explore the house, get dressed, and head to the party as a group.

"Did you sleep last night?" Mallory asked as they drove to the office.

"About five or six hours, but I feel good this morning. After you left, I did think that we should have just stayed the night together. I mean, we were already together. It would have been easier to leave this morning from one place."

"I thought that, too. When I went home after work yesterday, I took a shower and changed clothes. While I was picking out something to wear over to your place, I packed my bag. I thought about just adding another set of clothes and spending the night with you. But, we hadn't talked about that and you were asleep. I didn't want to …impose."

Jacqueline looked at her. "Never."

"What?"

"Oh, you're never an imposition." Jacqueline stopped at a coffee shop and ordered Mallory's favorite.

"Thank you, but you didn't order anything for yourself."

"I have tea at work. Besides, I have sworn off drinking and driving." Jacqueline smiled and headed off to work.

Jacqueline hadn't planned to do a lot of work. She dressed casually knowing that she would only be in the office for a few conference calls and a meeting with Jack. He had come to the office to discuss filling the department editor positions.

"You've done a great job executing the company's new direction. I couldn't be happier. I hope you called the bank this morning and noticed exactly how happy I am."

Smiling, Jacqueline said, "As a matter of fact, I logged in from my phone this morning to check my balance. The bank was very happy."

"Well, I'm glad. The Board's happy. I'm happy. And, you look pretty happy. I think that this is going to work out very well for everyone." Jack said pouring a bourbon at nine in the morning. "By the way, don't worry. While you are away, I'm going to come into the office every other day. Just a show that management is present."

"Jack, before we start celebrating, maybe we should formally fill the department editor positions. Each candidate has had two interviews, one with two existing members of management, and one with just me. The existing managers passed suggestions on to me of who they think would be best suited and I have made recommendations as well." She passed him an envelope.

He placed the envelope on the end of his desk and said, "Okay. Well, who do you want to hire?"

Confused, she said, "Don't you want to do your own interview?"

"Absolutely not," he said as he finished his drink. "Whatever you think is best." With that, he went and laid on the couch in this office.

Jacqueline retrieved the envelope from Jack's desk and she sat down in the chair beside the couch. She opened it and began to read the suggestions she had made. "Okay, so, Paige is the existing Production Manager. I don't know that there is any reason to remove her from that spot. She has done a bang up job."

"Short, fat one with the artsy fartsy office. She's nice and she bakes cookies at the holidays," Jack replied.

"She's fluffy, but I don't know that she's fat," Jacqueline tried to defend her.

"Oh, she's chubby, but a sweet girl. Who's next?"

"Bob is the Politics Editor. If you remember, we discussed incorporating national and international news with politics. If that's still the plan, I think that Bob can handle all three under one umbrella," she passed Jack papers that showed information on how the three areas were interconnected and an overview on Bob. Jack held his hand out to receive it, then he placed it face down on his chest.

With his right hand behind his head, he scratched his neck and repeated, "Bob? Bob? Bob?"

"Tall man. Maybe late fifties. Wears glasses." Jacqueline tried to help.

Starting to remember, Jack roared, "Bean pole Bob!"

Jacqueline stared at Jack for a moment wondering if she should go on. Realizing that this may have been a bad idea, but one that she couldn't abort, so she continued, "I think Guy Flynt would be great for Sports Editor. He's a former Olympic wrestler who has amazing sports connections all over the world. His last two pieces get picked up by the AP wire." She waited. She was expecting some comment from Jack, but he was silent. She uttered, "Uh, no comment about Guy?"

"Hell no. That man's huge. Have you seen him? Next."

Jacqueline chuckled and continued. "Okay, I have Nelson Prime down for Metro Editor and Mia Steinbach for Business Editor." She handed him the paperwork on Guy, Nelson, and Mia. After he added those papers on his chest as well, she added, "Nelson was a copywriter and a staff writer for years. His work is impeccable. It rarely needs editing and is well cited. Then, there is Mia. She has corporate and Chamber of Commerce contacts that we have used as sources or leads for years. She can oversee Business with ease."

Jack was starting to drift off. He had slipped his feet out of his loafers. He spoke through his yawn, "That woman is a beast. She drank me under the table at last year's Christmas party. We had had two bottles of champagne in an hour. I was lit. My whole life had become a blur, but there she was still applying her lipstick and checking her mascara."

When Jacqueline removed the last paper from the envelope, she held it in her hands and stared at the name. She didn't look at Jack. This was the moment that she needed him. She wanted him to give her the third degree, to ask probing questions that would guarantee that Jacqueline had made the best business decision without prejudice. In a whisper, she said, "I think Mallory is perfect to lead Lifestyles. She has the accolades and the track record. She had success writing pieces outside of arts and entertainment, so I think she would be great handling the new direction we want to explore with the department. As you know, I think that the department has real potential to grow from being film, restaurant, and show reviews to something more substantive and engaging for a new cosmopolitan audience. I think Mallory has the talent and leadership to oversee the expansion of the department to include tech, some science, and health news." As she passed him the information on the Lifestyles department and Mallory, she stared at the empty envelope that sat in her lap. She didn't notice that he had turned his head towards her.

Softly, he agreed, "Yeah, I think she's up to it. You know, you've done a wonderful job." He placed the papers on the floor beside him, rolled over, and faced the back of the couch. Reaching for his suit jacket, he said, "Now, take your hard-working ass on vacation. When you get back, we will send emails to all the candidates who weren't chosen and make the chosen ones very happy. We will let HR handle salary and all that other nonsense."

"Okay, Jack," she agreed, helped cover him with his jacket, and headed to her office. She spoke to Grant for a few minutes, cleaned off her desk, and walked out of her office to collect Mallory for the long drive. Unbeknownst to her, Mallory was waiting on the elevator as Jacqueline was riding down. They nearly collided into one another when the doors opened.

Mallory spoke first, "I was coming to get you."

"I was coming to get you."

"Why the long face? We are heading out of town for fun in the sun." Mallory said.

"Oh, it was a long few hours. I'm ready to leave and not think about work anymore for a week."

Mallory smirked, "Come on. Let's go now or you will be thinking about this place the entire ride to Seaborn Island." She hooked her arm in Jacqueline's arm.

Jacqueline felt anxiously delighted. Trying to appear relaxed, she found her sunglasses in her bag. Exchanged them for her glasses, she said, "Then, you'll just have to keep me distracted.

CROSS YOUR FINGERS

10

Heading south on I-75, Jacqueline drove at a calm pace. She and Mallory enjoyed moments of great conversation coupled with comfortable silence. Jacqueline had brought along a varied CD collection that Mallory had sifted through and acted as deejay only playing the best of the best. As the ride began to dull, Jacqueline noticed that Mallory had drifted off to sleep. Steering with one hand, She nabbed a blanket from the backseat and did her best to cover Mallory. She lowered the radio, so it would not disturb her and they traveled quietly for almost an hour.

When she exited the interstate, Mallory awoke, "Where are we?"

"Almost there. I'm gonna go ahead and fill up. Do you want anything from inside the store?"

Mallory was checking her makeup in her compact. "I'm going inside to use the bathroom. I'll bring you something back." Jacqueline watched as she stretched and stumbled inside.

After she finished pumping gas, she decided the weather looked nice enough to drop the top. She removed the windows, unlatched the fabric rooftop from behind the visors, and pulled it down from the over the door jams. As she was starting to lower it behind the back seat, Mallory reappeared with a bag from the gas station.

"Finally!"

"What?" Jacqueline wasn't sure she heard her right.

"I was wondering when you were going to take the top off."

"I wasn't sure that you wanted to drive seventy miles an hour without the top up. The wind can get intense."

"I can handle intense," quipped Mallory. Jacqueline finished with the top and jumped in. She started the engine and headed west towards the island. Putting on her sunglasses and turning the music up loud, she finally felt as if she was on vacation. The two drove along the highway jamming to Jacqueline's hip-hop mix.

As they traveled along the state road towards the island, the air became cleaner and crisper. The cars that had exited the interstate with them soon began to decrease. The trees that crowded the exit were replaced with lower lying bushes and shrubs. The two took the state road to its end. Once there, they turned right and drove along the gulffront highway. As the road winded through residential and business areas alike, Mallory became more and more interested in the scenery. She turned the music down and folded her arms under her head so that she could better rest it on the door and gaze outside. From time to time, Jacqueline would hear her say, "This is so beautiful," a comment to which she never responded. She didn't mind the absence of conversation. She was happy to be with Mallory and to be out of the office for a while. As they crossed the final bridge, they saw the sign announcing that they had arrived.

Seaborn Island had a single entrance for non-boating visitors. The island was known for its sugary white-colored coastline, green waters, and island-size parties. It was a vacation spot for national and international visitors. Often, film directors for both movies and television shows used the island. The island's size and atmosphere were its biggest draw. It was so small that the sound of the waves and the visions of a dynamic sunset were only a few blocks away in every direction. Because of that, people navigated on foot or by bicycle. That familiarity and quaintness gave Seaborn Island the culture of relaxation and fun that Jacqueline needed. When her travel agent told her about a villa for rent, Jacqueline jumped at the chance to view it. She knew before ever seeing it, that she was going to leave a deposit, but when they walked through the house, her expectations were exceeded.

At the light that led into town, Jacqueline saw Alex and Paige in the rearview mirror. They were two cars behind the Laredo. She had been worried that they would be at the Stevens' house preparing for the party for so long that they wouldn't arrive in enough time to tour the house before it was time to leave it and head Brandon. Excited to see that their plan was going to work, Jacqueline beeped and waved. The car between Jacqueline and Mallory waved as did Paige and Alex.

Driving past beach goers, Mallory let down her hair and let it blow in the breeze. Jacqueline stared at this transformation for too long and, she nearly drove off the road. Mallory smiled, but never mentioned the swerving or sudden braking. After about ten minutes of maneuvering through town, Jacqueline pulled up to a two-story villa. Within minutes, Alex and Paige arrived. All the women stood outside the vehicles and stretched in the shadow of this large, Italianesque home. After gathering all the bags, Jacqueline unlocked the door and invited everyone inside.

The foyer was eleven feet high with Brazilian Cherry flooring underfoot. The women ventured in different directions. Paige went to the kitchen. She scuttled around looking in cabinets and opening doors. She squealed with delight when she found the fully stocked wine fridge.

Alex headed for the backyard. She passed through the large living room area that had a seventy-inch television and wall-installed surround sound. Overlooking all of that, she walked towards the back of the house. She exited through one of the two sets of glass French doors into the backyard. She marveled at the oasis that lie behind the house. She slipped off her sandals and dipped her toes into the massive pool. She made a mental note to enjoy many nights in the six person jacuzzi. Surveying her surroundings, Alex noticed the thatched roof cabana and outdoor grill. In the middle of the high hedges, Alex saw the glimmer of wrought iron. She wasn't sure what why it was there. Squinting and blocking the sun with her hand, she went to inspect it. As she ran her fingers over the cold metal, she realized it was a gate door covered in hedges. Sliding her fingers the metal, she found the latch to open it. She pushed it open and stepped upon the soft, white beach. Standing in front of the Gulf, she jumped up and down in celebration and belted out, "Hell yeah!"

Since Jacqueline and Mallory had been to the house before, the two did not tour it again. They proceeded upstairs to lay claim to their bedrooms. Jacqueline took the first room on the right. It was the only room with a king size bed. Mallory laid claim to the room next door. Each bedroom had its own bathroom. There would be no reason to share or be delayed by any other occupant needing to get ready for an evening out. While Jacqueline was giving Mallory her bags, Alex and Paige came upstairs.

"This place is amazing." Alex said while Paige nodded in agreement. Both of them chose a room on the left side of the hall. However, neither chose rooms directly across from Jacqueline or Mallory. Paige was across the hall from

Mallory but a room down. Alex went further down the hall and chose a room near the end.

With all the room doors open, Jacqueline yelled into the hallway, "We leave in one hour." With that announcement, all the doors closed.

Jacqueline lay across her bed for a few minutes. She knew that it would take her the least amount of time to prepare for the party. Lying in the bed, she was happy to be under the same roof with all of her friends. She looked forward to the time that they were about to share. She wasn't sure what they would do, but she was certain that there would be plenty of hanging out, talking, drinking, and laughing. That was reason enough for her to be happy. She felt sleep coming to her. While she would have loved to take a nap, she decided that it was a far better idea to go prepare the Laredo for the drive to Brandon. Retrieving her keys, she leapt from the bed, walked downstairs, and back outside. Not looking back, she didn't know that Mallory had opened her door when she heard Jacqueline's door open.

It only took Jacqueline a few minutes to collect all the trash, organize the CDs, and place the top back on the YJ. Admiring its charm, Jacqueline stood back against Alex's car and thought of possible upgrades to make. Part of her wanted to look for a bucket and soap and give it a quick wash, but she knew that there was no time for that. Instead, she adjusted the fog lights and headed back in the house.

Climbing the stairs, Jacqueline noticed Mallory in the hall in a bathrobe with a towel on her shoulder, "Where'd you go?"

"Oh, I was outside."

"Well, I noticed that. What were you doing?"

"Nothing."

"Nothing?"

"I didn't want to tell you, but I was talking to Tania. I gave her the address to the house and told her to come by tomorrow." Mallory didn't respond. She blinked rapidly a few times. Jacqueline had only been teasing. She had no idea that Mallory might have this response. Taken aback, it took Jacqueline a few minutes to realize how this had affected Mallory. "I was just kidding. Relax." Mallory hit her with the towel. "Ow! I didn't realize that you felt this strongly about her." Mallory went into her room and closed her door.

Jacqueline tittered and went into her room to quickly shower and get ready.

They were only twenty minutes behind schedule when Jacqueline cranked the Jeep to life and backed out away from the villa. The hip-hop mix that Jacqueline and Mallory had been listening to was still in the CD player. With a crank of the engine, they were in the middle of a song. Jacqueline reached to turn it down, but she stopped when she noticed that they were rapping along while teasing their hair, applying lip-gloss, and spraying perfume. Instead, she just drove into the night with her chorus singing along to any, and every, song.

When they arrived at the party, only a few guests were there. Alex jumped out and hurried inside to see if Jo needed more help. Inside, the house looked amazing. With white flowers and a banner that read HAPPY 40th ANNIVERSARY, Alex was without words. She was staring at the decorations when Jo appeared in a white and gold jumpsuit. Her ponytail was gone and her long, relaxed tresses rested on her shoulders. It was times like these that Alex remembered how she always wanted to look like her older sister when she was young. Josephine said, "Well, it came together nice, huh?"

"It sure did, Jo. It's amazing."

"Go, look out back. It looks great. The guys really did a great job."

The back porch and the backyard had been transformed. The back porch had high back chairs covered in white chair covers arranged on the porch. The railings were decorated in white tea light candles and orchid leaves.

Each side of the yard had a large, white tent strung with stringed clear lights. The center of the yard was left uncovered. There was a parquet dance floor surrounded by tiki torches, which were wrapped in a white toile cloth. The tent on the left was set up for food. It had serving tables draped in white cloth and a table for gifts and the cake. On the right side, the other tent was filled with tables of varying sizes that were also draped in white cloth and a centerpiece of orchid petals floating in clear bowls of water. It was spectacular.

As Alex stood on the back porch, she could hear Jacqueline, Mallory, and Paige entering the house and talking with Jo and Dom. She was so busy eavesdropping that she didn't notice that someone had joined her on the porch.

When she felt cool breath on her back, she turned quickly into Elet's chest. He hugged her close. "Hi, baby. I feel like I haven't seen you in forever. I don't know what I'm gonna do next week."

Smiling, she said, "You'll get through it." She pulled back from his embrace to see him standing there in black pants, black loafers, and a button up white shirt. "Don't you look nice?"

"I wasn't sure if I should have worn a tie. I brought one just in case you wanted me to put it on."

She slapped him on the butt and turned back towards the yard. "Are my parents here?" she asked.

"No, your Uncle William is supposed to have them here in forty-five minutes. Jo wanted them to be wowed by the decorations. I'm sure that they will."

Kissing him on the cheek, she turned and walked inside to start receiving guests. Within minutes, the house and yard began to fill with distant family and close friends. The caterer came with food and Dom started a playlist of music from a speaker in the dining room window. Within minutes, Alex and Jo's parents arrived with their Uncle Will to a round of applause. They were thrilled at the outpouring of people who had come to celebrate their anniversary. As they walked among their guests to thank them all, they shared what a wonderful job their children had done with the decorations.

Alex buzzed around the tent welcoming people, hearing how wonderful she looked, and how proud people were to see her name in the Sun. She hugged and kissed more times than she could remember. Jo was busy on the porch welcoming people and talking about how big the boys were getting. Elet stood in the corner of the porch drinking punch and being introduced by Dom as Mr. Alexandra Stevens. He smiled shaking hands and being asked how old he was, where his family was from, what he did for a living, and when they were getting married. At the request of Jo, Paige, Mallory, and Jacqueline assisted the caterer or guests as needed. In most cases, there wasn't much to be done, but they were happy to help.

There came a lull in the party after everyone had finally arrived. The Stevens' were mingling among their guests and their family.

Elet had found Alex and they were slow dancing in the grass to the croons of Jazz greats. He said, "This is an amazing night. I hope that we have a party like this in forty years."

Joking, Alex said, "Except we'll have hip-hop playing in the background of our party, not jazz and Motown classics."

"You left out rap. We have to have booty-shaking."

"Now, that's a party," she said still swaying in the breeze.

Unaware of the outside world, the eyes of the guests were on them. Jo and Dom were standing side-by-side on the porch looking down upon them. Each was remembering what it was like to have young love. Mr. Stevens was sitting amongst the surviving members of his naval platoon. He warmed at the sight of his youngest daughter laughing in the arms of a man he liked. Her mother was surrounded by her sisters who wanted to know if Elet was the one. Paige smiled sweetly as Jacqueline tried to point Mallory in their direction. Yet, no one spoke above a whisper. No one wanted to interrupt this moment that they had been privileged to witness.

Levi interrupted the tranquility. He'd been playing on his iPad throughout most of the party. Josephine had lost that battle with Dom. Levi had been allowed to bring it as long as he played with his headphones on. It was not the sound from the headphones that interrupted the party. The moment was disrupted by Levi's triumphant scream "Touchdown, suckas!" The yard, the porch, Elet and Alex erupted in laughter. Josephine screamed his name, but Mr. Stevens told her to leave the boy alone. And, so, Levi was left to play.

Elet left Alex to mingle as he went to talk on the porch to Jacqueline who stood alone for the first time that evening. He said, "Hey, stranger, how the hell are ya?"

"Hey, man," they hugged. "I'm good. I mean, I haven't proposed to anyone this week, but I'm good. How are things with you?"

"Better than I deserve. I noticed that you've had a companion all evening. I wanted to come over and talk, but I didn't want to interrupt."

"What? With who? Mallory? Oh, come on, you can come over and talk no matter who I'm with. You know how much I love you. Besides, you know Mallory."

Pointing to himself with his drink in his hand, "Oh, I know her. I think the world of her, but it looked like I might interrupt something if I walked up. That's all I'm sayin'."

"What? Nah, just us talking about people. You know, what's funny, though? All night when I introduce Mallory to friends and family, they ask me how long we've been together. I laugh and say that we're just friends. Just because I like girls doesn't mean I can't be friends with one."

He'd been nodding while she spoke, then he said, "Well, it could be that the two of you kinda look at each other like there might be something going on."

"Do not."

"Yeah, you do, Jacqueline."

"And, that's fine by me. I would like nothing more than for you to be happy, but what's going on. Are you falling for her? Is she falling for you? Is this sex or a relationship? You can tell me anything. Even if you aren't sure," he put his arm on her shoulder. "We've been through a lot together. I'm not trying to get in your business. Hell, maybe you don't even know, but it sure looks like you like her."

Jacqueline stepped from under his arm. "I swear it's nothing. Just two friends hanging out. You remember how much Alex and I hung out before you two started getting serious. It's the same thing."

Shaking his head, Elet said, "No, Jacqueline, it's not the same. You look at her like you don't know that the rest of us are around. You tease her in flirty little ways. You never did that with Alex. You could look past Alex to look at some other woman. You don't see other women when Mallory's in the room. Look, if you like her, then cool." He placed his arm back around her, looked her in the eyes, and poked her in her chest as he made his point, "Figure out what you want from her and if you can have it. Figure out, even if you can have it, if it's worth it if things go bad."

When he stopped speaking, she wiggled free from him. She walked to the edge of the porch as if she was going to walk out into the yard. She walked down two stairs and sat down. She placed her head in her hands. Elet was watching from the porch. He was confident that he had gotten through to her.

However, his confidence was quelled when Mallory came out of the house, walked behind Jacqueline, and placed her hand gently on Jacqueline's shoulder. Jacqueline removed her head from her hands and sat upright.

To himself, Elet said, "See, this is what I mean."

The music was turned off. The kids were gathered as all the guests sat to eat. Mr. and Mrs. Stevens sat facing their guest and family. People laughed as they enjoyed the warm, summer evening, good food, and good company. Before the cake was served, many friends and family members stood, told stories, and made speeches. At the end, Uncle Will stood to give his speech.

"Ladies and Gentleman, on behalf of my brother, Henry, and his bride of forty years, Mary, my niece, Josephine and her husband, Dominic, and my other niece, Alexandra and her young man, Elet, let me thank you all for joining us to celebrate tonight. Having been a man long since widowed, I'm happy that my little brother and his wife still enjoy the day-to-day joy that love has to offer. I hope that they, and all of you, experience that kind of love for many years to come."

The yard filled with applause and cheers. Alex had been listening to all the stories of people recalling moments in the lives of her parents. She was touched by the stories and the fondness so many people shared for her parents. She was sitting at a table with Dominic, Jo, and Elet. She and her sister had wiped away tears on many occasions, but they were tears of happiness. She was enjoying this evening more than she thought she might. And, she was happy that Elet was here with her.

There came a break in the speakers. She was going to lean in and tell Elet that they should slip away from the party. She was going to propose that they take his truck around the block for a quick getaway. But before she could say any of that, she felt Elet rise to speak. She wondered if he had prepared something. She thought that maybe Jo had suggested it.

Elet stood and the crowd turned and looked at him. The yard fell silent. He started to speak, "I have a story that's close to my heart that I want to share as well. Alex and I had been dating for a few months when she said that the upcoming weekend was her mother's birthday and that she was going to come down here and take her mother and father to lunch. While Alex and I were out shopping for her mother's birthday gift, Mrs. Stevens called. Mrs. Stevens wanted to know where they'd be going to lunch. Alex hadn't planned any location, so I threw out a few places. After three or four places, Mrs. Stevens picked one and asked who it was that was with her. Alex told her my new boyfriend, Elet. Mrs. Stevens must have told Alex to bring me along to lunch since it was my pick. Now, I gotta admit I was nervous. I'd been told that I was the first white boy that Alex had ever dated but I was eager to meet Alex's parents. I had my truck detailed, got a shave, a haircut, and bought a new shirt the morning of the lunch. We drove here, to this house." Elet held his hands up and pointed to the house. "I was so nervous when I walked up to the porch and knocked. Even more so, when Mr. Stevens opened the door, looked and at me, and said we don't want none of what you're sellin'. He was just about to close the door when he saw Alex. Then, I could see his mind work, he realized, that I was the new boyfriend. He said *sorry young man everybody's selling something* and opened the door. I gave Mrs. Stevens the flowers I'd stopped and bought her. She pulled me in and hugged me. She told me that she couldn't reach the vase and Mr. Stevens was too old to be getting up on stools. So, she grabbed me by my hand and led me to the kitchen to get it for her. Mr. Stevens was standing by the sink quizzing me on my family, my education, and my profession. I felt good until he asked about military service and football. I had nothing good for either. But, I was able to tell him that my father, who had passed away, was in the Army and that I like baseball far more than football. In fact, I have a brother, Silas who plays in the minor league. Helping arrange the flowers for Mrs. Stevens, he and I talked about baseball. Outfielders. Pitchers. Catchers. Teams. Designated Hitters. When we were ready to go, I helped Mrs. Stevens into the front of the cab and Mr. Stevens and Alex rode in the back. We talked all the way to lunch. It was a good lunch. We talked about family and more baseball." The crowd laughed. Most commented on how Mr. Stevens did love sports talk.

Elet went on, "When we got back to the house, Mr. Stevens took me to the backyard and told me - *son, your daddy would be proud. It looks like you've grown into a good man and that's all a father wants from his son. You're welcome around here, as long*

Alex wants it. I thought he wanted to shake my hand, but he pulled me in and hugged me. In the years since that lunch, Mr. and Mrs. Stevens have treated me like a member of their family. Ever since that meeting, I have tried to be a good man for my father, my mother, and for the Stevens and I just wanted to say Happy Anniversary to such wonderful people."

As he ended, Alex looked up at him with tears in her eyes. He looked down at her with tears in his eyes and reached for her hand. She grabbed his outreached hand, pulled him down, and kissed him. Mr. and Mrs. Stevens had stood up and walked to Elet. Mrs. Stevens hugged, kissed him, and told him that she loved him. Mr. Stevens hugged him and said, "You're a fine man."

While still in his embrace, Elet whispered in his ear, "I asked Alex to marry me. She said yes. I wanted you to know, but I didn't want to make the party about us, not you."

Mr. Stevens pulled back, looked at his wife, and then to Alex, but neither of them had heard what Elet had said. Then, he pulled Elet in for a tight, strong hug. He said, "Nonsense, son. We ain't waiting. We're gonna tell everybody right now."

Mr. Stevens leaned down and whispered the news to his wife. She covered her mouth in happiness.

Jo leaned over to Alex and said, "Are you pregnant?"

Alex said, "What? No, I'm not pregnant. I have an IUD."

Jo said, "TMI!"

Then, it hit Alex. She was stunned. As she looked at him in anger, he squeezed her hand and tried to kiss her forehead. Hastily, she pulled away. Mr. Stevens led Mrs. Stevens back to their table and said, "I have an announcement. We've loved Elet like a member of this family for years. We've just found out that he's about to become one. He's proposed to Alex and she's said yes. There's gonna be a Stevens wedding." The crowd began to cheer and congratulate them. Mr. Stevens finished with, "and you're all invited."

Jo leaned over and said, "Why didn't you tell me?"

Scowling, Alex said, "Elet and I agreed not to tell anyone until after the party." She looked at Elet with fire in her eyes, but her anger was unknown to him. He was enjoying the outpouring of love and congratulations that they were receiving.

Alex stood up from the table and walked towards the house. Jacqueline met her on the porch. Before Jacqueline could think of something reassuring to say, Alex said, "I need a drink."

"Yeah, I bet. I thought you weren't gonna tell them tonight."

"Uh, yeah, we weren't supposed to tell them tonight, but Captain Tears got caught up in the moment. I'm so ready to get out of here."

"I don't think that you can just go. They're your parents and it's their party." Jacqueline said.

"Jax, this is a nightmare. My entire family just found out and I didn't get to tell them. Elet told them even when I said not to do it. I want to kill him."

Just then, Elet walked up. "Babe, I know that you're mad, but look, it all worked out. No one's calling me names. It's okay. Everyone's happy."

Angrily, she said, "Do I look happy Elet? Do I?" Her eyes were piercing into his face. He didn't dare reply. She walked away. Without speaking to him, the two sat side-by-side as they received well wishes for the rest of the meal.

After the cake was cut, Alex inhaled her piece. She found Jacqueline and announced, "We're outta here."

Paige said, "I'm still eating."

Alex leaned into her face and said, "Pack it in your purse or you're staying here. We're leaving NOW." The women said their goodbyes quickly and were in the Laredo heading back to Seaborn Island within ten minutes.

<u>11</u>

The drive from the party to Seaborn Island was silent. Alex was stewing in the front seat. Jacqueline mustered, "I'm sorry that this didn't work out like you planned."

Alex grumbled, "It worked out exactly as I didn't want it to."

"Yeah, I know, but what'd you really think was gonna happen. Elet's excited. He is bursting at the seams to tell the world. You're trying to keep a lid on him, and I don't know if you can."

"No shit."

Uncertain of what to say, Mallory and Paige sat in the backseat quietly listening. That was the last talking that would happen on the drive to the house. Jacqueline drove quietly for about twenty minutes when she realized that Alex, Mallory, and Paige had dozed off. The vibration of the world passing underneath had calmed them all into a peaceful slumber.

She removed the CD and searched for the local public radio station. Enjoying Vivaldi's *Four Seasons*, she drove along in the darkness replaying the night's most interesting moments. Jacqueline smiled to herself as she thought of their pleasant faces. She thought of how beautiful the house was decorated. She thought how amazing it was when Jo and Alex got along. She laughed to herself when she remembered Levi's touchdown cheer. She felt warm by the love that was obvious that Elet and Alex share; but, then she thought of her conversation with Elet. She was certain that Alex had said something to him that started his intervention. She wasn't mad at him. She wasn't mad at Alex for asking. She just wasn't sure why everyone had been asking.

She looked in the rearview window at Mallory. She thought about all the time that they had spent together. They were fond memories of seeing movies, having dinner, going on mini-trips, shopping together, birthdays, and holidays. None of them felt out of the ordinary. Nothing unusual had happened during any of those times together. She thought, *it's nice to have someone that you can be yourself with. It's nice to have someone that wants to be with you and go places with you and share experiences with you.*

She had not said any of this aloud when anyone asked. Surprised by her own thoughts, she looked at herself in the mirror. She realized exactly what Alex, and now Elet, were asking. Was she feeling something more? Was it just her? Was it Mallory as well? And, if Mallory felt something, what was it she felt? And, worse, what did she want to do about it?

She inched into the driveway of the villa hoping not to wake them, but as she crept up the incline of the driveway, Mallory awoke. Garbled, she said, "Where are we?"

Without thinking, Jacqueline replied, "Home."

"Are you going to come in for a bit," Mallory asked still groggy.

"Yes, of course, since I'm staying here, too," Jacqueline enjoyed teasing her in her bleariness.

"Good, I've been wanting you to stay over," Mallory responded. Jacqueline didn't say anything. She just sat in her seat and stared at a sleeping Mallory. She looked around to see if the other women were awake. She thought that none of them were. She was wrong. Paige was awake. Her eyes had remained closed, but she had heard the exchange. She would have made her herself known, but much like Jacqueline, she wasn't sure what to say or think after Mallory's sleep confession.

Hoping to avoid any more sleep talking, Jacqueline opened her door causing the interior light to cause the sharp return to reality for her sleepyheads. The women drug themselves out of the Laredo, into the house, and to their respective rooms without much conversation. Four women went to four separate bathrooms to begin their nightly routines.

After a half hour, Paige stepped into the hall and wished everyone a peaceful slumber; and, so began five minutes of each saying good night in turn to one another from behind their closed doors.

After Jacqueline settled into bed, there was a knock at the door. As it opened, she saw Mallory standing in the doorframe with wet hair in red and white, silk pajama pants, and a red, camisole-like top. With the hall light behind her, the outline of her body was apparent. Jacqueline thought that she should look away, but she couldn't.

Mallory spoke, "I can't go back to sleep. I noticed your light was on and thought that you might be awake, too."

In a whisper, Jacqueline said, "I was reading." Mallory apologized for disturbing her and headed to return to her room. Jacqueline continued, "But, come on in. I don't know if I really thought that I'd finish this on vacation." She tossed the book aside and pulled herself up in her king-sized bed.

Like an excited child, Mallory said, "Good," jumped onto the other side of the bed and got under the covers. They had touched many times, but lying in bed together under the covers felt different. So different, for a few moments, they stared in each other eyes not saying a word. Then, there was another knock

118

at the door. This time, it was Paige. Jacqueline and Mallory knew that because Paige announced herself.

"Jacqueline, are you awake? It's Paige. I really wanted to talk to you about something that was on my mind." When Jacqueline agreed, Paige opened the door, but she was obviously surprised to find Mallory in Jacqueline's bed. Jacqueline could see the surprise in her face.

Trying to ease Paige's concerns, Jacqueline said, "Looks like there is a slumber party in my room tonight." Mallory sat up and patted the middle of the bed as if to invite Paige to join them. Paige approached the bed, but she sat nervously at the foot of it.

Jacqueline said, "What do you want to talk about? I'm all ears."

"Oh, nothing important. I just wanted to chitchat. It was such an emotional day."

Chiming in, Mallory said, "It really was emotional, wasn't it? I wonder how Alex and Elet are."

Paige responded, "Oh, I know. Alex looked so...exposed when he made the announcement."

Mallory said, "I don't know if I can blame him. He's obviously very excited. He loves her. He wants to tell the world. I mean, what do you expect? She's not knocked up, so he can't figure out why he can't tell the world."

"Because we agreed not to," Alex said as she walked in the room. With a cotton nightgown on that said, ALWAYS ON, across the front, Alex slid into bed pushing Mallory next to Jacqueline.

Lying on her back, Mallory said, "But, come on, Alex, you're just scared. He realized nothing bad was going to happen and took a shot and told them. Now, you're all pissy, because he didn't do what you wanted. Well, tough shit, welcome to marriage!"

"Well, that's not reassuring," Alex, said hugging a pillow.

Paige had stretched out across the bottom of the bed. Jacqueline passed her two pillows. Paige stood up, straightened her flannel nightgown, and got under the blanket but not the sheet. She asked, "Have you spoken to him?"

"Yeah, I finally called him back. He's apologized about a hundred times. I know that he feels bad, but I'm still pissed. I wasn't ready to tell them yet. I wasn't ready to deal with their shit. I told you, guys, why couldn't that be enough?"

"Well, I guess we should plan for a long engagement," Jacqueline said snuggling further down in the bed. In doing so, she realized that Mallory had intertwined their feet. Jacqueline didn't move hers and Mallory didn't face her. It was obvious that the closeness was to remain unspoken.

Alex said, "Somehow, I doubt it." After a long pause, she sat up with a big smile on her face, "Let's not talk about this anymore. We are on vacation. What are we gonna do? Tomorrow, Olive's boat arrives, but other than that, tomorrow is our oyster."

"Well, location was one of the big draws of this place. We have the Gulf in the backyard. We can walk down to the bars, restaurants, and clubs on the boardwalk. When Mallory and I came to scout the place out, the realtor said that things are open all night every night." replied Jacqueline.

Reminding her of things she didn't mention, Mallory added, "Jax, remember you said that we can also take the boat out of the marina. And, we can leave the island and go into town and shop. Remember, you said that we'd shop."

"Oh, a boat. We definitely have to do that," Paige was excited.

Alex added, "I wanna get a new bathing suit. We definitely have to go shopping. I need some new things for all these nights that we're going out."

Turning to face Alex, Jacqueline felt the weight of the back of Mallory's body as the back of Mallory pressed into the front of Jacqueline. She fought all temptation to put her arm around her. Mallory said, "Didn't you buy a bunch of things before we left town?"

"Yes, but those are Tampa clothes. I need Seaborn Island clothes."

Everyone laughed. Paige started to yawn. Looking for a clock, she yawn-spoke, "What time is it?"

Jacqueline pulled away from Mallory to check her cell phone, "Almost three."

Paige stood and stretched, "I've got to get some sleep, or I won't be worth a shit in the morning." They stared at her. She rarely, if ever, cursed. Knowing exactly why there were staring, she said, "A saint has a little bit of sinning in her," winked and walked out.

From the bed, they all said, "Good night."

To which she replied, "Night Night" and closed her door.

Jacqueline placed her phone on the nightstand and retrieved the remote. She turned on the television. Flipping past the music videos that Alex wanted to watch, Jacqueline stopped on the news.

"Oh my God, when'd you get so old?" Alex said as she got out of the bed and walked out the door. Jacqueline and Mallory told her goodnight. With just the two of them in the room now, Jacqueline thought that Mallory was going to leave or, at the very least, roll to the other side of the king-sized bed. Mallory did move further to the middle, but she didn't go fully onto the far side of the bed. Instead, Mallory laid there talking to Jacqueline about the news segments and anchors. Then, after ten minutes or so, Jacqueline noticed that Mallory breathing had slowed and she'd stopped talking. She lifted up on one arm and tried to look to see if Mallory was asleep. She couldn't tell, but she assumed that since Mallory didn't responded that it was safe to assume that she had dozed off. Aloud Jacqueline said, *humph*. For the first time, she began to wonder what was happening between them. But, alone in the room, she was happy to have Mallory there. She turned the TV down and the light off so as not to wake her.

CROSS YOUR FINGERS

·

12

At seven-thirty, Jacqueline awoke to Mallory snuggled beside her in bed. Lifting her head to get a better view of their meshed bodies, she replayed the night's events just to verify in her own mind that nothing regrettable had happened. Once she was secure in her own innocence, she slid out of bed. Always the productive early riser, she prepared herself for the morning and leaped downstairs into the gourmet kitchen.

She'd paid for a well-stocked kitchen; and, it turned out to be a sound investment. The pantry, the wine cooler, the refrigerator, and the freezer were packed. After surveying all the contents, she began preparing a buffet of breakfast items. With coffee brewing and muffins baking, she began to make bacon and sausage. The smell traveled throughout the quiet house. Listening overhead at the sounds of her friends moving about, she smiled and turned on the kitchen radio. One by one, women stumbled down the stairs and into the kitchen.

Dressed casually, in shorts and a T-shirt, Paige was the first to appear. "Sorry to wake you. Of everyone in the house, I wanted you to be able to get some sleep," Jacqueline said.

"Oh, girl, I slept like a log. It was the first time in a while that I've got the chance to just sleep without listening out for little feet or cries," Paige admitted. She looked refreshed and awake. She peeked her head into the oven. "You need any help?" she asked.

Jacqueline shrugged, "I think I've got everything under control. Do you think I'm missing anything?"

Paige looked around. She checked out the meats, the muffins, the eggs sitting in the bowl, and then she whirled around and said, "Grits." She grabbed a pot and looked for grits. "Did you run to the store this morning? You bought so much food for a few days?"

"No way. I can't carry this much stuff. My trunk is the size of a lunchbox. The realtor gave me the option of having the house stocked for our vacation. I paid extra for all of this," Jacqueline explained swirling the spatula in hand.

"You should've let us help pay for all of this. You know we do make money." Paige said.

"Yes, I know. I approve your timesheets," Jacqueline winked at her.

"Yeah, you do." Paige stared at Jacqueline for a few minutes. She didn't say a word, but Jacqueline could feel herself being watched.

Finally, Jacqueline said, "Come out with it."

Paige stepped in close. "You know, I love you. We're friends and I respect you. I'd do anything for you. For all of you. But, I have to ask. Are you and Mallory messing around?" Jacqueline hung her head. She thought, *this is like an epidemic.* Before she could answer, Paige went on, "If you don't want to tell me yet, that's fine, but you should know that it's starting to look kinda obvious."

With bread in her hand, Jacqueline stopped cooking, walked closer to Paige, and said, "There's nothing going on."

"But, you look like there is."

"But, there's not."

"Do you want there to be? Do you like her *that way?*"

"You know, I don't think so." Jacqueline was going to turn back to the stove and continue cooking, but she couldn't. She hung her head down and held onto the counter for the support she felt like she wasn't getting anywhere else. "I don't know what's going on. Everyone keeps asking me 'what's going on.' Well, absolutely nothing is going on. I'm not being coy or secretive. You guys could be with us every waking minute. There's nothing going on, I swear. But, you guys have made me start questioning things myself. But, there really isn't anything going on. I don't know what to tell any of you." She'd had enough of everyone asking. She'd kept her cool, but now, it was pissing her off. "I promise that I won't let the pariah that my life apparently is spill all over and destroy the lives of innocent bystanders." Jacqueline said defensively.

She was mad and Paige knew it. "I didn't mean it like that."

• "You did. Everyone does. You, Elet, and Alex are all warning me not to hurt her or not to hurt our friendship or not to make her feel uncomfortable because of the *way* I am. I get it. It's all duly noted. I understand." Jacqueline abruptly went back to breakfast. Paige moved the grits she'd been making from the burner. Jacqueline had turned her back to her.

Paige walked behind her and placed her head on Jacqueline's shoulder and her left arm around her neck. "I'm sorry, friend. I never meant it that way. I really didn't. I'd love to see you happily dating or in a relationship with someone who loved you and cared about you the way that you love and care about everyone else. I just didn't want you to bark up a street that might be a cul-de-sac."

Jacqueline's anger was overcome by a belly laugh. "What does that even mean?" Paige started to laugh at Jacqueline's laugh.

Mallory entered the kitchen to the two of them laughing. She said, "What's so funny?" The two didn't stop laughing long enough to answer her. Grabbing a slice of bacon, she began to chomp.

Jacqueline slapped her hand with the bread she was still holding, "Hey, don't eat that. Wait til it's time to eat."

Playfully, Mallory turned away, "If you want it come and get it." Jacqueline was staring at Mallory, still dressed as she had been in Jacqueline's bed an hour ago. Paige was staring at Jacqueline staring at Mallory.

From the hall, Alex said, "I'm in the hallway. Should I go back upstairs until the freakiness is over?"

Jacqueline said, "Get in here. Breakfast is almost ready."

"If it's a freaky breakfast, I don't want any part of it. I can wait and have a non-freaky breakfast with Paige."

Paige said, "I'm in here. It's okay."

Alex peered around the corner. "Paige? Just had to check." As Alex reached for bacon, Jacqueline pushed her out of the room and pointed towards the dining room table.

Mallory said, "It's nice out. Let's eat outside by the pool. There's a table out there." Ushering all the food, the women walked onto the back patio and set up. They had a smorgasbord. They ate and drank sherbet mimosas, an Alex recipe from years prior. After they had finished their breakfast feast, the table was devastated. Plates were empty. Sherbet was melting on the glass tabletop.

With her leg thrown over her chair, patting her belly through her robe, Alex begged, "Jax, please, please, go get Olive for me? Please."

Jacqueline was ready to agree, but before she could, Mallory rushed to her defense. "What are *you* going to be doing?"

Alex didn't answer. She still had her hands closed like the steeple of a church with pleading eyes.

Paige asked, "Who's Olive?"

Alex swung around to look at her. "I've answered this question for you a million times. Olive's my old friend. We grew up together. She works for a cruise line, remember?" Paige nodded, but she didn't remember.

Finally answering Mallory, Alex said, "I thought that I'd call Elet, clean my pores, and get dressed, so that when Jax and Olive got back we could all go shopping before we go out tonight."

"When'd we agree that's what we were doing today?" Mallory didn't recall any of those plans.

"Oh, that's right. We talked about it after you fell asleep with your head on Jax's chest." Alex teased.

Mallory blushed and looked at Jacqueline. Jacqueline nodded her head denying that any of that happened - just in case Mallory wasn't sure if any of that had happened. All Mallory could reply with was, "Shut up."

Jacqueline stood up and started gathering plates. She said, "I love Olive. I'll go get her." Balancing a few plates on top of her plate, she joked, "I guess I should've paid for a maid." After the porch and kitchen were cleaned, Jacqueline ran back upstairs. She was closing her door behind her as Mallory came in.

"Want me to ride with you?"

"Sure, if you want. You've never met Olive, have you?"

"No, I haven't had the pleasure."

"Well, she's….a character, a free spirit." Jacqueline laughed, "Just remember that she doesn't mean any harm." Jacqueline pulled a pair of shorts from the closet and threw them on the bed.

"I guess I can't wear this," Mallory said tugging at her cami.

"No, probably not your best idea." Jacqueline was busy gathering her clothes.

Mallory walked in and sat on the bed. "Are we okay?"

Removing her shoes from the closet, Jacqueline said, "Yeah, of course, why wouldn't we be?"

"Well, things feel different. I don't know. Different."

"It's fine. You fell asleep in my bed. That's all. It's no big deal. Nothing more happened. It didn't mean anything. It was like a sleepover."

"It didn't mean anything? It didn't mean anything. Right, it didn't mean anything." Mallory got up and walked out of Jacqueline's room. With shoe in hand, Jacqueline stood up and looked in her direction. She heard Mallory open her own door and close it. She sat on her bed, holding her head in her hands. She wasn't sure. There was something definitely happening, but Jacqueline didn't know what it was or what it meant. Moreover, what was worse, judging from Mallory's concerned face, Jacqueline knew that Mallory didn't know either.

Jacqueline decided that she wouldn't read anything into it. She went to the bathroom and splashed water on her face. Looking at herself, she thought, *everything is just fine. We're good friends. That's all. Good friends. Don't let them creep you out.* She dressed and went outside to prepare for the ride to the port. As she was lowering the top, Mallory showed up in tiny, white shorts and a sleeveless, blue cut-out top. She tried not to gawk, but she had a feeling that she might have been. Mallory smiled and got in the front seat. Jacqueline finished putting away the top and jumped in. After putting on her shades, Jacqueline said, "We're off." And, off they were.

With the top down, a deep conversation would be too hard to have; and Jacqueline knew it. She wasn't sure that she wanted to talk about whatever it was that everyone thought was going on. The two smiled and sang as they drove down the state road. It was a beautiful ride on a sunny day. They were smiling and enjoying being in one another's company. Jacqueline thought of how well they got along, how easy things were between them, and how she loved things as they were.

When they arrived, Jacqueline parked the Laredo and got out. Jacqueline had begun walking towards the terminal when she realized Mallory was not with her. Mallory was still sitting, so she returned to the Jeep and walked right to the passenger's side. She noticed that Mallory was checking her makeup.

Jacqueline said, "Trust me, you don't have to fix your makeup for Olive."

Finishing up, Mallory closed her compact and said, "Maybe, it's for you."

"You don't have to fix it for me either."

"Don't you want me to look nice?"

"You always do." Jacqueline opened the door with her right hand and rested her left hand on the top. Mallory slid out between the door and Jacqueline's left arm.

Mallory rested in the doorframe. For a few moments, they stood still facing each other in silence. Mallory said, "Thank you," bit her lip, and slid out from between Jacqueline and the doorframe.

Jacqueline closed the door, but she did not immediately follow Mallory. She rested her head against the door and took a deep breath to reorient herself, and thought, *Fuck*. When she turned around, Mallory was heading towards the docking ship. Jacqueline didn't rush to catch her. Instead, she walked behind her enjoying the look of her legs peering from under her shorts as they moved along to the beat of a song that only played in Mallory's head. The reorientation had failed.

When Mallory noticed how far back Jacqueline was, she stopped, and put her hands on her hips and waited. Jacqueline jogged to catch up. Then, the two walked side by side towards the towering cruise ship, laughing and joking.

Mallory said, "Am I going to like Olive?"

"Probably not. She has to grow on people and that's always hard for you."

Swatting at Jacqueline, "Don't say that. Alex grew on me." Just then, Jacqueline stopped walking and bent her knees. Looking confused, Mallory said, "What're you doing?"

"Getting ready," Jacqueline replied. When Mallory turned to look in the direction that Jacqueline was facing, she saw a woman in a long, tie-dyed skirt, a tank top, and foam, green flip-flops running towards them. In full steam, the woman was gaining ground quickly. For a moment, Mallory feared that this stranger was crazy and planning to hurt them.

As the woman got closer, she could hear that the woman was talking, "Hey, it's been so long. I'm so happy to see you. Oh my God, you look great. Woo hoo."

When she got within a few feet, she leapt into the air. Jacqueline caught her. The woman wrapped her arms and legs around Jacqueline and bounced in her arms as if she was riding a Bronco.

With the woman in her arms, Jacqueline turned to Mallory and said, "Mallory, this is Olive."

After giving Jacqueline a firm, peck on the lips, she slid down Jacqueline's body onto the ground. Immediately, Olive whirled around and faced Mallory. Looking slightly afraid, Mallory received an Olive hug, a bear hug that involved Mallory being lifted up and bounced around. Being held in the air by Olive, Mallory could smell the mix of alcohol and patchouli in Olive's hair. Letting her go, Olive said, "Hey, girl. I'm Olive."

Backing away, Mallory said, "Uh, hi, I'm Mallory."

Jacqueline picked up Olive's duffel bag off the ground. As they were returning to the Jeep, Olive was waving and talking to the vacationers heading to their cars.

Mallory said, "Were you on vacation?"

Jacqueline answered for a busy Olive, "No, she works onboard."

When they arrived at the Laredo, Olive took over the explanation, "Oh, yeah. That's my job. It's what I do and I must say it's fuckin' incredible. It's like a never-ending community of people trying to get away from all the shit that's back here on land. Man, it's the best."

Jacqueline smiled. She was enjoying watching Mallory get to know Olive. Olive opened the passenger's door and angled for Mallory to get in the back of the Laredo. Since it was their first meeting, Mallory complied. Jacqueline already had the Laredo roaring and backed out of the parking lot as soon as the two resolved their seating options.

Olive slipped out of her shoes and sat on her feet. She turned to face Mallory who was sitting behind Jacqueline. "So, Mallory, who are you?"

"Who am I?"

"Yeah, what's your story? Who are you? I think you really get to know a person if you ask who they think that they are. Then, you know what they think is important about them." Jacqueline laughed audibly. She knew what was ahead.

Mallory wasn't certain how to answer. "Let's see, I work alongside Alex at the Sun."

"Oh, is Alex your boss?"

"No, we're co-workers. Jax is technically our boss."

"Oh, I like that. Jax. That sounds hot just like you." And Olive winked in Jacqueline's direction and touched her arm, softly. Turning back to Mallory, she asked, "Hey, did you apply for that big job, too?"

"Yeah, we both did. Well, us and some other people." Mallory didn't want to talk about this with Olive. She was scared of where it might go.

"Did you apply anywhere else like Alex did?" Olive asked. Jacqueline met Mallory's eyes in the rearview mirror. She motioned for Mallory to keep her lid. Jacqueline wanted to give Olive all the space in the world to talk. So, Olive went on. "I told her, Alex, don't sit around waiting to get the axe. Use your contacts, get out there, and drum up some opportunities. But, shit, I'm glad she got that interview with that magazine so quick or I would've felt like a real jackass for suggesting some shit that didn't happen." Jacqueline's eyebrows were raised. Mallory smirked.

As Olive continued with Mallory's interview, Jacqueline grew angry and felt betrayed. She was upset about being placed in a position to choose the best candidate when two of the possibilities were her friends. She had stressed over this. Now, she found out that Alex had been pursuing opportunities outside of the Sun. Jacqueline had stopped listening to Olive's inquisition of Mallory and her ex-husband, daughter, college major, and neighborhood. She was seething. *I thought we were friends. I thought we could tell each other anything. I can't believe that she kept this from me.* She felt feverish with anger.

Then, something Olive said caught her attention. They had been working on *who* Mallory was, but now, Olive wanted to know *what* Mallory was. Even Jacqueline wasn't sure where this new line of questioning was headed. Olive explained. "You know, gay, straight, bi, monogamous, polyamorous." Pointing to herself, "Me. I'm a polyamorous hetero. That doesn't mean that I haven't been with women." Olive winked at Jacqueline. "I've definitely enjoyed the company of women, but, you know, it just never clicked with me and women the way it does with me and men. That's why I don't consider myself bi." Olive said all of this with such ease and confidence as if she was a sex therapist. Mallory looked astounded, but little did she know that there was more. "But, Jacqueline, on the other hand, she had fun with sex for a long time. Alex tells me she's cooled down. But, she's gay. I mean, there were some guys, but she's the opposite of me. I told Alex the other day that I think Jax here, is probably monogamously gay. Just watch. I think she's 'bout ready to settle in. Aren't you, honey?" Jacqueline shrugged. Olive nodded as if to convince Jacqueline. Turning back to Mallory, she said, "So, what are you?"

Almost offended by this entire conversation, Mallory said, "Didn't I tell you that I have a daughter named Zoe?"

"Yeah, and that means that you were with a guy at least once. I'm talking about love. I'm talking about what makes your toes curl. I'm talking about giggling all night. I'm not talking about getting married and doing what the world tells you to do. Girls get caught up in that shit before they really get to know themselves in this great big world. I'm not sayin that there's anything wrong with being a plain ole monogamous hetero. I'm just saying that people pick it before they know that they even have options. People are scared of options. Aren't they, Jax?" Again, Jacqueline nodded assuming that that was her role. "I'm saying, you gotta know what does it for you. Fuck that. Who does it for you? Figure that shit out, and then, you're really living." Mallory got her own Olive wink.

Praying that they were close to the house, Mallory mumbled a stunned "I don't know." To Jacqueline, it sounded like a desperate attempt to get to end the conversation, but Olive believed that Mallory really was not certain. Jacqueline shook her head as if to tell Mallory that her attempt to end this conversation had failed. Olive reiterated, "Well, baby, you better figure it out. That's the shit that makes life worth living." Then, finally, they didn't say anything for a long while.

Jacqueline just drove in silence. She was still stewing in the news of Alex's interview with a magazine. Olive was strumming on the dashboard to the classic rock CD she put in the player. Mallory was rubbing her forehead.

After awhile Mallory spoke, "Olive, what do you do when you aren't on the boat?"

"Oh, I usually spend it with my kids."

Surprised, Jacqueline turned to Olive, "I didn't know you had kids."

"Shit, yeah. I got four. They're with my momma back in Brandon." The strumming stopped. Olive faced forward and looked out her window, "When I'm off the boat, I usually go home to them. Try to catch up on their lives. Spend time with them, teaching them the things I've learned, so that they can have a little piece of me other than just my good looks." She laughed to herself. Olive was subdued. Sitting there in the Laredo on a hot, summer day, Olive seemed transported from the Laredo back home in Brandon surrounded by her children.

Mallory said, "I couldn't imagine."

"People always say shit like that." Mallory apologized for possibly offending her, but Olive didn't hear her. She went on talking, "They ask me 'shouldn't I be home? Wouldn't the kids be better off with seeing me every day?' Shit, no, they wouldn't. Hell, I wouldn't. I know me. My momma knows me and my kids know me. I'm just glad that I got a momma who knows the truth."

Mallory asked, "Where's their father?"

"Fuck, I don't know. If you see one of them, catch his ass and hold him for me."

Mallory laughed and Olive laughed with her. As Jacqueline turned back onto the island, Olive let loose her hair and stood up on the floorboard. Holding onto the windshield, she roared, hollering at anybody in the street. It continued all the way to the villa. Jacqueline braced her at every turn. The roar was so loud that when they reached the driveway Alex ran outside to greet her saying she heard them coming down the road. As the two hugged, Jacqueline lifted her seat forward, so Mallory to could get out.

Jacqueline reached up and placed her hands at Mallory's waist to help her out of the Jeep. Mallory whispered in Jacqueline's ear as Jacqueline eased her back on the ground, "Did you ever sleep with her?"

Jacqueline smiled and said, "I've never been <u>that</u> lonely."

CROSS YOUR FINGERS

13

Olive asked, "Hey, where's Jo at? I thought she'd be here this week."

Rolling her eyes, Alex responded, "She'll be here tomorrow." Alex was busy putting the final touches on her new outfit. They had all gone downtown to the touristy stores for a little shopping. Alex was in heaven. Having her friends was like the relationship she'd always wanted to share with Jo. They went out shopping and tried on outfits. They picked out accessories for one another. They'd had lunch, then they headed back to the house to get dressed for the evening.

Other than Jacqueline, who was waiting downstairs, everyone was upstairs with their doors open running back and forth from room to room giggling and getting dressed. Alex had no need for Jo to come. She had everything she needed in her friends, but she'd been invited. And, now, Jo was coming. Alex decided not to think about it. Instead, she made a perfume cloud to walk through. Once she'd paced through it sufficiently, she yelled for the others.

"Where's my bitches?" she screamed as she walked out of her room.

Like prostitutes, they appeared in their doorways. Paige was wearing a belted, lace, red and black tulip dress, and black heels. Mallory had curled her hair, so that it looked like waves. Olive had applied a face full of makeup. As Alex talked to Paige in the hall, she thought back on the quiet, maternal Paige that she had grown used to, but told Paige "This," pointing to her outfit, "is the Paige that I want to see more of."

Paige blushed and told her, "Stop it." As Paige left to join Jacqueline downstairs, Alex swatted her on the butt. Olive was in Mallory's room watching her finish her hair. Olive stood in the doorframe of the bathroom barefoot in a black leather strapless dress. Her wavy hair had been washed, dried, and mousse applied. It was dry but had the look of being wet. Alex reached out and touched.

Olive grabbed her hair and said, "Hey, don't mess it up."

"Is that possible?" Olive swung like she was going to hit her. Alex dodged her hand.

"Oh, look at you limber in heels!" replied Mallory .

Strutting around, Alex said, "I can do anything in heels."

Teasing her, Olive said, "I bet you can. I bet that's why Elet gave you that big ring." Olive went to grab her hand and noticed that Alex wasn't wearing her engagement ring. Olive asked, "Um, where's the ring?"

"I'm not wearing that thing tonight. It's a mood-killer."

"Whose mood is it killing? Ours? Yours? Or the guy you're waiting to talk to?" Mallory asked as she finished with her hair.

"Shut up. Let's go." Alex walked out the room.

Downstairs, Jacqueline was outside sitting in a lounge chair. Alex walked up and said, "See, you look nice. Aren't you happier with that than whatever you were going to wear?"

Jacqueline stood up in her long, black skinny jeans and polka dotted fitted button up. She did look nice, but she wouldn't dare admit it. She knew if she did, then they would try to do more shopping for her. She was about to answer Alex when Mallory appeared. Jacqueline saw her approaching. She was looking over Alex's shoulders into the house at Mallory walking towards them. She couldn't see the heels, but she knew that she was wearing them. She thought, *women have this indescribable way of teetering in heels. Between four and six inches, it's sexy as hell. There's no way to explain it, but if you catch a beautiful woman walking towards you in a pair of heels at the right moment, it's magnificent.* Alex noticed that she had lost Jacqueline's attention.

Noticing Jacqueline, Mallory spoke first, "You look amazing. I knew you could wear those pants." Mallory walked right to her and tugged on her pants.

Jacqueline didn't shy away from the tug. She replied, "Everything's so tight."

Alex said, "You gotta show people the goods."

Mallory reassured Jacqueline that things would loosen up some as the night went on. Alex noticed that no one had responded to or looked at her at all. Alex cleared her throat, but neither Jacqueline nor Mallory looked in her direction.

Jacqueline told Mallory, "You look nice too." Mallory spun around. Her wrap blouse swung in the breeze she made.

Alex was fake coughing. When they still didn't look, she said, "Don't I look nice?"

Without looking at her, Jacqueline said, "Yeah, you look great."

"Whatever. If you two are done complimenting each other, then let's go." Alex walked inside the house. Mallory followed her and Jacqueline brought up the rear. Olive and Paige were already outside the house eager to go. The women decided that there was no reason to drive since they could walk from the villa down to the sidewalk to the boardwalk.

They passed bars, restaurants, and beach accessories stores that they promised to check out over the next few days. They laughed and joked usually ignoring the comments of the men they passed. However, the attention they garnered helped Alex forget how no one in the house had complimented her. When they passed a club called the Honey Pot, Alex yelled back over her shoulder at Jacqueline, "I'm taking you there."

Olive chimed in, "Hell yeah. We're gonna get you laid before this vacation is over." Jacqueline was looking inside the club when the door opened. Out walked a tall, dark-haired woman in leather pants, Jacqueline held the door.

The stranger looked at Jacqueline and said, "Thanks. Are you going in?"

Jacqueline said, "No, I was walking by and I thought I'd help you out."

The woman replied, "That's sweet. You'll have to come by later and let me buy you a thank you drink."

Alex had stopped. She noticed that Jacqueline wasn't with them. She was heading back to see what was happening and overheard the woman's offer. Before Jacqueline could respond, she said, "When will you be back? Let me know and I'll make sure that she takes you up on it."

Still looking at Jacqueline, the woman replied, "I'll be back later tonight."

Alex said, "Then, it's a date."

The woman said, "Well, we'll have to see about that," and walked on.

Alex put her arm around Jacqueline's neck and said, "I love it here." The two caught up to the rest of the women.

Mallory asked Jacqueline, "What was that about?"

"Oh, nothing. Alex loves to help you even when you don't need help."

"No, with that woman. Are you going to go back there tonight to find her?"

"I doubt it. I'm sure it was just a little pointless flirting. Women in bars on a Saturday night. You know how it is."

"Oh, okay," Mallory said with hesitance in her voice. Jacqueline noticed the hesitance, but she didn't acknowledge it.

As the women walked further and further down the boardwalk, they heard the thumping of music. Alex said, "That's where we're going." Paige and Olive began to dance on the sidewalk. Mallory was singing along to the tune. As they got closer and closer, they saw the strobe lights out on the sidewalk. Immediately, everyone went to stand in line. Alex did not. She walked around the line to the bouncer. The other women looked to see what she was doing.

Jacqueline said, "Watch a master at work. She'll be back for us." As Jacqueline said that, Alex reappeared and told them to follow her. The women skipped the line and entered Dazzle.

The black carpet was decorated with confetti. Some of the strobe lights overhead were black lights and as they hit the carpet, the confetti carpet would glow. Trying to talk over the music proved too challenging, so Alex just pointed in the direction of the high top tables on the right side of the dance floor. The women formed a line and walk-danced to a large, circular table in the far end of the bar.

Alex said, "How do we wanna do this? Separate drinks? Rounds? Or bottle service?"

Mallory said, "Shots." Dancing where her chair once was, Olive nodded in agreement. She high-fived Mallory to reflect that as her true vote of agreement.

Jacqueline said, "Let's go ahead and order some drinks. There's no sense getting a bottle if we aren't staying here all night."

Alex screamed, "Oh, we're staying here." Then, she and Olive left the table and went to the dance floor.

Paige looked at Jacqueline, "What are they drinking?"

"Don't worry. I got it." Jacqueline said. Mallory had been dancing at the table. Jacqueline leaned into her and said, "Why don't you take Paige and join them on the dance floor?"

"I'm fine right here."

"I know you are, but, come on, Paige needs to have a good time. Those two aren't gonna wait for her. Besides, you'll be all back over here as soon as I get some drinks." With that, Mallory reached out for Paige's hand and pulled her towards the dance floor. Jacqueline perched up on the bar stool and watched them slither through the crowd to Alex and Olive. Jacqueline could see Alex dancing in a circle of men. Olive had made an instant connection with just one man. She was jumping offbeat to the song, but she appeared amazingly happy doing so. Mallory looked like Paige was her toddler and she was trying to teach a child to twist to the beat.

Jacqueline was laughing at them when she heard a familiar voice.

"Maybe, I'll just buy you that drink now and we won't have to wait until later." Jacqueline didn't know her name, but she knew the voice. It was from a few minutes ago outside Honey Pot. It was the woman at the door.

Jacqueline said, "How about you let me buy you the drink?"

"Can't," the woman said. Even in the strobe lights, Jacqueline must have looked confused, because the woman continued, "I'm working. I can't stop and have a drink with you...even though, I'd like to."

"Oh, okay. How 'bout this? I place an order for six shots of tequila. You get those and come back. Then, I will place an order for more drinks. I'll think long and hard about that second order and it will give us some time to just stand here and talk. When you bring back the second order, you will have to clear away the shots and we can talk some more. By the way, I'm Jacqueline."

"Well, Jacqueline, you ordered six shots of tequila, but there are only five of you."

"One's for you," Jacqueline said smiling.

"Nice move. I'm Shannon."

"It's nice to meet you. Very nice."

"I was thinking the same thing." And, with that, Shannon walked back to the bar. Halfway there, she turned around to see if Jacqueline was looking. And, she was.

When Shannon returned, she had the six shots of tequila. She and Jacqueline took their two shots. Shannon said, "I thought you were going into Honey Pot. I was going to be late getting back from my lunch to hang out with you."

"No, we had just started down the boardwalk. My friends were teasing about taking me in there before we leave next weekend."

"Ah, you're on vacation."

"Yeah, we're down from Tampa."

"Oh, that's not far."

"Far enough," Jacqueline said.

"So, what made you pick Dazzle?"

Jacqueline pointed to them out there dancing it up on the dance floor. Now, they were in a circle dancing together. Paige looked like she was having a good time. Jacqueline chuckled, "I suppose they were dazzled by the strobe lights."

"Fucking strobe lights give me a headache most nights." Jacqueline got off the stool and stood beside Shannon. She was petite. Sitting on the stool, Jacqueline hadn't noticed how small she was. She was tall, slightly taller than

Jacqueline at five foot seven, but she was thin. She was a size four at the very most. Jacqueline noticed that she had a full sleeve tattoo on her left arm. Jacqueline wanted to see it, but it was too dark in the club. They were talking about tattoos when Paige, Mallory, Alex, and Olive returned to the table.

Pointing to them one by one, Jacqueline said, "Alex, Olive, Paige, and Mallory, this is Shannon."

Olive said, "Ah, you found the Honey Pot. Good job, Jax." Then, she passed out the shot glasses. Olive, Paige, and Alex took their shot. Mallory was holding hers.

She leaned in and said to Jacqueline, "Where's your shot?"

Jacqueline said, "Oh, I already had mine."

"Hmm, have you had anything else while we were out on the dance floor?" Mallory said under her breath. Over the music, no one heard her comment. She realized it. She didn't say it for volume. Stepping closer to Jacqueline, who was facing Shannon, Mallory said, "Have you ordered the drinks?" Jacqueline and Shannon laughed.

"Oh, I'm sorry. No. I used the second round of drinks as a ploy to get to talk to Shannon longer."

"It was a horrible ploy," Shannon said.

Mallory said, "We need an Appletini, a screwdriver, a rum runner, and two margarita on the rocks."

"Uh, okay," Shannon said to Mallory. Then, looked at Jacqueline and said, "I guess you'll just have to think of another way to make me stay when I get back."

As she left, Alex, Olive, and Paige were celebrating. High-fives and hugs were abound. Mallory sat chair dancing. When Shannon returned, she passed out all the drinks and said, "I'll be back. I have to check on some of my other tables."

Alex said, "Don't worry. We'll be here all night."

Jacqueline grabbed her drink and walked around the table to stand behind Mallory. In her ear, she asked, "What don't you like about her in ten seconds?"

"She's trash."

"You're probably right. I should kill her and put her out of her misery." Mallory smiled. She found it hard to stay mad at Jacqueline for too long. The first few beats of a song came on and Mallory grabbed Jacqueline's hand and said, "Come dance with me."

Jacqueline didn't have time to respond before Mallory reached for her hand and tugged her onto the dance floor. Jacqueline wasn't certain what Mallory was expecting or where any of this was leading, but she decided that she'd just enjoy the moment. When Mallory had found the perfect spot for them, she began to dance. Her slow, smooth moves gave Jacqueline confidence that all was going to be well. Feeling calmer, Jacqueline felt comfortable dancing as she would with any friend. She danced her normal two-step with her eyes closed while she bit her lip in total enjoyment of the music and energy of the floor. As Mallory danced and sang around her, Jacqueline began to loosen up and enjoy herself more.

Then, the bass dropped and the crowd roared. Mallory turned from facing Jacqueline to standing inside Jacqueline's outstretched arms and against her body. At first, she was shocked and stopped dancing; but, after a few seconds, the dancing came natural. As the rhythm took over, Mallory placed her arms were around her neck. They were dancing without regard or restraint. The rest of the room had melted away. As they began to move in unison, Jacqueline's hands moved up on the backs of Mallory's arms. Each had her eyes closed and they had intertwined in the guise of dance.

When the song ended, they stood there for a moment. Mallory pulled her arms from Jacqueline's neck and turned to face her. Standing on the dance floor, surrounded by heaving bodies, they were forced to stand face-to-face within inches of each other. Once again, they found themselves staring into each other eyes, unaware of the world around them. They were so close that Jacqueline could feel the rapid exhales of Mallory's breath on her face. Hoping to calm her, Jacqueline reached out and put her hand on Mallory's cheek. Mallory placed her hand over Jacqueline's hand, smiled, and closed her eyes. Her breathing calmed. When she reopened her eyes, she saw the sweetness in Jacqueline's face. Still holding her hand, Mallory led Jacqueline off the dance floor and back to their table.

When they returned to the table, no one was talking. Jacqueline picked up her drink and took a long swig. Mallory perched herself on her bar stool, reached for her margarita, sipped it slowly, and stared at the dance floor.

14

Alex, Paige, and Olive watched Jacqueline and Mallory return to the table. As soon as they returned, the women shifted their attention from them and returned it to watching the crowd. Jacqueline looked around the club nervously. She was trying to avoid making eye contact with anyone.

Trying to break the silence, Alex said, "Hey, did you notice that I ordered another round while you guys were out there. And, I made everyone wait to take their shots until you two got back."

"Cool," Jacqueline replied. The women took their shots. After which, the silence resumed. Olive was making motions toward the man she'd been dancing with earlier.

He walked over to the table. "Hey, ladies. You don't mind if I steal her away, do ya?"

Paige spoke on their behalf, "Make sure you bring her back."

"Oh, I ain't promising that." Just like that, Olive was whisked back into the sea of writhing bodies.

Dancing at the table, Alex said to Paige, "Let's go back out there." Paige downed her drink and followed Alex.

Jacqueline said to Mallory, "Did you see that?"

"Olive and the guy?"

"No, Paige. How many of those has she had? She has never been too much of a drinker. She's gonna be in bad shape in the morning."

Mallory turned toward Jacqueline. "Let her have a good time. That's why we came here, right? To have a good time." She was resting her head in the palm of her hand.

Jacqueline brushed a curl from her face and said, "Yeah. That's why we came." They were smirking at each other when Shannon returned.

"What are you guys up to?"

Mallory stared at Jacqueline, "Having a good time."

Not sure how to respond, Shannon said, "I'll grab you another round."

Before she could leave, Mallory said, "We're going back on the dance floor, but when you bring the round switch that screwdriver out for a Long Island." Shannon wrote it down and walked away.

Jacqueline said, "Are you trying to get me fucked up?"

"Now, why would I do that?" Mallory responded slyly. Then, she stood and held her hand over her shoulder. Jacqueline reached out and allowed herself to be led back to the dance floor.

The bass from the music was vibrating the room. There wasn't half an inch between Mallory and Jacqueline. The world took notice of how enthralled they were in each other's presence.

Dancing with her new friend, Olive leaned back to talk to Alex, who was dancing near her, and said, "What's going on there?"

Also, now dancing with only one man, Alex shrugged her shoulders. When she finally leaned to look for Jacqueline and Mallory, she said, "Wow! Well, I guess we'll all have stories next week." Using her head, she pointed in Paige's direction and said, "Even Paige has found a few dance partners." Olive threw her hands around her dance partner's neck and screamed with elation. The crowd screamed back.

After four pounding songs, a slow song played. Most dancers left the dance floor, including Olive, her partner, and Paige. Jacqueline was heading back to the table when Mallory pulled her back by the tail of her shirt. Jacqueline turned to face her. Mallory leaned forward and said in Jacqueline's ear, "Don't go. Dance with me." Jacqueline pulled her close, closed her eyes, and they danced. They were unaware that half the eyes in the club, including Olive, Paige, and Shannon, were on them. Alex's eyes were not. She and her most recent dance partner were caught up in a passionate kiss.

As they danced, Mallory rested her head on Jacqueline's shoulder with her arms around her neck. Jacqueline focused solely on the music, the lyrics, the weight of Mallory's body, and the smell of her perfume. She was engrossed in the moment. It was one that she knew that she'd want to savor for some time to come. Satisfied with just being in the experience, Jacqueline's eyes remained closed, but Mallory had opened hers. She'd done so with the intention to reorient herself. As they dance around, she moved her arms down from Jacqueline's neck to her arms. She saw Paige smiling at her. She could see Olive staring intently at the guy she'd danced with most of the night. As she lifted her head to look for Alex, she saw Shannon looking at her and Jacqueline. The two made eye contact. Shannon shook her head at Mallory. Mallory turned her face from the crowd and returned her arms to Jacqueline's neck. She stood up on her tiptoes and whispered into Jacqueline's ear, "Do me a favor."

"Anything," Jacqueline replied.

"Don't bring that girl back to the house. I couldn't be next door and hear the two of you …"

Before she finished, Jacqueline responded, "I wouldn't ever," and drew Mallory in tighter. Mallory turned her head back toward the crowd and winked at Shannon. In response, Shannon gave her the finger.

When the song ended, Jacqueline said, "I need to go to the restroom." Mallory nodded and pointed that she was going to return to the table. Cutting through the crowded dance floor, Jacqueline felt a little wobbly. She wasn't sure if it was from the dancing, the heat, or the emotion of the evening.

Determined, she didn't notice that Shannon was approaching her. "Hey, what's the deal? Is that your girl?" Shannon said as if she'd been manipulated.

"No, what?" Jacqueline couldn't hear her. ""Oh, Mallory. No, she's not my girl."

Shannon looked relieved but skeptical. "Does she know that she's not your girl?"

"What, of course, she knows? We haven't...I mean, we aren't....No, she's not my girl. We're just friends."

Making air quotes, Shannon asked, "Friends?"

"No, plain ole friends."

"Yeah, I'm pretty sure that's not true, but you're only here on vacation, right?"

"Right."

Feeling more confident, Shannon said, "Then, that's your drama when you get home, but we can have fun while you're here." Shannon rapped her fingers against the drink tray and continued making her rounds. The delay increased Jacqueline's need to get to the restroom more urgent.

At the same time, back at the table, Paige had finished her last round and was waiting on Shannon to return to order another.

152

Mallory said, "Be careful there, sailor. You're outta practice." Paige's once carefully coiffed hair had untangled. Sweat had pasted her roots to her scalp. She disregarded Mallory's cautions and looked for Shannon.

Mallory turned to Olive. "Looks like you've found someone."

Olive said, "Yeah. He's nice. He's an engineer. He's so great. He and his friends are here for a friend's bachelor party. They're staying at the resort. Do you know that he didn't even ask me to come to his room? He said he'd like to see me tomorrow. Can you believe that? Tomorrow!" Olive was over the moon.

Mallory said, "I'm happy for you. From the look of things, you two really hit it off."

Olive said, "Paige told me how everyone has been giving Jax a hard time about you. You know, what I think?"

"I don't think I want to know."

"I think that they're wrong. I think it's you that they should give a hard time. Jax isn't tempting you. She isn't coming on to you. She isn't out to run some old game on you. It's you that's playing the game."

"What? You're crazy."

"Girl, people just think I'm crazy. They think I'm dumb, too. I ain't crazy or dumb. But, you know what's great about being overlooked, misunderstood, and ignored? I get to do what I want without fear of whether anyone'll say anything." Pointing at Mallory's chest, Olive went on. "You aren't playing a game. You like her. It's natural. You ain't forcing it. You just like her. I think you may even be falling for her. And, that scares the shit out of you. You don't know what to do with yourself. You wanna run from her and run to her at the same time. I get it. You don't have to agree with me. You don't have to say nothing. But, you better figure some shit out. How long do you think she's just

153

gonna stay available? How long can she turn down girls who want her to see if you might?"

She pointed to Shannon who was talking to Jacqueline near the restroom. Mallory didn't say a word. Olive walked behind her chair and rubbed her shoulder. She said, "It's gonna be fine. Happiness is messy. Don't think about all the consequences and possibilities and all that bullshit. Just be happy. The whole world would be better if everyone just worked on their own bullshit instead of worrying about other people's." Olive hugged her.

From behind Olive, Mallory heard a man's voice. "You can't have all the pretty women." It was Olive's friend, the engineer.

Olive whirled around and hit him on this arm, "Hush up."

"Mallory, this is Drew."

"Hi, Drew." Mallory shook his outreached hand.

"I was only joking about the comment. I could tell you and your girlfriend are really into each other."

Olive screamed, "SEE!" then, she pulled Drew back to the dance floor. Paige followed them. Mallory saw Shannon pass by and she ordered another round. She kept looking for Jacqueline, but she couldn't see her.

After running into Shannon, Jacqueline made it to the bathroom just in time. As she washed her hands, she heard other girls talking about a guy and girl making out in the bathroom. Jacqueline snickered to herself and thought back on some things that she'd done in bathroom stalls in her past.

She was drying her hands when she recognized the voice coming from the bathroom stall. Peering through the crack made by the wall and the stall door, Jacqueline saw Alex sitting on the sink with her dancing partner standing between her legs. Alex was only partially dressed. Jacqueline knocked on the stall door. Alex lifted her head to look, but she quickly discarded the notion of trying to investigate. Jacqueline noticed that her disruption was minor and Alex had no intention of making her new friend stop. Hearing Alex's moans coupled with the conversations all the other women were having, Jacqueline knew something had to be done, so she opened the unlocked door and stormed in.

"What the fuck are you doin'," Jacqueline demanded to know. The guy stopped, but he didn't remove his hands from under her dress.

Alex replied, "Me? I'm having a great time on vacation! Just like you were on the dance floor!"

"Unbelievable!" Jacqueline walked out of stall. After hitting the stall wall, the door flung open revealing Alex to the other women in the bathroom. Feeling exposed, Alex pushed back against the guy, hopped down off the sink, and chased after Jacqueline. Alex caught Jacqueline before she left the bathroom.

"What are YOU doing?" Alex asked her.

"What am I doing? What are you doing?"

"I was having a good time with my friends on vacation. I was enjoying the moment. Just like you've been doing. Except my fun isn't going back home with us."

Jacqueline ran her hand through her hair. She screamed and punched the paper towel holder. All the women waiting in line watched the two argue in silence.

Alex said, "Exactly," and followed the guy out the restroom. The guy headed to the bar and Jacqueline and Alex headed to the table. Alex was still talking to Jacqueline as they crossed the club, but Jacqueline was no longer listening.

When they arrived at the table, Mallory was sitting there alone. "You were gone so long I thought you went back to the house to use the bathroom."

Jacqueline smiled at her and said, "I shoulda." Jacqueline downed her drink. Mallory noticed that something was wrong and cocked her to ask. Jacqueline said, "I'm fine."

Mallory said, "Do you feel like dancing some more before last call? Or, would you rather hang over here by the table? I'm okay with whatever you want to do."

Trying to shake off her anger, Jacqueline said, "No, let's go have a good time. We're on vacation."

Overhearing, Alex said, "That's what's I'm talking 'bout. I'll make sure to get drinks before last call." Alex ordered two more rounds and met her dancing partner at the bar. He was busy talking to his friends. Rather than pull up a stool, she sat on his lap. She finished her drink and scanned the crowd to locate Paige. Alex found her on the dance floor enjoying herself dancing with Olive, Drew, and his friends.

Mallory asked, "Jax, are you okay?"

"I am now." And, the two danced until the DJ announced it was last call.

At last call, they all wandered back to their table. Jacqueline helped Paige get back on her stool. Mallory found Paige's shoes and help get them back on her feet.

Drew was standing at the table. He asked, "Olive, can I take you out to breakfast in the morning?"

Olive ran in place. "How's about you come to the house and I'll cook and we can eat out by our pool."

Jacqueline suggested, "Maybe we should make that a brunch. I think some of us are gonna need to sleep in." She was bracing Paige at the table.

He said, "Are you guys gonna be okay going back to the house?"

"Oh, yeah. We're fine. We're walking." Olive gave him the address, her cell phone number, and the directions. He hugged her, wished them a good night, and left.

"Well. Well. Well. We have a man coming over tomorrow?" Alex said like Olive's mother.

"An engineer.," Olive replied, blushing.

"Um, a professional. And, do we like this gentleman?"

"Maybe, maybe," Olive said waving to him as he walked out of Dazzle with his friends. When lights came on, the entire club looked like an interrogation room at the police station. Under the fluorescent lights, Jacqueline noticed that everyone looked a little dazed and worse for wear. It was three in the morning and Paige was very nearly passed out.

Alex said, "Drink up, bitches. We gotta get Cinderella home."

Jacqueline downed the last of her drinks. She left the table and walked to the bar where Shannon was. Mallory watched, but she didn't say a word.

"Hey, Shannon, I wanna cash out the table."

"Um, your wife already took care of it. She gave me a good tip, too. I wonder if it was money to just keep me away." Jacqueline turned on the stool and looked at a smiling Mallory.

"Did it work?"

"What?"

"Did the tip keep you away?"

Shannon leaned closer to her. "Do you want me to stay away?"

"Depends."

"On what?"

"How close you wanna be." Jacqueline stood up and walked back to the table. Shannon was still looking at her, but Jacqueline never looked back. She walked right to Paige and said, "I think it's time we get you to bed." She stood her up and waited on her to steady herself. With her arm around Paige, Jacqueline started walking out of Dazzle. The rest of the women followed.

When they arrived at the house, Olive helped Jacqueline get Paige upstairs and into her room. Paige fell across her bed. Jacqueline turned and walked to her own room as Mallory was entering Paige's room with a trashcan, a bottle of water, and some ibuprofen. Laughing, Jacqueline went into her room and closed the door. She didn't bother to gather pajamas from the drawers. She walked straight into the bathroom, peeled off her clothes, and stepped into the shower. For a few moments, she just stood there in the shower letting the cool water hit her in the face. She thought for a long time about Alex and Mallory. Then, aloud she said, "Enough."

When Alex arrived at the house, she walked straight to her room. She saw that Paige was under control and figured that there wasn't much more that she could add. She walked into her room, closed, and locked her door behind her. She stood for a few minutes with her back against the door in the dark. Standing alone, in the dark, tears rolled down her face. She wasn't sure what was causing them, but she was sure that she couldn't stop the them even if she tried. She thought back over the night. She smiled that Paige was able to let loose and that Olive met some man who seemed nice. She shook her head about Jacqueline and Mallory. But, then, in the dark, she thought about her own night; and, quietly, she sobbed.

Something inside her said *call Elet*. She turned on the TV to check the time. It was almost four in the morning. Part of her thought against it, but she wanted to hear from him. She found her phone in her purse and called him. The phone rang and rang.

She was about to hang up when she heard, "Hey, babe. You okay?"

"Yeah, I just wanted to hear your voice. I'm sorry I woke you up."

He could tell she'd been drinking. "You crying in the dark?"

She laughed. He knew her too well. "No," she said, lying.

"Of course, you are. You always cry in the dark after you've been out drinking. It's okay. Don't worry about it. You know, I miss you so much."

Melting, she said, "I miss you, too."

"You guys must have had fun if you're just getting in. Gees, what is it like three?"

Sniffling, she said, "Try four."

"Nothing good happens after three."

She said, "Tell me about it. Get some sleep, baby, I'll call you tomorrow. I love you."

"I love you too. Call whenever you want." Beep. He was gone and she realized exactly what she'd done tonight. She drug herself to her shower, so she could really cry.

When Jacqueline stepped out of the shower, she felt rejuvenated. In fact, the feeling was far better than she had expected. She'd been standing in there rinsing off her feelings for so long that tiny bathroom had become a steam room. She dried herself as best she could in a room full of steam. When she opened the door, her naked brown frame was chilled by the cool air. What she found more shocking was Mallory lying in her bed.

15

Quickly, Jacqueline tried to cover all of her most personal parts with her arms and hands. Mallory hadn't expected to catch Jacqueline exposed. She was as embarrassed as Jacqueline was. Blushing, Mallory said, "I'm sorry I scared you."

"No, I'm not...scared. I'm surprised." Jacqueline pulled out panties and a T-shirt from her drawers. She said, "I didn't expect you to be in here."

"I'm sorry. You were in the shower for a long time. I had time to take my own shower, change clothes, and come into your room. I was scared that I might fall asleep waiting to talk to you."

"Talk to me?" Jacqueline pointed to herself. She feared what Mallory wanted to talk about and decided to try to change the subject. "Is Paige okay?"

"Oh, she's fine. She's thrown up and is passed out for the next few hours. We'll deal with the rest of it tomorrow." Mallory was staring at Jacqueline walk around the room in her T-shirt and panties. Jacqueline could feel her looking at her.

"I'm sorry. I can't find my shorts."

Still blushing Mallory said, "No, it's fine. I guess I never would have thought..."

"That I wore underwear?" Jacqueline said stepping into her shorts.

"Lace hi-cut panties," Mallory replied.

"Wow. You got a lot of detail in a short period time." Jacqueline said trying quickly to put her shorts on.

"Yep." Mallory was biting her lips and watching Jacqueline. "I mean, I'm sorry that I scared you."

Jacqueline snapped in front of Mallory's zoned out eyes. "Yeah, you said that." Jacqueline appeared to be walking around her room without purpose.

Mallory noticed and said, "Do you want me to leave and go back to my room?"

"No, it's fine."

"It can be our little secret."

Jacqueline slipped into her bed. Mallory had been lying on top of the covers, but she hesitated to get under the cover with Jacqueline. Trying to break the ice, "Well, I guess I don't have any secrets left."

Mallory responded, "Oh, I'm sure that you do."

"Do not."

"Did you have fun tonight?" Mallory changed the subject.

"Parts of it were incredible."

"Which parts?" Mallory said teasing her.

"Well, that Shannon was something." Mallory hit her with a pillow. Jacqueline said, "I'm only joking. Who knew you were such a good...dancer?" Jacqueline leaned out of the bed and picked the pillow up off the floor. While she was reaching for the pillow, Mallory got under the covers. When Jacqueline sat back up, she continued, "Sometimes, I wonder if I'm done going to clubs. I wonder if I've outgrown the scene. I like to have a drink. I like to be with my friends and have a good time. I can still handle the club, but I'm so tired of it."

"Really?"

"Really. Why don't you ever believe me?"

"I believe you. I just don't want you to feel like you have to say things."

Jacqueline said, "I don't. I know what I've done. I spent years in a club with my friends proving what I could accomplish, proving who I could get; but, in the end, what do I have? Friends who rave about my stupid antics? The legend is overrated."

"Okay."

"Okay? That's all you have to say. I just admitted something to you that I've never admitted to anyone. And, all you say is okay?"

"I'm sorry. Okay, I'm sleepy. Turn off the light."

Jacqueline leaned over and turned out the light. Mallory turned on her side facing away from Jacqueline. Jacqueline scooted up behind her, wrapped her arm around her, and held her close. Mallory held her breath. She hadn't expected this, but she didn't want Jacqueline's arm to move. Slowly, she started to breath. Then, she realized how this was the perfect ending to the night. She put her hand on Jacqueline's arm and said, "Good night."

Jacqueline said, "Night, baby." She called her *baby* before she realized it. It fell out of her. She opened her eyes and waited for something - an argument, for her to wiggle from underneath her arm, for her get out of bed and leave the room. None of that happened. Instead, Mallory smiled and dozed off.

Jacqueline was awake by nine. She put on a sports bra and walked downstairs tracking the smell of burning bread. In the kitchen, she saw Olive surrounded by burnt waffles and smoke. Jacqueline walked up behind her and said, "Need some help?"

"Oh my God. I'm so glad someone's up. I want Drew to like brunch, not for us to need the fire department. Things keep burning. Help!"

"It's cool. We'll make something to impress him. Pass me those bananas." Jacqueline diced bananas to add to the waffle batter. "So, you really like the guy?"

Olive smiled, "I think so. He texted me after we got to the house. He wanted to make sure that we got in safe."

"Well, that's sweet." Jacqueline began to scramble eggs.

"We were texting so long that I told him to just call. And, he did. He didn't say one wrong thing in the whole conversation. He asked about me and what I did and what I wanted and if I had kids and where I saw myself in five years. We talked and talked. He told me all about himself. I didn't even have to ask. He never said anything crazy or rude or sexual."

Jacqueline was impressed. She had stopped whipping the eggs and was staring at Olive. She was glowing. Jacqueline had never seen her look so happy. "I'm really happy for you. He sounds like a nice guy who is really interested in you."

"I know. Isn't that amazing?" Olive took out bacon and sausage.

Jacqueline gathered some new pans as Olive cleaned the ones that she had burned. She walked behind Olive, held her hair back to expose her ear, and whispered, "No, you're great. You deserve the best."

"You know, you do too."

"Thanks."

"Oh, don't give me that bullshit thanks. I didn't give you some fake compliment. You're pretty great. You should be with someone who loves you as much as you love the rest of us." Jacqueline began frying the meat. Olive found some champagne. Struggling to open it, Jacqueline took the bottle from her and Olive took over making the bacon and sausage. Looking at Jacqueline making mimosas, she went on, "Are you working on it?"

"Almost got it." Jacqueline grunted.

"Not the mimosas. Are you working on reeling her in?"

"Who?" Jacqueline was on her tiptoes looking through the cabinets.

"Come on, Mallory. Are you close to getting her?"

"You guys are killing me. I'm not trying to do anything to anyone. I'm just hanging out on vacation," she said as she located a pitcher.

"You can't tell me that you didn't like being out there on that dance floor with her." Olive pointed at her with the spatula.

"No more so than I enjoyed getting kissed by you." Jacqueline teased.

"What? When?"

"How quickly you forget that you kissed me at the dock." Appearing hurt, Jacqueline stopped making the mimosas to look at Olive. "I came to pick you up and you ran to me, jumped in my arms, and kissed me. Maybe, I was waiting on you and you went and found some dude. Maybe, I'm heartbroken." Jacqueline batted her eyes.

Playing along, Olive said, "Oh, honey, I'm sorry. Things between us would never work out. I just couldn't make you happy, but I will always love you."

Jacqueline dropped her head to her chest, "Then, I must go and be sad upstairs. Make sure he loves you the way you deserve."

Olive laughed. "You seriously better not let Mallory hear this or she is gonna come beat my ass." Jacqueline laughed it off. Then, she showed Olive how to make the waffles so that they would be a warm, crispy brown. With Jacqueline's help, Olive had prepared a nice brunch, complete with eggs, sausage, banana waffles, and mimosas. When the doorbell rang, Jacqueline gave Olive a hug and scurried back upstairs.

Before re-entering her room, Jacqueline checked in on Paige and Alex. Upon entering Paige's room, it was obvious that she had gotten sick in the night. It looked as though she had tried to clean up. Jacqueline pulled the covers up over her and cleaned up as much as she could without waking her.

Before Jacqueline opened Alex's door, she could hear Alex snoring loudly. She opened the door to find Alex laid out across her bed. Jacqueline grinned and closed her door quietly.

She went back into her room. Mallory was still asleep. She was lying on her side facing the wall. Jacqueline slid softly back into the bed behind her and wrapped her arm around her. Closing her eyes, she knew that she wasn't going to fall back to sleep. She thought it would be rude to turn on the television. In truth, she was quite content to lie awake in bed with Mallory in her arms.

Trying not to think about the last night, Jacqueline's thoughts fast-forwarded to a quickly approaching future. In a matter of days, they'd return home. Mallory would go back to her house, her life, and her bed. Since it would still be summer, she thought that she could still see quite a lot of Mallory, but she feared that it wouldn't be like it was right here, right now. This wasn't ideal. They'd been enjoying each other's company, but being at the house on vacation may have heightened their feelings.

Holding her close, she imagined a relationship. She thought of life with Mallory and Zoe. She imagined dinners and parties. She wondered about their families and friends. Lying in bed, she was holding someone who led a very different life that she did. Jacqueline was very aware of what a relationship with her would affect her life and her daughter's life. Then, her mind drifted to last night and she wondered what would have happened if she'd tried to kiss her. She realized that it might not be just her own fears with which she had to worry. Looking at Mallory, snuggled beside her, she wondered what Mallory might be dreaming.

Mallory must have sensed someone staring at her, because she began to stir. She rolled over and draped her arm around Jacqueline. Now, the two were interconnected, holding one another. Jacqueline thought Mallory was still sleeping until Mallory spoke.

"It was sweet of you to go downstairs and help Olive."

"Do you have psychic powers?" Jacqueline said lifting her head to look down at her.

"No, silly, I felt you get up. I saw you put on a bra and walk out of the room. I was headed after you, but when I got to the hall, I could hear you trying to help Olive. I'm not much of a cook, so I came back to bed," Mallory admitted.

"Yeah, she was in the weeds. I got her set-up and came back to bed."

"I'm glad. The bed's cold without you."

Jacqueline wanted to ask her what that meant, what was happening between them, where things were going. But, then, lying there in bed with her was nicer than she could have imagined and Jacqueline grew scared. She feared that Mallory's response would not be one that she wanted to hear or that if she made Mallory aware of all that had happened that everything might change. Instead, she was reserved and responded with, "Mmm Hmm."

Mallory spoke, "I think Olive really likes him. She and I had time to chat."

"Chat? You chatted with Olive?"

"Yes, we chatted at the club."

"You…chatted with Olive…..at a club? Do you even know how that sentence doesn't make sense?"

"Yes, I do. I'm a journalist." That's when Jacqueline's stomach dropped. She was a journalist – one who was about to get a new promotion, one who was lying in the arms of her boss. Mallory kept talking, "She gave me an entire speech about being happy." Mallory sighed.

"It might be a little soon for Olive to declare herself happy. She just met the man."

"Yeah, I think she was talking about me."

"Oh, are you happy with Olive?" Jacqueline teased.

Mallory tickled her. Jacqueline giggled and squirmed. "I didn't know that you were ticklish." Mallory continued. The two scuffled in the bed as Mallory tickled and Jacqueline tried to twist away. Eventually, Mallory got the upper hand and rolled on top of Jacqueline. Poised to tickle her, Mallory teased and Jacqueline begged for mercy.

In the ruckus, they were oblivious to the door opening. Neither noticed Olive's presence until she spoke.

16

"Should I even ask?" Olive said with her arms folded.

Alex had joined her, "They'd deny the whole thing."

"You know, I don't think that they're lying to us. I think they're lying to themselves."

Jacqueline rolled Mallory from on top of her. She interjected, "Thank you, peanut gallery." Paige's door opened and Alex and Olive turned to look in her direction. She inched out of her room holding her face.

Olive started, "How ya feelin'?"

Looking angry, Paige lashed out, "How do you think?" She sounded like she had a sore throat in addition to a hangover.

Alex asked, "Honey, can I get you anything?"

Paige walked into Jacqueline's room and sat in the chair in the corner. Removing her slippers, she curled into the fetal position. "Yes, I'd like new friends." They giggled, but Paige was angry. "I'm not laughing. I can't believe that you guys let this happen to me. I spend all of my time thinking of you, trying to help you, and this is how you repay me?"

The women looked shocked. Mallory spoke first, "Um, I tried to slow you down and you insisted that you were okay."

Paige retorted, "Way to listen to a drunk person."

"Listen, I know you feel like shit, but we didn't let any harm come to you. We looked after you. We let you have a good time in a safe place. We let you have fun. I promise, you didn't do anything that you should worry about. You didn't dance with, touch, or do anything inappropriate. When I thought you were in danger of passing out, we brought you here and put you to bed," Jacqueline tried to soothe her.

"How could you know what I was doing? You were busy grinding on your friend, weren't you? You had your hands full chasing after two women, so how could you know what I was doing?" Jacqueline had never heard Paige speak this way. She was taken aback. She didn't know what to say.

Alex broke in. "Look, you danced with me. You danced with Mallory before she and Jax danced. You spent the rest of the evening with Olive and the guy she met. You're fine. We tried to let you have a good time without having to worry about Brett and the twins."

"Thanks. Thanks for that. You know, we aren't all trying to avoid being a wife and mother. Some of us really don't mind finding someone who loves us."

Offended Alex said, "What does *that* mean?"

Paige rattled off. "Jacqueline wasn't the only one who had to pee." Alex slumped away. "I'm just saying. I can't believe that my friends wouldn't know me well enough to know that I gave all of that stuff up to be a wife and mother."

Jacqueline had overlooked what Paige said about her. She still wanted to make this situation better. "You didn't do anything that a wife or mother shouldn't do. Yes, you had more drinks than you have had since you've been married and had kids, but you were safe. We thought we were letting you have a good time. I'm sorry," Jacqueline walked over to her and put her hand on her shoulder.

Paige started to relax some, "I know. But, I didn't want to be that kinda mother. You know, the one that's different when her husband and kids aren't around. I know I was single once and we got drunk all the time, acted liked fools, and did crazy things. But, that changed for me when I got married. I was ready to get married. I was ready to just be a good mother and a good wife." Paige held her head and began to cry.

Olive said, "Paige, you're a great mother and a great wife. I didn't know that you wanted to have a good time, but within reason, I promise that I kept an eye on you. It's okay to have a good time and not get plastered. I get it." Paige was in tears.

Mallory went to her. "It's fine. It'll be our secret."

"We certainly have a lot of them," Alex said under her breath.

Jacqueline lost her temper. She walked to Alex and said, "I've had enough. We shouldn't have all these secrets. Let's just say it. Let's spill it all. Who do you wanna start with? Me or you? It makes me no difference."

Alex pushed off from the door and Jacqueline and Alex were nose to nose. Their arms were swinging by their sides. Paige thought that they might actually punch each other. Even as bad as she felt, she was starting to feel more like herself, she said, "What's wrong with you two? We're all friends."

Looking at Alex, but talking to Paige, Jacqueline said, "Don't pretend to be a saint now. We know what's inside. Let's get everything out in the open."

Cleaning from under her nails, Olive said, "This is why I don't have secrets."

"Guys, cool it. Everything's fine. We're just tired." Mallory said.

Alex, still nose to nose with Jacqueline said, "I bet she's well rested. Huh, Jax? Did you rock *your friend* to sleep?" Jacqueline pushed her into the door. Alex's head hit the door and gave her a striking sense of whiplash.

Olive said, "Enough." Jacqueline walked away from Alex. Starting to feel as though she has been in an accident, Alex was holding her neck. Jacqueline didn't say another word for minutes. She paced around her room. Everyone stared at her and stayed out of her way. She found a pair of jeans in the closet and put them on over her sleeping shorts.

"I can't take another fucking minute of this. If this shit keeps up, I'm gonna ruin a few friendships and not the one that Alex thinks. I've haven't done a thing. I'm not hypnotizing her. I'm not tricking her. I didn't put anything into her food. You know the problem. I figured it out." She walked back to Alex. Alex backed away from her this time. "You've known me for years. You've heard and seen all the shit I've said about other girls and you think that I'm still that way. You want to defend Mallory like I'm a predator, like I'm out to get her."

Alex said, "Aren't you?" Walking back to her bed, Jacqueline didn't say a thing. She wasn't sure what to say.

Shaking her head, "I like girls. I do. You got me on that one. I like them the way you like guys. I don't like them all. They don't all like me. But, it's not a parlor trick. I don't conjure them to like me back and I'm exhausted trying to explain that I'm not any different than any of you. You wanna accuse me of something, then fine, but know this - I'm a grown ass woman. I'm done playing games. I've figured out who I am."

They stared at her as she pulled a shirt over her nightshirt, stuck her feet in her shoes, and picked up her wallet and keys from the dresser. As she walked out of her bedroom door, she yelled, "Maybe if you took some time figuring out who you were and what you wanted, then you could leave me the fuck alone."

Then, Jacqueline jogged down the stairs and slammed the front door. She passed Josephine on her way out.

Mallory got out of bed and headed to her own room. Olive followed her. "Mallory, just let her go blow off some steam." Alex and Paige headed downstairs.

Slipping into her own sweats, Mallory said, "Thanks for the suggestion, but I'm going after her."

"To say what?"

"Are you kidding me?" Mallory stopped getting dressed and said, "Did you see what just happened in there? I'm going after her to find out what's wrong."

"Seriously, Mallory, you don't know?" Olive pulled her sleeve and yanked her downstairs into the living room where everyone else had gathered. Speaking to Alex and Paige, she said, "Okay, tell her what you have been saying to Jacqueline."

Alex spoke first, "Look, everyone can see what's going on. You're getting invited to dinners. She took you out of town. You're sleeping in her bed. She's dancing with you out on the dance floor. Jax and I have been friends for a long time. This is the longest I've seen her pursue a girl."

Mallory didn't let Alex finish. "Is that what you think? Do you think that she's pursuing me?" Mallory looked around at all of them. "Have you been telling her to leave me alone?"

"Well, yeah. I don't want her hormones to ruin our friendship." Alex said.

Josephine laughed. "I'm sorry. I don't mean to get involved in this, but I can't help it. Do you think that Jacqueline is manipulating Mallory into liking her?"

Alex turned to Josephine and said, "None of you know how good she is. Only me and Paige and Elet were around back then. She's amazing. We used to go into a bar or a club and she'd tell us who's number she was gonna get or who she was gonna take home that night. And, she could do it. I mean, she got the girl most of the time. It was fucking amazing. This cute, little girl that you never thought would sleep with or run after some gay girl was doing it."

Mallory looked sick to her stomach. Olive tried to hush Alex.

Finishing her thought, Alex said, "I'm just saying. She can get whoever she wants. She really can."

Josephine said, "I can't believe that she's friends with you. She can't convince people to sleep with her. They had to already be interested. She's not tricking girls anymore than you are tricking Elet."

"And, I bet that it's Mallory who's doing more of the misleading," Olive added. Mallory fell back on the couch and started to rub her forehead. Olive sat beside her.

"It's not like you think. I like being with her. I don't really invite myself over. I mean, in the beginning, we'd talk and I'd ask what she was doing, and I'd ask if she wanted company. She never said no."

"And?" Olive said.

"And what?"

"We're past seeing a movie or shopping together." Alex added.

"What? I don't know. We talk. She talks to all of us about what she can cook or what she'd like to see or do. I don't know. I just tell her we'll do it."

"Uh huh, so..." Paige was waving her along.

"Alright, I may flirt with her a little bit, but she never comes on to me."

"Are you teasing her or do you like her?"

"I don't know." Mallory put her face in the pillows.

Olive pulled the pillows from her and sat her upright. "I think you know."

Alex asked, "How do you keep ending up in her bed?"

"I come in there and get in bed with her."

"Shit!" Alex said.

"Have you *done*...anything?" Paige asked.

"No. Not really. She's checked me out. I've seen her. I mean sometimes I catch her looking at me but she looks away when she knows that I'm watching. And, I guess there was the dancing last night."

Josephine asked, "What happened last night?"

Alex, Olive, and Paige said, "Oh my God," in unison.

Mallory answered, "We danced together."

Alex and Olive demonstrated. Olive said, "It got me hot and I don't want either one of them."

Looking surprised, Josephine said, "Well, how'd that happen?"

Mallory started to answer and Olive jumped in. "Jealousy. You see, there was a cute waitress paying Jax a little too much attention and Mallory got jealous. She amped up her game, pulled Jax onto the dance floor, and was all over her. Mallory was scared of what might happen if she didn't do something drastic. Classic crazy girl move."

Finally, figuring out the truth, Alex said, "Lemme get this straight, you flirt with her, you used to invite yourself places, you tickle her, you gave her a nickname, and you took her to the dance floor." Rubbing her chin and thinking about all of this, "I yelled at Jacqueline, but, maybe I shoulda yell at you. You're the one messing with her head."

Josephine said, "Wrong, again, little sister." Alex was now angry and confused.

Paige tried to help. "Alex, Mallory likes Jacqueline. She may not have admitted that to herself yet. Jacqueline is the one being pursued. If she didn't already know it, she knew it as of last night."

Alex said, "Okay, but if that's true, then why hasn't Jacqueline told any of us that that's what she thinks is happening."

Josephine said, "Because you've all been horrible friends. She can't figure out if Mallory is seducing her or just being friendly flirty the way you all are with her. You guys use her like your fake man. You ask her to carry things, pick things up, smell things, and how you look in things. And, she couldn't tell any of the rest of you what she thought Mallory might be doing, because you've all been accusing her of giving Mallory a magic seduction apple, warning her that it's a bad idea, and threatening her to leave Mallory alone."

Alex responded, "Then, I gotta go after her."

Mallory said, "No, I do."

Olive said, "You can't."

"Why not? I'm the only one who can."

"You can't help her. She's scared to ask you what's going on. You've gotta figure this out before you go after her," said Olive.

"She's gonna come back here and know that you've talked to us more than you've talked to her," warned Paige.

"But, we don't know where she is," Mallory said frantic.

"Of course, we do. She's at Honey Pot," Olive said calmly.

"Why would she go there? Do you think that she went to look for Shannon?" Mallory looked scared.

"What is it with you and Shannon? No, she didn't go looking for Shannon," Olive responded.

"However, that should tell your ass something about how you feel," Josephine said.

Paige tried to explain, "Mallory, it's easy. She went where she could be herself. She went where she could be surrounded by people she didn't have to pretend with. That's why flirting with Shannon was easy and fun. She didn't have to watch what she said or wonder what Shannon meant. Shannon was flirting because she liked Jacqueline. And, Jacqueline knew it. Why are you flirting? Why are you worried that she's at Honey Pot?"

"I don't know," Mallory admitted.

"Yeah, you do," Olive pressed.

"I don't know why any of this is happening. It's never been this way about anyone else."

Josephine said, "Well, tell her that you aren't sure. But, tell her something."

Olive disagreed, "Don't tell her that you aren't sure. You're sure that you don't want her to be with anyone else. Right?"

"I really don't. I even asked her not to bring Shannon back to the house." Mallory said.

"What? That's a bold bitch move," Alex was proud of her. "Did Jacqueline agree?"

Embarrassed, Mallory admitted, "Yeah. She promised she wouldn't."

"Good move." Alex tried to high-five Mallory's weak hand.

"Shut up, Alex!. Mallory, go tell Jacqueline that you like her. That you like being with her. You want to sleep in the bed with her, you don't want her to be with anyone else, and you don't want to be with anyone else. The two of you can figure the rest out." Olive fell silent for a few second, then she said, "Did she try anything last night?"

"You already asked me that, but no, nothing happened" Mallory mumbled as she rubbed her face.

"Actually we ask if you'd done anything."

"She said no." Paige came to the rescue.

"No, don't you see? Mallory is sad when she gets asked if they have done anything. She's not mad at me for asking. She pulled Jax on the floor. She danced all over her. She got in her bed afterward. She was on top of her when we walked in. Mallory wanted her to do something. A kiss, at the very least. Isn't that right?"

Mallory stood up and said, "I don't know what I expected. I had a great night. One of the best of my life, but I thought we would've...something. I guess I better go get her." She ran upstairs to get dressed.

Paige said, "Is this gonna work?"

Josephine said, "Absolutely. Jacqueline likes her. She's just needs a sign."

Alex said, "It's gonna be weird."

"Not really. They've been all over each other for a while now," Paige reminded her.

Josephine crossed her legs and said, "You guys need to prepare for sucking up. You owe some big apologies."

CROSS YOUR FINGERS

17

The Honey Pot might be an amazing bar after dark, but just after noon on a Sunday, it's dead. Jacqueline was sitting at the bar eating peanuts from a bowl and watching a rerun of last night's ballgame when Mallory walked in. Hoping not to find Jacqueline flirting with another woman, Mallory was nervous as she opened the door. When she saw Jacqueline alone at the bar, her heart warmed. She walked over to her, "Whatcha doing here?"

"Where else should I be?"

"At the house," Mallory said.

"Nope. These are my people'" and she raised a fist in the air to them, "these seven strangers understand me better than everyone in that house."

"Oh, I didn't know that." Mallory started eating the peanuts. "Well, how long are you gonna sit here?"

"As long as I can."

"You're gonna be drunk soon."

"Doubtful." Jacqueline passed her drink. Mallory shook her head. "Come on, taste it."

"You know that I like fruity drinks, not your bitter ones."

"Just try it. You'll like it." Preparing for something strong, Mallory closed her eyes and took a sip. The taste was unexpected. She opened her eyes and said, "It's ginger ale. You're sitting in a bar drinking ginger ale and watching last night's game?"

"Yep. I knew you'd come. I knew you'd want to talk and I couldn't be drunk. I figured that when I left and they'd tell you everything about my past. Then, they'd probably send you to talk to me. To set me straight, but lemme just say. You don't have to say anything. You didn't do anything to be worried about or be embarrassed about. We didn't do anything that changes who you are or what you are. You slept in a bed with me. You were dressed and I was dressed. It was fine. Girls sleep in the same bed all the time and no one thinks anything of it. We can still be friends. We just won't do anything alone until you feel more comfortable. And, that's okay too. I completely understand." Throughout Jacqueline's entire speech, she never looked at Mallory. She just ate the peanuts and watched the game.

With her head almost in the peanuts bowl, Mallory tried to make eye contact with Jacqueline. "That would be a great speech if I was coming to say that I felt conflicted or confused."

Jacqueline looked at her. "Well, what'd you come to tell me?"

"Well, dummy, I came to say that you haven't been seducing me anymore than I've been seducing you. That I have enjoyed everything that we've done. And, I do like you. I like you a lot."

Sarcastically, Jacqueline said, "Yeah, I like you, too."

Mallory became stern with her. "Stop watching the damn TV and listen to me. I'm here trying to tell you that I want to see where this goes. Don't you understand? I'm happy being with you. Are you happy when you're with me?"

"Yeah."

"Yeah? That's all you've got to say."

Jacqueline noticed that her answer wasn't what Mallory was expecting. She tried to explain, "I'm apprehensive. Scared, even."

"Scared of what?"

"I know how hard this is going to be. I know that people will talk about you, the friends or family you will lose. I'm scared of getting involved and watching you leave, because you hate how liking me makes everyone else feel. See, I've already lost the closed-minded people in my life. I know what it's like. I don't want you to hate me for that." Mallory was quiet. Jacqueline said, "You hadn't thought of that, had you?"

"Of course, I had. I know exactly who will talk about me. I know the people who won't support my choice, but I'm happier with you than I ever was with them. So, I'm here to say let's try. But, I have to ask you. Why haven't you tried anything? I've given you plenty of chances."

Jacqueline looked away, "What if I'd been wrong? It was better to hold you in my arms quietly than to try something and you run away."

"Did you want to last night?"

"Yeah, I wanted to kiss you."

Mallory looked disappointed. "That's all?"

Jacqueline laughed, "Yeah, anything more would have been wrong. Besides, we are in the house with our friends. I'd been drinking. I mean, the first time…should be special. It'd be our first time together. And, it would be your first time with a woman. It couldn't be here." She pointed.

"Well, I wasn't thinking the Honey Pot, but I don't know that a gulffront mansion is such a bad idea."

"Did you want me to try last night?"

"Everyone keeps asking me that. I guess I did. You were paying such close attention to Shannon that it was pretty obvious that you thought about spending the night with her. I just wanted you to feel that way about me." After she said that, Mallory was embarrassed. She dropped her head and played with the drawstring on Jacqueline's pants.

Placing her forefinger under Mallory's chin, she slowly lifted her head. "I wanted more in Key West. I wanted more plenty of nights when you were at my house and when I was over at yours. Oh, I've wanted more. I just didn't want you to think that's all I wanted. Think of how many times I asked you if you just wanted to spend the night. You always turned me down."

"I was scared to death that you were gonna escort me to some spare room on the other end of the condo. I couldn't figure out how to get into your bed."

Laughing, Jacqueline said, "Well, you figured that one out." Mallory hit her arm.

"I guess I knew that I felt something. I'd known for a while and it scared me. I'm sorry but I have to admit that I really wanted the feelings to go away. They just wouldn't. And, then we started doing things together, just us. You know, after Paige got married and Alex started dating Elet, it was just us. It was just us or just us and Zoe."

Surprise ran over Jacqueline's face, "Zoe? What's she gonna say?"

"She already loves you more than me. She wants us to move in. She told me that you bought a couch for the patio just for her." Mallory looked disapproving.

"When you're working late, we eat out and, then, she likes to go on the balcony. Well, I thought she'd like to see the stars, so we bought a telescope. But, it was too science project-ish. She told me that she wanted to lie down and look up at the stars. Well, blankets just weren't working. That cold concrete was killing my back. So, before she left for the summer, we were together, just she and I, and we went and found a round outdoor couch with a pillow. I had it delivered, but she doesn't want me to use it until she's back. So, it's waiting in the back bedroom until she gets back and you work late." Jacqueline explained.

"You never told me anything about this."

"Was I supposed to? It's not a big deal. I'll make sure she doesn't get sick or stay up late."

Mallory was tearing up. "It's very sweet. She told me all about it on our way to the airport. She said 'Mommy, I know you will see the couch, but it's mine and Jax, not yours.'" Mallory laughed.

"It's hers. I got it for her. I love her."

"And, she loves you."

"Your ex won't."

"Not my problem."

"What about work? Should we try to keep it quiet?"

Mallory leaned in, "I think they know."

"Grant knows."

"Grant, how?"

"He came in my office a few weeks back to tell me that you had a crush on me. He said that he could tell by how you acted around me."

"I don't act any kinda way around you."

"Nope. None at all," Jacqueline said smiling. They were out of peanuts and the Rays were losing.

Looking around, Mallory asked, "Where's Shannon?"

"I don't know. What is it with you and her? You're caught up on her."

"I guess I'd never seen you flirt with anyone. I mean, you were seriously flirting with her."

"Look, we were out. I haven't been quite sure what you were doing or what I should be doing. I've been giving it a helluva lotta thought. It was nice to just talk and flirt with someone and not have to think too much about it." Jacqueline tried to explain.

"Well, I didn't like it at all. I wanted to rip her arm off and beat her with it. And, I had this whole fantasy of you bringing her back to the house bumping into things, kissing, falling all over each other, giggling, making noises from your room with me lying in bed mad, angry, and alone. Then, I stormed in and grabbed her by the hair and threw her out."

"Um, that is, once again, very detailed. Maybe I should reconsider getting involved with you."

"Too late, now," Mallory winked.

Jacqueline sat up straight and said, "There's something you should know. I'm gay, but that doesn't mean that every girl I'm looking at I'm checking out. Just because I don't wear dresses doesn't mean that I want to be a man. Just because I'm gay, doesn't mean that I don't like kids. It doesn't mean that I don't believe in monogamy or I don't like or want a serious relationship. I'm just like everyone else. Most of my days are spent doing everything that everyone else is doing. Laundry, cleaning, shopping, watching TV, listening to music, pretending to exercise, drinking, biting my nails, texting, and eating too much. And, then a couple times a week for about an hour, I like to do something that makes me different than ninety-eight percent of the population. Which is small in comparison. I mean, I'm different only a hundred and four hours a year which is only about one percent of the year."

Sarcastically, Mallory asked, "Did you prepare that speech here?"

"No, this morning when I wanted to kiss you."

"It was a little too much." Mallory turned around, "Where is Shannon?"

Jacqueline sighed, "Again, you have the wrong come back." Jacqueline looked around for Shannon. "You know she doesn't work here. She came here last night on her break. She's probably at home. We can ask around if you wanna see her."

"I'll beat that bitch's ass."

"You know, I didn't sleep with her, right? Like, you imagined that whole thing?"

"Yeah, I know. But, you were gonna sleep with her."

"Seems unlikely. However, you only asked me not to sleep with her at the house. I could have gone to her place." Mallory hit her in the arm again. "Ow, I guess we are exclusive, then." Mallory hit her again. "Listen, you can't keep hitting me or they are gonna call the cops."

"Come on. Let's go."

"Where are we going?"

"Let's go get our friends, get changed, and take the boat out. Remember how excited you were when you found out about that boat?"

Jacqueline was excited. She'd forgotten about her boat rental. She stood up from the bar, took a ten from her wallet, and left it to cover her tab. Mallory picked up the ten, exchanged it with a five from her own wallet. She put Jacqueline's ten in her pocket and said, "You have a girlfriend now."

Jacqueline laughed and opened the door for her. "Do you think it's going to be weird back at the house?"

"Nah, we've been unofficially dating for months. Besides, you have no plans of having sex this week, so that won't be an issue."

"What happened to the flirting? We've been dating for like five minutes and shit's already real." Jacqueline said opening the Laredo door for Mallory.

Mallory smiled at her and pulled out her phone. She sent a text:

```
I got her. We're heading back to the house. Get your
swimsuits on. Jax wants to take us out on the boat.
```

All the responses were smiley and winky faces. They matched the faces Jacqueline and Mallory were wearing.

<u>18</u>

The drive from the Honey Pot to the house took less than five minutes. When they pulled into the driveway, Jacqueline didn't move.

"What's wrong?"

"Do we have to go in there? We can go check into a hotel room and come get our bags later."

Turning towards her, Mallory said, "It's gonna be okay. I promise." As she opened her door and got out of the Laredo, Jacqueline watched her. She walked to driver's side and opened the door. "Come on. Let's get this part over with."

Jacqueline stepped out. She placed both of her hands into the warm pockets of her sweatpants. She unlocked the door and opened it for Mallory. Before she was inside the house, Paige, Alex, and Olive had her surrounded. Josephine was standing in the entrance to the kitchen watching the mob attack.

Jacqueline could not make out any of the individual apologies. Paige and Alex were speaking at once. Mallory came to Jacqueline's rescue, "Can you let her into the house? Gees."

Jacqueline smiled and walked past everyone into the kitchen. As she passed Josephine, she said, "Hey, I'm glad you made it. Sorry about earlier. Things are a little crazy right now."

"Yeah, it looks like I came just in time for the drama."

Before Jacqueline could ask her how she liked the house, Paige spoke, "We're all really sorry for everything we said to you and how we treated you. It really wasn't fair."

Jacqueline held her hand up, "You know, it's okay. I mean, it happened. I'm over it. I'm sorry that I blew up. Oh, and pushed Alex into the wall."

"Door," Alex said, correcting her.

"No one mentioned that there was violence. Damn, I wish I had seen that part," remarked Josephine.

"Yeah, I'm sorry. By the way, I'm no angel in all of this. Mallory might have flirted with me, but I'm sure that I flirted right back. During the months that we were spending together, I was reacting to her in ways that I wouldn't have reacted to any of you. No offense."

"None taken," Alex said.

"Uh, what's wrong with me?" Olive asked.

"I just didn't want you guys to think that I was some poor victim. I enjoyed all the attention and I certainly gave some mixed signals myself. I'm just saying there was a lot going on." Jacqueline admitted.

"Why didn't you tell me or us or one of us?" Alex asked.

Jacqueline snickered. "I know what you think of me. All of you. It's my own fault." She walked into the living room and sat down. Everyone followed her. Mallory came and sat next to her. "Look, I know that I have never really brought anyone around you guys that I was seriously involved in. You have seen me only be casual at best. I get that. I do. But, something hit me when everyone I knew started getting serious. You know? I guess I started thinking that I wanted to get serious, too. Anyhow, you wouldn't have believed me, so I just didn't tell you." Jacqueline leaned back against the couch.

"I would have believed you," Paige said.

"Me too." said Olive.

"Not me. I would've talked you outta that shit. I would've taken you out and reminded you about all the fun we had," Alex added.

Jacqueline laughed. "And, that's why I didn't tell you."

They all laughed. Josephine said, "I kinda wish that I had come tomorrow."

"What? Why?" Mallory turned to her and asked.

"So, I could have missed all this therapy shit." The room erupted in laughter.

"You're right, Jo. Go get your suits on. Let's take out this boat." Jacqueline stood up and turned to pull Mallory off the couch. "Are you ready?"

"Well, of course not, I have to go get my suit on." Mallory teased.

"Okay, well hop to it. I'm looking forward to staring at you without shame."

"You're the one choosing to wait." She winked and said as she walked out of the room.

After all of the women were upstairs, Jacqueline walked into the backyard and sat in one of the lawn chairs. She extended her legs and slouched down in the chair. With her eyes closed, she enjoyed the feel of the sun against her face. She kicked off her shoes and ran her toes in the grass. She thought of selling the penthouse and buying a small house at the beach. She thought of an oceanfront bungalow. She imagined a small, cozy place with a big deck, normal ceilings, and a kitchen that looked out at the water. She thought of white hurricane shutters and an outdoor kitchen. She thought of a dog lying beside her in the grass. In her mind's eye, she saw Zoe collecting seashells right beyond the fence and smelled dinner on the grill. She could hear Mallory talking from inside the house. She wasn't sure what she was saying, but the tone etched a smile over her face. The dream ended when the sweet sounds of Mallory were replaced by Olive's voice.

"It's nice to see you smile."

"Sorry, you caught me daydreaming." Jacqueline admitted. She sat up quickly. Olive was standing over her with the sun behind her. She was a talking shadow.

"I get a feeling that you might be falling in love a little bit. Huh?" and Olive nudged her with her knee.

"Probably not yet, but we'll see. Are you gonna yell at me about that?" Jacqueline shielded her eyes so she could better see Olive. She noticed that she had her suit on. She wasn't wearing a cover-up or any clothes over her yellow two-piece. She stood outside inches from Jacqueline with her crimped, dirty blonde hair falling from behind her ears.

"Nope. Not at all. I came to tell you that you may not be good at this yet so you're gonna need a few pointers. Never wander out of earshot of your girlfriend." Jacqueline leaned forward and turned toward the house. She could hear the faint yell of her name. "Girls like it when you respond to their calls."

Laughing, Jacqueline said, "Got it." Jacqueline stood up from the chair, picked up her shoes, and headed inside. When she reached the porch, she turned and walked back over to Olive who was walking towards the back gate. Jacqueline tapped her on the shoulder. Olive turned around and Jacqueline hugged her, "Thanks."

"Get in there!" Olive barked. She went back to looking out over the clear water but could overhear Jacqueline respond to Mallory's bellows.

Dressed in a t-shirt and a pair board shorts, Jacqueline was the only member of her party not in a swimsuit. When they arrived at the marina, heads turned to see them walk past people and headed towards the end of the dock. They passed anglers on small boats, families loading into pontoons, and young men carrying kayaks past them.

When they reached the end, they stood near their boat. It towered over them. Jacqueline turned her head and guessed that it was, at least, sixty feet long. She'd been born and raised in Florida. She had driven and been on tons of boats of varying sizes. But, this thing was huge. She walked past Alex and Jo who were standing back staring at it. She skipped ahead of Olive who was slapping the side of it. As she walked along its side, the other women noticed how Jacqueline's head was only as high as the rails.

"Are you sure that you can drive this thing?" Mallory asked.

Jacqueline wasn't about to admit that she wasn't sure. She responded confidently, "Hell yeah." Then, she jumped aboard from the stern. Seeing her standing aboard, the other women joined. Jacqueline stood there helping each of them come aboard. Once they were all together, the women began to scout out the boat. Alex wandered up to the forward and sat down.

Having experience with much larger boats, Olive was not impressed until she came upon the galley. From below deck, she yelled, "There's a fully stocked kitchen in here. There's a stove, oven, microwave, freezer, and a washer and dryer."

"Is there any food?" Alex yelled back.

"Hell, yeah. It's fully stocked. There's alcohol in here, too."

"Thanks, Jacqueline," Josephine yelled. She was stretched out on the seats along the stern. All of the other women thanked Jacqueline in echo.

Standing at the helm, Jacqueline was excited. Still Anxious, Mallory said, "You can tell me if you can't do this."

"Of course, I can."

"This thing is big."

"The Gulf is bigger."

"Thanks for that. That didn't make me feel better."

"Go out there and have fun. We are about to pull out." With that, Jacqueline turned on the engine. The boat began to purr. She verified that it was full of gas and checked all of her dials. She was headed to untie from the dock, but she saw Olive and Josephine taking care of it. When they signaled that they were free, Jacqueline withdrew the anchor from its watery home and pulled the boat out to sea.

As they slowly headed away from the marina, Mallory's anxiety started to fade. "Look at you."

"Oh, ye, of little faith. Of course, I can drive a boat." Mallory headed to the starboard side. Looking out through the glass, Jacqueline could see Mallory remove her cover-up and stand onboard in a white, two-piece string bikini. Jacqueline remembered that she wore the same one in Key West. Still trying to look at Mallory without being seen, Jacqueline squinted her eyes and slouched her posture to get a better look at Mallory holding onto the metal rails with her hair blowing in the wind.

Staring into the cockpit from the stern, Josephine could see what Jacqueline was trying to do. She yelled, "Mallory! Mallory, go inside. Jacqueline can't see you from where she is." The boat broke out in an uproar.

Mallory turned and walked back into the cockpit. "What are you doing?"

Looking at the panel, pretending to be making adjusts, Jacqueline replied, "Nothing."

"You know, we don't have to play that game anymore." She tapped Jacqueline on the shoulder. When Jacqueline turned around, Mallory turned around and around with one hand on her hip and the other arm, bent at the elbow, on display like a mannequin.

"I'm sorry," Jacqueline said bashfully.

"Why?"

"I don't know." She said in almost a whisper.

"It's quite alright." Mallory sat down in the captain's chair. "Where are we headed?"

"Well, we have left Seaborn Island and I thought we'd just head down the coast for a bit."

"That sounds nice," said Mallory.

"You look nice." Jacqueline said.

"Thank you." Mallory swatted Jacqueline on the butt, got up, and left the cockpit.

Jacqueline engaged the autopilot, set a course for the autopilot, and turned on the radio. Alex sprang onto the deck when she heard music come out of the speakers. "Oh yeah!" She stood up and started to dance. Pulling Paige to her feet, Alex and Paige danced on the forward. Olive, Josephine, and Mallory quickly joined in. They were dancing and singing when Jacqueline appeared on deck with a tray of drinks.

"Now, this is a party." Olive took the tray from Jacqueline and began passing out glasses.

Jacqueline took her glass to the stern of the boat. Dragging her feet in the water, she had an idea. She walked into the cockpit, disengaged the autopilot, dropped anchor, and stepped down into the warm water. The deck party ended when they caught site of Jacqueline treading water behind the boat.

"Look at that." Alex said, "You don't see one of those every day."

Paige looked around for a dolphin or manatee. When she couldn't figure out what marine miracle Alex had seen, she asked, "What'd you see? I don't see it."

"Paige, look right there. Have you ever seen one of those?" Paige stared in the direction Alex pointed. Realizing that Paige didn't catch the joke, Alex pointed Paige's head in Jacqueline's direction and said, "A black girl who can swim."

Mallory corrected Alex, "A hot black girl who can swim." And, Mallory stepped down off the stern until she could maneuver into the water. Jacqueline treaded over to her. She put her arms around Jacqueline's neck, "This is better, isn't it?"

"Yeah, it is."

Alex was sitting on the stern with her feet in the water. "Are you two gonna make out?" Jacqueline splashed her. Olive jumped overboard into the water and swam where Jacqueline and Mallory were.

"This is great. Isn't this great?"

"Yeah, it's pretty incredible." Jo replied.

The women relaxed in the water for hours.

After an afternoon of cruising, which was complete with food, drink, music, and swimming, the women were exhausted. Jacqueline made sure that the boat was back into the marina as the women headed for Josephine's Yukon. Their bodies were still warm from being sun-exposed for hours; but, as they sat down on the cold, leather seat each of them began to tremble. To help warm them, Josephine turned on the heater.

From the third row, Alex said, "Thanks, Jo," she sounded like a little sister.

Paige said, "Aw."

As the women began to adjust to the temperature change, Jacqueline arrived. Josephine had saved the passenger's seat for her. When Jacqueline opened the door, she was hit with a blast of hot air. Still standing outside in the Florida sunshine, she said, "God, it's hot in here," and reached for the air conditioner. All the women screamed in objection. Looking back at them wrapped in towels, she quickly realized how the truck might seem cool to them. Teasing she said, "Well, I guess we all learned that board shorts are not just cute, but hold in heat." And, with that, Josephine headed to the house.

When they arrived, Jacqueline jumped out and opened the side doors for Mallory and Paige, while looking at her phone. As Jacqueline held out a hand to help Mallory out of the truck, Mallory said, "What are you doing on your phone?"

"Looking for the game time."

"Do we even get the right channel at the house?"

"Shit. No, we don't." Jacqueline was disappointed. She shuffled into the house. She went upstairs and laid down across her bed.

Mallory came in, "I wonder if that sports bar...What's its name? Anyhow, I bet it'll show the game."

"Yes!" Jacqueline hopped up and started undressing. "I bet that it will. I'll change and go up there and watch the game while you guys nap. Or do whatever."

Mallory closed and locked the bedroom door. "Two things. One, I'm going with you. Two, stop changing clothes in front of me if we're waiting. We haven't even kissed yet, but you keep getting naked in front of me. You've never seen me naked."

Jacqueline stopped changing clothes. "I have seen you naked. It was on accident. I followed you home after work, so we could have dinner. You told me that you were going to take a quick shower. You went into your room to change, but you were trying to talk to me from your bedroom. It was my first time inside your house. You were giving me a verbal tour. Look at this, see that. You were naked in your room when you passed in front of the mirror on your dresser. I could see your reflection from where I was standing. There, now, we're even."

"I can't believe that you never told me."

"Uh, why would I? And, you saw me naked when I thought I was in my room by myself. Standing here, right now, in a t-shirt and my panties doesn't count as naked. You can only see my bare feet and thighs." Then, Jacqueline went into her bathroom and closed the door.

Mallory followed and opened the door. "What are you doing?"

"Taking a shower."

"To go see a baseball game up at a sports bar?"

"Yes."

"Are you hoping to meet someone?" Mallory teased.

"Yeah, maybe Shannon goes by there too." Jacqueline teased back.

"And, that's why I'm going," Mallory replied.

"Well, you better go get dressed, then. Unless you're wearing your bikini."

"Maybe, I will," Mallory teased. "I have to do something to keep your attention."

By the time, Jacqueline made it downstairs everyone in the house was dressed. They weren't dressed like they were in for the night. They were all dressed casually like they were heading out.

Hoping that they might be going shopping, Jacqueline said, "Where are you guys going?"

Mallory, who was sitting on the couch, said, "We're all coming with you. Paige asked where I was going, I told her and, she thought it might be fun. And, then we all got to talking about going up there, shooting darts, watching the game, having a few drinks, playing pool. It felt like a nice, fun night after a long day."

"Yeah, it should be something." Jacqueline said, but she thought, *damn it.*

The conversation stopped as they heard a ringing. Everyone checked their own phone, but the electronica ringtone could only be one person. Alex answered her ringing phone.

"Hey, honey. We were on our way out. What's up?"

"Oh, I'm sorry. Where you headed today?" asked Elet.

"We're just going up to Scoreboard."

"Scoreboard? That doesn't sound like your kinda place."

"No, Jax wanted to go watch the game. We all decided to go with her."

"Oh. Okay. I'll make it short. I was calling to let you know that I told my family about us getting married and everyone is excited. Dee Dee wanted to come up here and hang out with you, but I told you were off at Seaborn having your girls' getaway. She wanted to head over there, but I told her that I should ask you first. So, what do you say? Do you wanted your little sister-in-law-to-be cramping your style?"

Alex was instantly enraged. This was just one more thing taking away the last surviving moments of her freedom. No, she didn't particularly want Dee Dee to come, but she couldn't think of anything she could say that would be the right response.

"Sure. That'd be cool. When's she gonna get here?"

The other women, who hadn't been eavesdropping, were now holding their hands in the air wondering who was about to join them.

"Oh, Tuesday afternoon sometime. She's gonna come from my mom's house, so I bet it will take her a few hours. I'll text her the address. Go, have fun, babe. I love you. Go Rays." Beep. Elet was gone.

Olive said, "Spill it."

"Elet's little sister is coming on Wednesday."

"Oh, that's not as bad as I thought." Olive said. "What's she like twenty? She'll be fine. We're like older sisters. I doubt we even see her. She'll probably spend all of her time down at Dazzle."

"You don't get it. I bet she's coming to spy on me."

"Spy on you doing what?" Josephine asked. "What's spy worthy? You've eaten, drank, went to a club, cussed out your friend, went on a boat, and now, we're heading to a sports bar. There's not a lot to tell. By the way, I'm putting my ID and cash in your little purse," Josephine said, holding the purse for Alex to acknowledge.

"This is the beginning of the end." Alex moped.

Ready to see the game, Jacqueline said, "Well, today is Sunday. Let's go make these days worth it before she gets here."

That re-energized Alex. She said, "Hell yea. Good idea." She got up from the couch.

As the women were passing by Jacqueline to leave, Alex stopped and said, "I'm sorry for everything. I really am. I want you to feel like you can tell me anything."

Jacqueline said, "I want you to feel the same way," and locked the house behind them.

Walking along the boardwalk, Jacqueline caught up with Mallory and held her hand. The sun was setting out over the Gulf. The air was clean and crisp as it blew off the water. Mallory and Jacqueline were happy together surrounded by supportive friends. When they reached Scoreboards, Jacqueline held the door for everyone as they walked in.

Scoreboards was like any other sports bar in any city around the country. The tables were wooden covered in sport memorabilia sealed under coats of lacquer. There were flat screen TVs mounted on walls and freestanding television tuned to various sporting events. The back corner of the restaurant had three pool tables, a jukebox, and four dartboards. There was a fully stocked bar that sat in the back near the kitchen and the aroma of fried food mixed with body splash.

Jacqueline directed the women to a long table set up on the right side of the restaurant. The table had a perfect view of a 70-inch plasma TV playing the Rays game. In addition, it was in close proximity to the pool table area. She had hoped that the women would find themselves playing rounds of pool while she sat at the table and enjoyed the game.

As the women started to settle at the table, a server appeared. Dressed in short black shorts and a low-hung, black tank top, Tiffany was ready to take their order. Acting as though, this was a Michelin four-star restaurant, Alex asked what Tiffany recommended.

Without hesitating, Tiffany said, "Beer and wings, beer or wings." Mallory grinned. Wanting them to order and simmer down, Jacqueline asked Tiffany to give them a few minutes. Indifferent, Tiffany went back to the bar. Jacqueline knew what she wanted. She had no need to check a menu, but the rest of the table perused it from cover to cover contemplating every dish.

"Oh, they have a fried macaroni and cheese appetizer." Olive read.

"And fried pickles," Josephine mumbled.

Alex had paid no attention to the list of foods. She had skipped right to the back of the menu to the special drinks section. She read the contents of various concoctions that the Scoreboard bartender was supposed to be able to make upon request.

"Oh, the Rodeo is tequila, sweet-and-sour mix, pineapple juice, and club soda. The Toasted Almond is coffee, amaretto, half-and-half, and cinnamon. I wonder if that's good. The Big Blue Shark might be good. It's got tequila, vodka, and a special mix. They all sound so good."

Throughout all of the talking, Jacqueline had been watching Rays' players stretch and warm-up. She'd seen the pitcher take the mound and throw out warm-up pitches. It was when the commentator appeared on the screen that Jacqueline realized that she needed to get this party started. She said, "Hey, why don't we get the Wing Bucket Special. That's sixty wings in different flavors with four orders of fries. Also, we will get two orders of onion rings. Why don't you all try one of the specialty drinks? Then, you can sample them all and decide on the next rounds based on what you like. Sound like a plan?"

Everyone complimented her good idea. Everyone except Mallory who stroked her arm and said, "Good plan to get them to shut up."

Jacqueline winked at her and waved for Tiffany to come over.

Tiffany came back, "Y'all ready?"

Jacqueline said, "Yep. I need six tequila shots, a screwdriver, all five of your drink specials on the back, the Wing Bucket special - all-breaded, in hot, medium, teriyaki, honey bar-b-que, and mild, and 2 orders of onion rings. Also, I need lots of blue cheese, ranch, honey mustard sauce, and napkins." Jacqueline felt that she'd been direct and concise, so when Tiffany began to ask questions Jacqueline was irritated.

"You know the Wing Bucket comes with fries?"

"Yep, but I also want the two orders of onion rings."

"You want carrots and celery?"

"Yep."

"Wet wipes?"

"Sure."

"What about baskets for the bones?"

"Absolutely."

"You want a tab at the bar for all of y'all or individual ones?"

"One is fine."

"You want the shots first or the drinks first?"

"Whatever."

"Do you want anything else?"

"Just a Rays win."

"Huh," said Tiffany

"Nothing. We're good." Jacqueline was happy to see Tiffany walked away.

Mallory rubbed her arm and said, "Relax. We will go to the Trop next week. Just me and you, okay?"

Jacqueline said, "It's a date."

The first inning proved to be a pitcher's battle. Jacqueline had enjoyed her shot and was working on her drink while the women were passing drink specials around the table and giggling. During the commercial break, she smiled at them drinking things they didn't like. Mallory had enjoyed the Purple Haze, the contents of which Jacqueline never heard. Mallory insisted that she try it. It didn't mix well with the tequila and vodka flavor that still existed on Jacqueline's tongue, but she smiled anyway enjoying how happy it made Mallory. As the second inning got underway, Tiffany came back with the food. Jacqueline leaned opposite of Tiffany to keep an eye on the game. The women started ordering more drinks, more sensible drinks based on what they really liked. Keenly aware that Jacqueline was running out of her screwdriver, Mallory ordered her a new one when she placed her Purple Haze order.

Jacqueline said, "Thanks, baby."

"That's twice."

Half-listening, Jacqueline said, "Twice what?"

"Twice that you've referred to me as *baby*. Once the night after Dazzle, you said *night, baby* as you fell asleep and just now."

"Oh, did you hear me that night? It just slipped out. I guess it slipped out again here. I'm sorry. I'll try not to say it."

"No. No. That's not what I meant. It's just twice now that you've let it slip out. It's okay, honey." Jacqueline stopped watching the game and looked at

Mallory. They smiled at each other and Jacqueline went back to looking at the game. "I want you to play a round of pool with me before we leave."

"Okay." Jacqueline said. "If the Rays pull ahead or fall behind by more than two runs, we will play during the game. If the game stays close, we will play towards the end. Deal?"

"Deal." Mallory was searching in her purse for something.

Jacqueline wanted the search to stop. She asked, "What are you looking for?"

"Money for the jukebox." Jacqueline reached into her pocket pulled out her wallet and handed it to Mallory who said, "You don't have to always give people your money. I have cash in here somewhere."

Josephine leaned over and said, "Always take the wallet."

Mallory rolled her eyes and took the wallet from Jacqueline's still outstretched hand. When Mallory left to go to the jukebox, Olive and Alex followed. The pool table area was empty. They decided to play pool and called for Josephine and Paige to join them. Jacqueline looked up and saw the other women laughing and playing pool. She thought of going over there, but the bases were loaded.

<u>19</u>

When Jacqueline felt comfortable that the Rays had sustained a good lead, she felt it was time to stop spending ninety percent of her time watching baseball and devote her time with her friends. During these past six innings, she'd walked over and talked to them. She'd even noticed that two men had joined the women at the tables. She even made sure to meet them, Marco and Tyler. Marco was a tall, thin man that Jacqueline thought was of Hispanic descent. Marco appeared to enjoy Alex's attention. Tyler, his shorter, rounder friend, appeared to be more along for the ride. He was talking to all the women equally. Jacqueline arose from the table, gathered her drink, and walked to the tables.

Mallory was happy to see her. "Is it my turn, now?"

"Yep, I'm ninety percent yours." Jacqueline responded with a smile.

"This game is almost over. It's taken forever." Mallory sighed. She pointed her cue in Alex's direction. Alex was in a corner, giggling with Marco.

"What's going on here?" Jacqueline asked Josephine.

"Jacqueline, come on, you know Alex. Every man wants her." Josephine scratched.

"I don't know why she'd want another man with a guy like Elet in love with her," Paige said after she hit the eight ball into the right corner.

Olive said, "Eh, let's cut her some slack. She's just having a good time." Jacqueline suspected that there was something more to what was happening.

Mallory noticed the distraction, "You said that you were ninety percent mine, so let's worry more about me and less about Alex."

Jacqueline winked. "Anything you say." Jacqueline ordered a beer and announced, "Hurry up and finish this sham of a game, so we can play some real pool. Alex, are you and Marco in?" Alex didn't respond. She just waved Jacqueline's request away.

Preparing to yell something to Alex, Jacqueline's mouth was pursed with a response. Before she could open it, Mallory passed her beer. "Don't say anything. Drink your drink."

Creating two teams of three, Jacqueline, Mallory, and Olive played against Tyler, Josephine, and Paige in eight ball pool. There was a good deal of laughing and drinking. Jacqueline spent a good number of Mallory's shots pressed against her from behind, flirtatiously assisting in the instruction of billiards. Amid catcalls and teasing from the other players, the two were wrapped in each other's company as everyone else had a good time around them. So, enthralled with their play, all of them missed the moment that Alex left the bar hand-in-hand with Marco.

After two hours of pool play and the end of the Rays game, Olive said, "Hey, where'd Alex go?" The group looked around the bar and didn't see her or Marco.

Jacqueline said, "I'm sure that she's fine. I bet they walked down to Dazzle or outside to talk or who knows what. Let's just hang out here and have a good time a little longer. If she's not back by the time we're ready to go, I'll call her."

Josephine said, "Um, she left with her purse. She has my money and ID in it."

"Don't worry about it. I'll cover you and you can get it back to me later," Paige reassured her. Olive had called Drew to meet them up at the bar. When Drew and his friends entered, Olive left the other women to sit in a booth with Drew and talk. Drew's friends began a game with Tyler, Josephine, and Paige. Mallory and Jacqueline switched to darts.

"I wonder where Alex really is," Jacqueline thought out loud.

"Out making a mistake, I'm sure," Mallory said. "Let's talk about us."

"Things are going good, aren't they?"

"Very good. Still worried?" Mallory asked, throwing her second dart into the wall next to the board instead of the board itself.

"Well, of course. But, it'll be okay. I'll either get hurt or I won't." Jacqueline responded.

"What?" Mallory crossed her arms surprised that Jacqueline would say that to her.

It was Jacqueline's turn, but Mallory continued to try to hit the board. Jacqueline stood by and let her. "It's gonna be fine. Don't worry." Trying to posture her hand in a better position, Jacqueline moved Mallory's body more in line with the placement of the board. Mallory hit the board and did a little shimmy that Jacqueline enjoyed watching.

"I saw you watching me."

Jacqueline winked, "I've been watching for a while now."

The friends moved from game to game talking and playing. Even, Olive and Drew joined.

Drew and Olive played a round of darts against Jacqueline and Mallory.

"Olive, are you any good at this?" Drew asked as picked darts for her.

"Absolutely."

Fearing defeat, Mallory whispered to Jacqueline, "We're gonna get beat."

"I doubt it. Olive is lying. She has to look good in front of him." Jacqueline said.

As the match began, Olive and Mallory took turns hitting the wall rather than the dartboard. Jacqueline and Drew smiled at their efforts.

"She's not good at this." He leaned in and told Jacqueline. This was the closest that Jacqueline had been to Drew. She took this as her opportunity to size him up. He was a tall, lanky man. His hair was short and his face was freshly shaven. She wondered if he had gotten a haircut this morning or one prior to vacation. He smelled of cologne, but the fragrance was not overpowering. His nails were jagged as though he bit them. He was not wearing a watch, but he had a watch tan. Yet, he did not appear to be tanned on his arms, neck, face, or legs. His deep blue eyes had the signs of slight wrinkling at the corners.

Trying not to wait too long to answer, she said, "No, she's not. I'm sure that she just said that to impress you."

"Ya think?"

"Sure, isn't that part of getting to know someone new? I faked knowing how to drive a damn yacht this afternoon. Come on, you've told her some half-truths?" He turned away from her. His ears seemed as though they were turning red. She thought, *I got him on the fence.*

"No, I haven't. Maybe, I should have, huh?"

"Well, what have you told her?"

"Anything that she's asked." He looked over at Olive and Mallory playing a horrible round of darts without them. "I'm not very good at dating. I don't do it very often. So, I told her the truth. I'm a hydraulic engineer who doesn't have kids, has never been married, who likes to build radio controlled model ships." He fiddled with this drink for a minute, then he added, "Oh, and I have four sisters."

Jacqueline stared at him. She thought that this was all a joke and he was going to say something funny or that he might laugh. He didn't. "Well, how's that worked for you?"

"Well, I thought it was going good until now." Jacqueline laughed. Concerned he asked, "Do you think that she doesn't like me? My buddies," and he pointed to them playing pool with Tyler, Paige, and Josephine, "think that I'm just her vacation boyfriend and she's just using me. But, I told them that we haven't done anything. I haven't bought her anything and we talk all night every night."

Jacqueline was taken aback. She wasn't sure what to say. She looked over at the girls who were still playing darts. They were smiling, laughing, and genuinely, enjoying each other's company. Then, she turned to the man that she didn't want to run away from Olive. "Drew, look at her." They turned their heads and faced the women. "She's the happiest that I have ever seen her. She's also the most honest person that I've ever met. Somehow, I don't think that either of those two can fake any emotion. I think if you feel like she likes you, then you're probably right. I will guarantee when she is upset with you that you will very certainly know."

"Do you think that we will really go out next weekend?"

"If she says you are going, then she plans on going. Count on it."

Drew took a deep breath. "Thanks for talking to me. That really made me feel better. I mean, I don't date a lot and it's been crazy to think that someone as great as her likes hanging out with me."

Mallory and Olive walked over to them at the table. Jacqueline continued, "Seems like you are both pretty great."

"I'm great, too," Mallory chimed.

"Of course, you are." Jacqueline answered.

After a few more rounds of darts and a game of pool, Paige announced that she was getting tired. It was nearly one in the morning.

Jacqueline said, "Shit, I forgot about Alex. Lemme call her." As Jacqueline reached for her phone, she saw that Alex had texted her. "My bad, guys, Alex sent me a text saying not to worry about her. She and Marco were going to Dazzle and that he'll bring her back to the house."

Tyler excused himself, shook hands with the guys, and left the bar. While Paige said she was ready to leave, they didn't immediately go. Olive and Drew walked to the booth where Drew and his friends had been sitting. Everyone followed. Jacqueline was tired. She leaned her long frame against the wooden booth. Mallory came and leaned against her. From their vantage point, they were looking down at Olive and Drew. Olive was sitting so close to him that it appeared that she sitting on top of him. With one arm wrapped around her, he was holding her hand with his other hand. Josephine and Paige were sitting across the booth from them. They were seated next to Ethan, the groom-to-be, and David, the other groomsmen. The guys had all known each other since college. At the table, they were telling tales of their college years. Each was trying to outdo the other with stories of bathroom pranks, illness, nakedness, and the usual college tomfoolery. The women chuckled at the stories.

Josephine thought of texting Dominic, but she thought against waking him. She knew he'd leave early for the base in the morning. She smiled at the thought of her husband and sons sleeping soundly under a roof that had always been a place of love in her family's legacy.

Paige thought of Brett. She did text him a few times. He was awake in their bed surrounded by their twins. The image of them melted her heart. The room was radiant with laughter of the past and adoration for the present.

The women walked back to the house with merriment in their steps. The house was as they had left it, dark and still, with the scent of various perfumes still mixing in the air. As each woman, headed to her room, they looked down the hall, secretly, hoping that Alex would be back. However, she wasn't.

Jacqueline was lying across her bed when Mallory came into the room with clothes in her hands. Without a word, Mallory brought all of her things from her room next door into Jacqueline's room. Jacqueline smiled but never said a word. Jacqueline moved from the bed and condensed her clothing to make room in the chest of drawers for Mallory. As Mallory brought outfits, Jacqueline hung them in the closet. When Mallory's empty suitcase appeared, Jacqueline placed it in the corner next to her own.

On the final trip, Mallory came with her cosmetics bag. They hadn't spoken a word. Jacqueline moved out of the way and lay on her side. She propped her head up on her hand and watched Mallory assemble her arsenal of beauty supplies. When things appeared to be in their final places, Jacqueline moved from the bed. She stood up, still fully dressed, straightened her clothes, and approached Mallory who was standing in the bathroom confirming all of her soldiers had successfully made the journey. When Mallory noticed that Jacqueline was standing in the door of the bathroom, she turned from in front of the sink to face Jacqueline in the doorframe.

Afraid that Mallory might speak, Jacqueline reached out and placed her hands on both of Mallory's hips. She smiled and looked into Mallory's sea green eyes. Without speaking, they both knew what was occurring. Jacqueline rotated her head slightly to the right and Mallory rotated slightly to the left and closed her eyes. Sight wouldn't be needed. The other senses would oblige their efforts. Each leaned forward just enough to feel the other's rapid breaths. Without hesitation, fear, or misunderstanding, Jacqueline placed her lips upon Mallory's lips. She could feel her quiver a bit at first touch. Giving Mallory space to become comfortable, Jacqueline kissed her gently. Within a matter of moments, Mallory's nerves faded away and their first kiss happened. When it was over, Jacqueline placed her forehead on Mallory's forehead and held her close for a few moments.

Jacqueline was breathy when she said, "Did you get all moved in?"

Mallory said, "Finally," as she smiled.

Jacqueline released Mallory from her grasp and walked out of the bathroom. She began to undress, not seductively, but in the manner in which couples that have been together for years often do. She was without self-consciousness and oblivious that other person may be watching. However, Mallory was watching. Jacqueline stopped undressing after she removed the lower half of her clothes. Standing in the room, in just the top half of her clothing, Jacqueline began to gather her pajamas and Mallory's.

As she crossed back to the bathroom, she said, "Join me?"

Mallory's stomach dropped. She was bewildered. While she had fantasized about seeing Jacqueline naked and kissing her, these moments in real life made Mallory very anxious. Jacqueline hadn't hesitated. She passed Mallory and stepped further into the bathroom. As Mallory still stood by the bathroom door, Jacqueline turned on the water to the shower and finished undressing. Standing completely naked in the bathroom with Mallory, Jacqueline tested the temperature of the water, and then she stepped inside the shower.

Mallory took a hard swallow, undressed, and stepped into the shower as well. Jacqueline moved to the back of the shower stall and allowed Mallory to stand in front of her. Jacqueline kissed her on her shoulder blade. Mallory became less anxious and the two began to bathe, assisting each other as needed.

Jacqueline exited the shower first and proceeded with the night's normal rituals. She brushed her teeth and cleaned her face. Once she was finished, she closed the bathroom door and headed to the bedroom. When Mallory finished bathing, she opened the shower door to a heart, finger drawn on the foggy, bathroom mirror. She dressed quickly and opened the bathroom door to find Jacqueline lying in bed with her book in hand. Mallory walked to the bed and stood over Jacqueline. Jacqueline moved over enough for Mallory to sit.

"That was unexpected and a little bit scary," Mallory admitted.

Putting her book down, Jacqueline said, "I'm sorry that it scares you. It scares me, too. We'll take it slow together." Jacqueline tucked Mallory's long, wet, red curls behind her ears.

Thinking hard, Mallory said, "Not too slow."

Jacqueline laughed, "I was trying to be understanding."

"Yeah, well don't understand so much that you misunderstand." Mallory stood up and walked to what was now her side of the bed. She climbed under the cover without thought of how to make the action inconspicuous. Jacqueline rolled over to see Mallory cheerfully moving into bed with her.

Lying in bed facing Jacqueline, Mallory said, "Tonight's been a great night. I loved every minute of it. Just because I was a little scared at times doesn't mean that I didn't have a great time."

"Do you wanna talk about why you're scared?"

"I don't know. I guess I imagined how things would be with you, but then when the things start to happen I get nervous. I guess I thought I had been preparing myself for what to expect, so I wouldn't seem nervous. But," she paused.

"But?" Jacqueline pushed her to finish.

"But, when the time comes, I'm nervous."

Jacqueline stroked Mallory's wet hair. "It's okay. I'm nervous, too."

"Why are you nervous? You've kissed a girl. You've showered with a girl. You've had sex with a girl."

"But, not with you. Listen, I kept myself out of a lot of my past relationships. I've never allowed a woman to come to my house. I've never shared very much of myself at all. I have a fine talent of listening to people, making them feel comfortable with me, but sharing very little of myself. Things are different with you. So, I'm nervous, too." Mallory smiled at her. "By the way, kissing is kissing. Showering with someone is showering with someone. And, don't worry about the sex. Sex always works itself out. It's the easiest thing anyone ever does. All you have to do is what feels right. Okay?"

"Is this what you tell all the girls?" Mallory teased.

"Nope. Just you." Jacqueline replied seriously. She leaned forward and kissed her gently.

"You know my favorite part of tonight?"

"The kiss?"

"Uh, well, I was gonna say watching you undress without having to pretend like I wasn't looking, but the kiss was nice, too."

Jacqueline chuckled and turned off the light. She snuggled down into bed, Mallory rolled over and placed her head on Jacqueline's chest as Jacqueline held her tight.

20

Paige was up early. She was already downstairs when Jacqueline came into the living room. Jacqueline jumped upon

seeing Paige sitting on the couch watching the news.

"Sorry, I scared you," Paige said quietly.

"No, I'm sorry. I'm used to being the only one up this time of morning."

"I thought you'd have slept in since you guys...you know." Paige said blushing.

Jacqueline was clueless for a second, and then she realized what Paige must have thought. "Oh, we had a good night, but Mallory and I haven't...you know. Gosh, I guess we're gonna figure out how much to tell one another since we're all friends. I mean, we will, but it just seemed that the first time shouldn't be here...with all of you in the house." She tried to explain without giving too many details. "I'm sure that it will happen as it should. You know, somewhere else...just the two of us." Jacqueline was stumbling to explain without oversharing.

"Aw, that's very sweet." Paige had noticed how uncomfortable this was making Jacqueline. "That would probably be for the best. I would imagine that it will be stressful enough without us teasing you both about it."

"Stressful?"

"Well, you know, the first time together is always...difficult. At least one person overanalyzes and feels a little awkward and vulnerable after it happens. I was a mess the first time after Brett and I were together. I was so self-conscious before it happened that I vomited all over his floor. He was so sweet trying to clean it up. But, even after it was over, I was so self-conscious. You can't really lie there in post-coital ecstasy if you can smell vomit in the room."

This was a story that Jacqueline had not heard. She laughed. "What the hell? You threw up on the man?"

With a straight face, Paige said, "No, on the floor. I was on my back." She leaned back against the couch to demonstrate. "I turned my head and threw up a little on his wall, his nightstand, and the floor between his bed and the nightstand."

Jacqueline was laughing. "And, he got up and cleaned it up? Then, the poor bastard came back and still had sex with you?"

"Well, yeah. I told you that he was very sweet about it."

"No, Paige, he is either a fucking saint or just got out of prison. Fuck, I hope that Mallory and I don't have that many problems. I swear if she vomits then I'm not trying again that day. Fuck. That week." Jacqueline had tears in her eyes. "Why haven't I heard that before?"

"I'm sure I told you."

"Uh, no, I would have remembered. That's some funny shit."

Trying to change the subject, Paige said, "But, wait who did I hear last night? I mean, I heard...bouncing around. And, since I saw Mallory move her things into your room. I just assumed that it was you two." Paige looked dumbfounded.

"Yeah, we didn't really talk about it, but I guess it didn't make sense for her to have a room since she's been in my room since we got here. But, no, it wasn't us. Maybe, Drew came over?" Jacqueline shrugged.

"She does seem to like him a lot. And, he really seems like a nice guy. A smart guy too. You know they've made a date for next weekend."

"He kinda hinted about that. I didn't know that, but it's awesome. I bet it was them." Jacqueline stretched out on the couch perpendicular to Paige. "Wait, why are you up so early? Everything okay?"

"Oh, yeah. I'm having a good time, but I miss Brett. Brett and the kids. But, I miss Brett. It's so funny. When things happen around here, arguments, discoveries," she pointed to Jacqueline, "I text him and tell him. It's like I just want to talk to him."

"You know, I've got a great idea. Why don't you ask your mom to keep an eye on the kids on Friday night? She can get them from daycare and have Brett come up for our last day. We got everything here. We should tell Jo to tell Dom to come up too." Jacqueline was just about to say that she thought Elet should come when the front door opened. She lifted her head and looked toward the door. From Jacqueline's vantage point, she could see out the door. She couldn't see the face, but she saw that it was a man. Then, she remembered his walk, his look from behind; she'd stared at it for part of the night at Scoreboard. It was Marco. Paige couldn't see who had left, but she knew someone had come in or out of the door and she could tell by the look on Jacqueline's face that she was surprised.

"Who was that?" Paige asked.

Jacqueline sprung from the couch and darted to the door. As she passed Paige, she said, "I think it was Marco." When Jacqueline reached the door, she saw the man's face. It was Marco driving away in a truck. He had placed sunglasses on his face, but it was him. He honked the horn as he drove away.

Closing the door, Jacqueline looked angrily at the stairs. She pounded up the stairs taking three or four at a time.

Alex was sitting on the side of the bed with her head in her hands. She was trapped inside of a cage of her own creation. Feeling as she did, the last thing she wanted to have happen was the one thing that she knew was about to happen. Someone, Jacqueline, Paige, or worse, Josephine, was going to come through her door any minute and want to talk. Alex was certain that she didn't want to talk to any of them. She had thought all the horrible things about herself that they were about to say.

The door opened with fury, but Alex didn't look up. She knew. Before Alex made eye contact with her interrogator, she heard the questions begin.

"Tell me exactly what we're doing." Jacqueline stood with her hands on her hips. Jacqueline had closed the door behind her.

"We?" Alex was going to delay the onslaught as long as she could.

"Can we skip the games? You and I have danced around this whole issue for long enough. And, I'm at a point where I don't even know that I care why you're doing what you're doing, but I would love to know what the fuck you're doing?"

Alex sighed with her face in her hands. She didn't have answers for any of this. There wasn't any plan. She was just moving through life with no set speed, reacting to the moments as they presented themselves. Becoming frustrated, Jacqueline began to shift her weight from one leg to another. Alex responded, finally, with "I don't have an answer for you."

"What the fuck does that mean?"

"It means what I said. I don't have an answer for you." Alex laid back on her bed. Jacqueline was beginning to pace and she could hear all the other women talking in the hallway outside the room. They were the father figure waiting outside for the mother to punish and report. She knew that they wouldn't sit still for very long. They'd have their own questions, accusations, and assumptions that they'd need to voice.

Jacqueline started to calm. She ran her hand through what would've been bangs if her hair were longer. Alex thought of how often she did this when she was thinking of a response. "Alex, I love you to death. I want you to be happy. We talked just yesterday about being honest with one another and supporting one another, but tell me what your decision is."

"Jax, there's no decision."

"What?" Jacqueline was completely confused. She hadn't thought that she was being cryptic or speaking in riddles. But, the women outside the door had decided that her technique was all wrong. They entered the room, like a joint front.

Mallory spoke first. "Look, you've been having a great time. You've been dancing, drinking, kissing, and sitting on laps with men since we got here. Jax is trying to ask you. Do you not want to marry Elet?"

Jo followed up with, "Or, are you just a whore?"

Then, the arguing started. Olive came to Alex's rescue. "Don't call her that Jo. That's not fair. If she doesn't want Elet, its cool. That doesn't make her a ho."

"Uh, sleeping with a guy she just met does make her a ho." Josephine and Olive were stating all the arguments that Alex predicted they would.

Then, it was Paige's turn. Alex knew what would happen. Paige sat beside her and said, "Why don't you just tell him that you aren't ready? Maybe you can have a long engagement. There's nothing wrong with that." Alex thought of how soothing and sweet Paige was at heart. She put her head on Paige, not because her words resonated with Alex; but Paige was comforting even amid the thunderstorm happening in the room.

After fifteen minutes of them bickering amongst themselves, Alex began to speak at a conversational level. The others stopped bickering at one another to listen. "Here's the thing. I don't know that I thought much about Elet while I've been here. I mean, I think of him when I get back to the room. But when I'm out there," pointing to outside the house. "I don't think of Elet. I think of me. I know what that sounds like. I know what you're all gonna say."

Josephine chimed in, "So, you're a dumb ho."

The group was starting to have another rumble. The crisis was diverted when Alex defended herself, "No, Jo, you're the dumb ho. You're the one who got pregnant in high school, not me. You've half hated me ever since it happened, but all the while you've pretended to look down on me." Alex stood and approached her sister. "Really? It's just jealousy. You lie and tell people that your family is the best thing that has ever happened to you. But, there's a part of you that hates me. You hate me, because I didn't get pregnant and have to get married to a man, I probably didn't want. You hate me, because I went to college. I have a career and an apartment all my own. I'm living the life you want. And, you hate me for it."

Josephine listened to all of this with her arms folded. Jacqueline noticed her flaring nostrils and saw Josephine's hand move toward Alex's face in slow motion. She was in time to grab Josephine and pull her back before contact was made.

However, Jacqueline wasn't quick enough to prevent Josephine from speaking her mind. "You're right. Of course, there are days when I wished that I had gone to college instead of going to hair school. Of course, there are times when I don't think what if I hadn't gotten pregnant, what if I hadn't married Dom, what if I had left Brandon. But, get this right, little sister, there's never a day in my life that I want to be the sorry, self-centered bitch you are." Josephine shook free from Jacqueline and stormed out of Alex's room and down the hall. Jacqueline followed her all the way to Josephine's room, but the door that slammed in Jacqueline's face was enough for her to end her pursuit and come back.

"She's such a fucking bitch. She's deserves what she got. I hope she stays in there and cries her eyes out." Alex was screaming from her room.

Paige said, "Alex, the horrible words that you and your sister said are a completely separate issue. You were in the bathroom with one stranger at Dazzle and, obviously, you spent the night with another stranger last night. We were outside in the hall when Jacqueline walked in. You weren't here jumping for joy. We could see you. You were sitting on the bed and you had your head in your hands. So, what's really going on?"

Alex began to clean up her room. She was picking up clothes and shoes off the floor. "I was trying to tell you. Elet's a great guy. I really do love him. When we get home and everything is quiet, I call him and we talk. He's like the only one I can talk, too. I tell him everything. I tell him everyone's business. I know he's a catch. His family loves me. I love them. I know I don't want to lose him." She stopped cleaning. She sat down in the wingback chair in the corner of her room. She was rubbing her hands. "But when I go out, I love how the guys look at me. I love it. I love the attention. I love the flirting. I love the drinks that they buy me. I love all that shit."

"Are you telling me that you're going to dump him, so you can party?" Mallory asked, stunned that this was the problem.

"I'm not dumping him and I don't want to party all the time. I'm not 20 anymore. When we are in town or usually when we are on vacation, I may flirt with other men. I may even get their numbers, but it has only been while we have been here that things have gotten out of control." Alex responded.

Now, the room was silent. Olive said, "Okay, I'm confused. What the hell, Alex?"

"I don't want to be Jo and Dom. I don't want to be my parents. I don't want to be Paige and Brett. No offense, Paige. Hell, I already don't want to be Jacqueline and Mallory or Drew and Olive. Marriage changes people. It makes them all about the other person. It makes them stop enjoying the attention of other people. It makes them...different. I don't want to be different."

There was silence. The women in the room didn't say a word. They looked at each other. They looked at her realizing that she had been sitting on top of clothes and shoes that had been in the chair.

Paige said, "I'm not offended. I did change. I chose to change. That's what you don't get. I wasn't popular in school. I didn't have many friends, and, then I met you guys. And, I was popular at work. I had friends who did wonderful things and it gave me a wonderful life. I'm grateful for that friendship. We have drank too much, partied too much, had one nightstands, but we were always safe together. You are my true friends." Paige looked at Alex more deeply than she ever had. "But, when I met Brett, I knew it was time to be something else.

Brett didn't say "stop looking at men.' Brett didn't say 'don't go out with your friends as much' or 'don't hang out with them without me.' I chose. I didn't want to look at men anymore. I didn't want to go out. I wanted to be with him and our kids. I still love you guys and I've been happy here, but I miss him. I want him here with me. I want to see him, lie in bed, and tell him all the things that are happening. If you don't get that, then you should just let Elet go. Maybe, you are too self-centered for marriage." Paige left Alex's room without saying another word.

Paige's words hurt Alex. Paige defends Alex and the world no matter what; and, now, Paige had told her that she couldn't do this. That she shouldn't marry Elet. Alex never expected Paige to think that there was something that she couldn't do.

Mallory said, "You know, you're full of shit." Jacqueline tried to flag her off. Mallory went on, "Do you think that you can hold onto Elet while dancing, making out, and fucking other men? I mean, really? Do you think that you're such a prize that he should put up with anything?"

Alex discarded Mallory's remarks as quickly as she said them. Mallory threw her hands into the air and left the room.

Alex thought that she was finished with this entire interrogation until Olive spoke, "Alex, here's the real deal. He's a good guy. A nice guy. But, he's not gonna wait on you to get it together. The moment you walk away to dance in the club with a guy whose last name you don't know, he will be with some other girl. She will be beautiful and she'll adore him. I guarantee you that his family will think that she is a better fit for him than you ever were. She will settle down, have little Elets, love his mom, and take his sister to the mall. And, you will be pretty, still rocking the clothes, still having the body, still dancing all night with boys half your age. I'm not telling you to stay with him if you don't love him, but I'm saying you're a damn fool if you walk away because you wanna go out. That shit gets old. It gets old the moment everyone goes home. Paige is going back to Brett. Jacqueline and Mallory are gonna try to make it work. Where are you going? Back to Dazzle? To Scoreboard? Where?"

Olive tossed Alex her engagement ring. Alex didn't realize that Olive knew she'd put it in her suitcase. "At least, have the balls to let the guy go. I'm gonna go call Drew. Do you know why? Because he likes me. I've told him everything and he likes me. He hasn't asked to sleep with me or touched me inappropriately. I'm gonna call him, because I like having him around. That's what it's all about." Olive walked down the hall and into her room.

Everyone had left Alex's room except for Jacqueline. Jacqueline was leaning against the doorframe with her hands in her shorts' pockets. Alex yelled down the hall, "I get what you're all trying to get me to do. You want me to realize that Elet's great and I'm shit."

"Nope, honey, we want you to grow up." Olive said from her room. "It really is time. This shit ain't fun or cute anymore."

"What if marriage changes me? What then, huh?" She kept holding on to them as they tried to pull away and stop talking to her.

"What change is going to happen?" Mallory screamed. "What's the change that you're scared of?"

"What if he and I stop having fun? What if he stops wanting me? What if things get dull?" she asked.

Josephine opened her door. She stuck her head into the hall and answered her little sister, "Then, that's what you fight to prevent. That's up to you and Elet, you little ho."

Alex threw a dirty towel at her. Alex said, "I do want to marry him."

Josephine said, "Then, you have to stop fucking everyone you meet." Alex did a fake laugh.

Jacqueline closed the door up some. "Sit down for a sec."

"Jacqueline, I really don't want your lecture."

"I'm not gonna give you one. It's just you and I and we're gonna sit here and talk. Okay?"

"Okay."

"What do you want to do? What's your perfect scenario?"

"I don't know. I like it that people show me attention."

"Okay, we all know you're an attention whore. I'm sure Elet knows that, too. Do you really still like the club?"

"Sometimes, not as much as I used to. It's all the same. The same songs. The same guys. The same drinks. The same girls. It's the same."

"I know. I like when we all go together, but it's not about the club. It's about being together. It's about being carefree and happy with your friends. But, I wouldn't go without you guys whether or not Mallory was in my life."

"When I go for work, I never dance. I get a drink. I walk around. I talk to people, but I don't dance. I think of myself as capturing the mood, not being a part of it."

"So, what's been going on since we got here?" Jacqueline sat on the edge of the bed next to Alex.

"I don't know. This feels like the last vacation we will ever have together where we can all be wild and free."

"We haven't been wild and free. Paige misses Brett. Olive has met a guy that she stays awake all night texting. Mallory and I have been trying to figure out what's going on between us. Our last trip when we were all wild and free has to go back a few years. Back before Paige met Brett. Those days were great, weren't they?"

"They were. Do you remember getting drunk in the mall in Miami and vomiting in the fountain?"

Jacqueline laughed. "Oh, my God, the water sprayed it all over my face."

"That was funny shit."

"Those were great times, but these are too. You've called Elet every night."

"And morning."

"Do you miss him?" Jacqueline asked.

"I hate to admit it but I do."

"Jo misses Dom. Paige misses Brett and Olive may leave us tonight to move in with Drew and his buddies. I told Paige that we should invite the guys up. Maybe, it's time we start sharing some of these great times with the rest of the people in our lives. Maybe, we will have even more great times, not less."

"Yeah. Maybe."

Getting up off Alex's bed, Jacqueline said, "Things change, but sometimes the change is cool. Let's just see where it goes. It could be great." Jacqueline got up and walked out of Alex's room. She left the door open.

From inside her room, Paige said, "Hey, clean up your room, go wash those disgusting sheets, and take a shower. It's like a whorehouse in there."

"Yes, ma'am." Alex chuckled and started removing the sheets from the bed.

CROSS YOUR FINGERS

21

It had been an emotional few days. When Alex awoke from her nap, she felt revived. She searched the upstairs and found it empty. As she crept towards the stairs, she heard music playing. Instead of running down the stairs in the direction of the music, Alex returned to her bedroom to make herself more presentable.

She called Elet, "Hey, baby!"

"Hey, babe! You okay? You sound shaky. Are you and Jo not getting along?" She loved how perceptive he was. Elet was in tune to the things that were going on in her life. Tears formed like a mist on her windows as she thought of the horrible things she'd done over the last few days. She knew that the things she had done would have hurt him. They would have truly changed his perspective about her and his love for her. She didn't want that to happen. Wiping her tears away, she said, "Oh, we're doing each other's hair and makeup right now."

"Uh huh. Sure you are. You know, if I could make one wish, I'd wish that you two could look past all the anger and hurt feelings and just see how much you love each other. All this fighting is about wanting something.."

She cut him off. "You wouldn't wish for peace, love, food for all the people of the world, freedom from war or disease? You'd use your one wish for me and my sister."

"Well, duh."

She laughed. "You're such a weirdo."

"But, you're marrying me." She'd decided that she was. She'd decided that it might be hard work and it might be scary, but she couldn't imagine life without him.

"If you're lucky." He laughed and then, started to cough. "You okay? Are you getting sick?" She stopped putting on her makeup to stare at her phone. Peering at it, she hoped she could see his face. She was concerned.

"Oh, yeah, I'm okay. It's just too much insulation in the air."

"I thought you were waiting on Silas and Reese to help with that part." She went back to putting on her face.

"They're here. Reese came Sunday night. We got a lot banged out. Kitchen is done. We got up in the attic. Finished the walls. Now, I wanna finish the floors and a few odds and ends."

She could hear him ruffling. Instantly, she saw his red face being wiped against the sleeve of his white t-shirts that she'd bought him. She knew he'd be standing there in the house in paint stained socks and jeans and the idea comforted her. "Ah, I wish I'd been there to see the guys. When does Silas have to rejoin the team?"

"Next week, he catches up with them in Greensboro. I think he's here til Monday or so. I'm sure that you'll get to see them. You know, I don't know if I can choose between them for a best man. Maybe, I should pick someone else."

With her makeup on, she picked up the phone. "Baby, that's up to you."

"Who will be your maid of honor? Paige? Jo? Jax? Olive? How can you pick?" She realized that she hadn't even thought about it. Worse than that, she'd purposely avoided it.

"Hmm, what about the lady who lives downstairs from me? She's nice and always so fashionable." Elet laughed. She laughed that he was laughing. She could hear another voice in the background. "Is that Reese? Tell him that I said hi." Elet did and she heard him say hi back. He was younger than Elet, but he sounded so much older. "Jax was talking about having everyone come up on Friday. Paige called her mom to get her to watch the twins, so Brett could come. I don't know what Jo is doing, but I'm sure Dom'll come. Why don't you come and bring the guys?"

"I'll see if they want to. We've had so many great nights of beer and hookers. I may not be able to tear them away." She could hear Reese say, "Bullshit." They both laughed. He said, "Get back to your fun. I love you."

"Love you too." She was refreshed after talking to Elet. She always was. She stared at the phone after he had hung up wanting to see his face. She threw on some clothes and ran downstairs.

There were speakers in the backyard. Jacqueline had played CDs from her Laredo on the stereo in the kitchen and turned on the outside speakers, so the music echoed outdoors. Jacqueline was grilling out meat and veggies. Everyone else was in their bathing suits. They were in the pool or the jacuzzi. It was nice. It was the kind of scene that Alex thought she'd like to live in forever.

Paige said, "Hey, sleepyhead. We were wondering how long it would take you to get moving."

Olive said, "Go put on your suit and get in the pool with us."

Alex responded, "Nah, not right now. Maybe after I eat, I will. I got up about an hour ago. I've been upstairs on my phone talking to Elet." Everyone stopped and stared at her. They were afraid of what she might have said or might have done. She noticed their reactions. "Don't look at me like that. I just called him to talk. I do call him every day."

"Did you tell him about what's been going on?" Paige asked.

"No, I mean. It would only hurt him. I'll fly right. I learned my mistake and I have more than enough people to keep me on course."

"You don't think he deserves to know?" Paige went on.

"I kinda agree with her. I mean, if she tells him, he really won't ever trust her. If she can turn this around and straighten up, I say we keep it between us." Mallory added.

"What happens on Seaborn Island. Stays on Seaborn Island." Jacqueline said amid the smoke and sizzle.

"I don't know, guys. How can they have complete honesty if she has things she's keeping from him?" Paige continued.

"I get what you're saying, Paige. From here on out, he can know everything. But, I don't want to hurt him by sharing some of the craziness I've done in my past." Alex agreed.

"Past? It was this morning?" Josephine said, laughing. Then, they all laughed.

"Oh, I invited him and his brothers to come down on Friday along with the other guys." Alex said.

"Do we have room for everyone?" Olive asked.

"Yeah, there are seven bedrooms. I have one. Oh, Mallory and I have one. Jo has one and Dom will be in there with her. So, that's two. Olive, you have yours. That's three. Alex has one; she can share with Elet. That's four. Paige has one for her and Brett. Silas and Reese can share one or have their own."

Jacqueline pointed to all of them with the turning fork. "Is Reese bringing Pam?"

"I doubt it. Who'd watch her kid? I thought we were doing adults only."

"Yeah, we are, but does Reese know that?" Mallory asked.

"Fuck. I'll call them back."

Alex was heading back to her room to call Elet when she heard Josephine say, "Alex, bring me my stuff out of your purse. I want to go to the store and buy some more champagne."

Over her shoulder, Alex responded, "Okay."

Back in her room, Alex decided to text Elet. She knew he'd make it clear. When she finished, she put the phone back on her dresser and started looking for her purse. Having cleaned the room earlier, there were far less places it could be. It wasn't under the bed; it wasn't in the suitcase; it wasn't in the bathroom; it wasn't on the floor or in the bed.

She looked everywhere. She stood up with her hand to her lips and retraced her steps. When she and Marco arrived at the house, she searched for the key to get inside. Marco held her purse when she moved flowerpots to find the one that had the key Jacqueline had left for her. She opened the door and turned off the alarm. Then, she led Marco upstairs, quietly into her room, and closed the door behind them.

Remembering this, her nightmare had gotten worse. The man, whose last name she didn't know, the man that she slept with last night, who helped violate the unspoken promises she'd made to Elet, had stolen her purse. She sat down on the side of her bed. She wanted to cry, scream, and vomit all at once. She thought about just letting him keep it. He had the purse, but she had her ID. All he had was some cash and the purse itself. She'd resolved to overlook it.

Then, she remembered that she couldn't. He took the purse and got her cash; but, more importantly, he stole Josephine's ID, her money, or whatever else she had placed in that purse. Alex knew that she had no choice but to go back downstairs and face all of them again with more unsettling news. She knew that Jo would never let her live this down.

With her hand in her pants, she slowly walked down the stairs. When she reached the kitchen, she turned off the music. The women screamed from outside for her to turn it back on. They were still threatening to kill her when she reached the backyard.

"Listen, guys, I have to call the cops." That was a bad opening line. It caused instant hysteria. Alex finished, "I think Marco stole my purse." The hysteria fell silent.

Josephine yelled, "Isn't this just great? I should've known this would only get worse."

"Listen, if it was me, I would let it go. He only got cash from me. About fifty bucks. But, he's got your ID and whatever else you put in my purse. I'm sorry, Jo. I know that you don't think that I am, but I am." Alex said with her head bowed.

"Oh, I think you're sorry now that the shit has hit the fan. I think that you just don't ever think about the consequences of your actions." Josephine was angry.

"Okay. We went over that part earlier. Let's not rehash." Jacqueline took the meat off the grill and took her phone out. "Josephine, what'd you put in her purse?" With her arms folded, Josephine admitted it was cash and her ID. "Okay, good. At least, it wasn't like your credit card or debit card. Let's call the cops and file a report. We will give the cops the information that we have and, then tomorrow we will work on getting Jo a new ID."

"It's my military ID. I can't just go get a new one." Everyone's face drew further down. Heads dropped, but Jacqueline still called and provided the information to the police.

While Jacqueline was on the phone, the rest of the women busied themselves preparing sides and drinks. The revelry became subdued. Things were heavier. It was their first night in the house that was spent inside the house. They didn't leave for the rest of the night. They watched movies, popped popcorn, and drank a bit. Eventually, one by one, they headed upstairs to their rooms. In the wee hours of the morning, Jacqueline felt herself getting sleeping. She awoke Mallory who had been sleeping in her lap for hours and ushered her off to bed.

CROSS YOUR FINGERS

22

Mallory heard the doorbell sound. She hoped someone else would answer it. When it rang through the house for a second time. She thought about getting up to answer the door. Before she made a final decision, Jacqueline began to stir.

Mallory rolled towards her and said, "Let someone else get it." Jacqueline was already out of bed. She was making herself presentable as fast as she could. Before she left the room, she looked back at Mallory and said, "Who?"

Jacqueline rubbed her face before she opened the door. To her surprise, there was a tall, leggy blonde at the door. She had on huge, round, black sunglasses, a tank top, and short jean shorts. When she threw her arms up to hug Jacqueline, she was surprised. Jacqueline hadn't expected a young woman at the door. She wasn't sure what she expected, but this wasn't it.

The young woman smiled and hugged her. Holding the girl in her arms, she remembered who this was, Dee Dee. Delilah was her name. She met her years ago when she wasn't quite a woman, when she was just Elet's baby sister. Now, here she was taller than Jacqueline, sun-kissed and stunning.

"Hey, Jacqueline. It's so good to see you." It was like her mouth held onto Dee Dee's words.

"My God, you've grown into an....adult." Jacqueline thought, *wasn't she just fourteen? When did this happen?*

Delilah was going on and on with the excitement that twenty-one year olds have. "This house is so amazing. I wish that I could just live here."

"Yea, Alex and I were talking about how it's like one, big sleepover." Jacqueline said.

"Oh, my gosh, that's so true. Gosh, I haven't had a sleepover in like five or six years." Jacqueline felt old. It was more than twenty years ago since she'd had a sleepover. It was like a shot in the chest when Jacqueline realized all of this. She fell over onto the couch.

Delilah went on, "Where's everyone at? I got up and left Mom's early. I wanted to make sure that I was here when you guys started your day. I'm so excited to be here."

"Well, everyone is still asleep. We camped out last night. We watched movies and drank. So, I think everyone is sleeping in a bit, but I'm sure that people will start stirring soon." Then, Jacqueline looked at the clock and realized that it was seven fifteen in the morning. "Okay, scratch that. We won't be up and stirring for a few hours. Jesus, girl, it's like seven fifteen. I'm going back to bed, but you can do whatever you like for a few hours." Jacqueline showed her around the house and, then she led her upstairs to one of the empty rooms. "The guys are coming down to join us on Friday, so we will be a full house. I forgot all about you being here when I was thinking about rooms. It doesn't matter. One of these rooms has two queen beds in it. Silas and Reese can just share that room."

"Exactly. Or sleep in Elet's truck."

"Ah, sisterly love," Jacqueline said.

"I'm the baby sister of all brothers. Do you know how much crap I've lived through with them? They can sleep outside for all I care." Delilah pulled her hair onto the top of her head in a bun in one, quick move.

Jacqueline stared at the movement in amazement. She slightly giggled to herself before saying, "I'm going to lie down for at least two hours. I'm sure things will be stirring by then."

Jacqueline was right. When she awoke for the second time that day, the house was stirring. Even, Mallory was out of bed. Jacqueline could see her in the bathroom drying her hair. She was singing. Rather than disturb the moment, Jacqueline just laid there and absorbed Mallory's moves. She was smitten, but felt it best to remain as cautious as her heart would allow.

When Jacqueline began to move in the bed, Mallory noticed. She came out of the bathroom and sat down on the edge of the bed, "I was wondering when you'd get up."

Jacqueline could smell perfume. "Where are you going?"

"Where are we going? We are going out shopping with the cute, blond twenty-one year old that's downstairs."

"Yeah, last time I saw Dee Dee she was a teenager. I mean, she was cute, then, but she was a kid."

"Yeah, she's not a kid, now. Anyhow, we are off to shop. Then, Alex promised to take her to Dazzle tonight."

Jacqueline rolled over. "Oh, no, I can't go back to Dazzle."

Mallory rolled her over. "You'll be fine."

With prompting and persuasion, Mallory coaxed Jacqueline into heading out for the day. Jacqueline's reluctance was wiped away when the sunshine hit her face. They drove from the villa, past the boardwalk, and into the small town's center. They stopped at a small diner and ate foods of gigantic proportions. After being properly stuffed, they meandered about looking into stores decorated with bright, ocean colors and worked by bright, beach town personalities. Women giggled as they tried on clothes. Women, who otherwise found themselves very attractive, felt a little less so when Dee Dee came out of her stall in a two-piece, striped, string bikini.

Mallory made sure that Jacqueline wasn't looking. Jacqueline wasn't looking; it seemed bizarre to think of looking. After all, in Jacqueline's eyes, she was Dee Dee, Elet's teenage little sister.

The women walked and talked. They smelled homemade soaps and lotions. They bought touristy gifts for the children who were not with them. They talked about the people that they had loved and lost and the ones they couldn't get rid of. They danced to the music of panhandlers. They pet the dogs who didn't know that they were as homeless as their masters were. They sat on park benches and recounted their day.

Alex said, "I brought my famous black dress."

"Oh, God, not the famous black dress." Jacqueline said.

"What's so famous about it?" Delilah asked

"Nothing really." Paige said

"Um, I was wearing the dress at a club opening down in Ybor City when.." Alex started to tell the story.

Delilah interrupted, "What club?"

Irritated by the interruption, Alex said, "That doesn't matter. It was a little shithole. It wasn't fun. It was in Ybor City without any Cuban flair. So, anyhow, I'm sitting at the bar trying to figure out what I'm going to say that didn't sound too mean. I can't figure out any good adjectives or kind words for the place. I stand up from the bar and the bar stool slips from underneath me. Now, I wasn't on it. I was safely on my feet. But, the damn thing fell. And, this'll tell you how bad the club was - you could hear the damn stool fall and hit the ground. The music didn't even mask the sound. So, I'm embarrassed. I wanna just pay the damn check and get out of here, before someone notices me..."

"No one noticed you, ever," Mallory interrupted.

Alex returned to the story. She began to talk faster. She was trying to prevent any other interruptions. "Anyhow, I bent down to pick up the stool. When I stand up, I feel a hand on my back. I was thinking it was some ugly, knight-in-shining-armor type. I was prepared to nicely reject him. But, when I hear him start to talk, I knew exactly who it is." Alex performed the rapper's dance as an ode to him. "He said, "Girl, that dress is too hot for you to bend over and pick up any damn stool.""

"Oh my God!" Delilah was impressed.

"Uh, try not to be too impressed. That's the end of the story. He made sure that she was okay. He walked past her, out the club, got into his limo, and left." Jacqueline said crushing Alex's moment.

"I can't believe that she chose Elet when she could have had a celebrity." Dee Dee was still swooning.

"Um, Dee Dee, I think you missed the point. There was no chance with him. He didn't buy her a drink. He didn't ask her for a date. He didn't stay and talk. She didn't even get an interview and she's a journalist." Mallory pointed out. "He just gave her a little line and walked away."

Alex reminded them, "And, he touched that dress." She gave them the bird and walked back to Josephine's SUV.

When they arrived back at the house, Jacqueline opened the wine they bought from a vendor. The women drank and got dressed for another night at Dazzle. Everyone, except for Delilah, was hoping for a less eventful night out than the past few nights they'd had. When everyone was dressed and ready, Jacqueline gathered them at the front door.

"Attention, ladies. I just wanna say before we go out tonight. Let's remember that we are coming back here together. Let's keep our wits about us, but have a great time." Her tiny speech was met with applause.

This time, they walked less leisurely down the boardwalk. This time, Jacqueline didn't pause to stare into the Honey Pot. This time, Mallory was holding Jacqueline's hand. And, this time, Alex was wearing 'the famous black dress." That meant, that there would be no return episode in the lady's room handicap stall. There was no way that the famous black dress could be defiled in such a way. They were recognized as regulars on the boardwalk and did not pay to enter Dazzle. They strode confidently to their table. Within minutes, they were met by their waitress.

"Hey, stranger. How come I haven't heard from you?" Shannon said.

Jacqueline thought, *Fuck*. She had so hoped that Shannon wouldn't be working on a Wednesday night. "Sorry. Things got complicated." Jacqueline said.

"Complicated? Did you get arrested or something?" Shannon asked like it might be a real possibility.

"What? No? I didn't get arrested." Jacqueline wanted her to disappear.

"She started sleeping with Mallory." Paige volunteered. All the women began to laugh. Jacqueline wanted to slip down under the table in embarrassment.

"Not like I didn't see that coming." Shannon said as she left the table.

Josephine pointed at Delilah and asked, "How old is she? Can she even drink?" Not waiting on anyone to answer for her, Delilah pulled out her ID and showed that she was, in fact, twenty-one. Recently, twenty-one, but she was twenty-one nonetheless. "You aren't gonna be that young drunk girl, are you?"

"No, I'll be fine. I dance more than I drink," Delilah said. Wearing a white tube top shirt and very short jean shorts, the table realized that she wouldn't be without a dance partner for most of the night.

Olive grabbed her hand and announced, "Let's hit the floor, then."

The table was emptied, except for Alex and Jacqueline.

"You can go dance with Mallory. I'm fine."

"You know, I think she only danced with me last time to reel me in. Now, that she's got me, she's fine out there on her own."

"I doubt that your time at this table lasts too long." Alex was forlorn. She was at odds with herself.

"You okay?" Jacqueline noticed that something was wrong.

"I just don't know that I should be here. I don't want to cause any more...drama." Alex was staring off into the space of the dance floor.

"Look, you can go out and have a good time. You can dance the night away as long as you know that you can't mislead anyone. That you should never behave in a way that you wouldn't with Elet around." Jacqueline tried to reassure her, but she understood. She wasn't certain her advice was right. "You can go out there and dance with all of them. Safety in numbers."

"Yeah, I'll go in a minute. Maybe, your ex-girlfriend will bring the drinks back as soon as she finishes peeing in yours."

"Well, at least the flavor will mix well with my vodka." Jacqueline smiled and leaned in and nudged Alex with her shoulder.

"I'm glad that we have this moment alone. There's something that I need to tell you." Alex played with her nails. "When I heard about the new direction at the Sun, I got nervous. I applied at *Upbeat* magazine. I've had two interviews. They called me this morning and want to make me an offer."

"Is this your resignation?" Jacqueline suddenly felt nervous.

"I don't know what to do. I figure that I'll talk to Elet about it, but I know that my chances are low to get editor for the department. I don't have the level of experience or the accolades that Mallory has. I just wanted to tell you what I should've told you before now."

"I already knew." Jacqueline admitted.

Stunned, Alex said, "How? That's not possible. The only people who knew about the interview were Elet and Olive. Elet had been telling me to tell you, but I could never find you alone for a moment."

"Olive thought you told me. She mentioned it when I picked her up. I didn't know what to say either. I was so angry. I was hurt, but I get it. I do. You gotta make the right choice for you and for Elet and your new life together. We're friends no matter where you work, right?"

"Yeah, I guess so. I made an appointment to go see them on Monday at lunchtime. That should give me time to figure things out. I just don't know. Also, here's this back." Alex slid the key to Jacqueline's apartment back to her.

"Well, this feels like a break-up."

"After everything that has happened here this week, I think it's pretty obvious that I shouldn't have a key to your place anymore."

"Nah, it's cool. It's not like we dated. You just came by to change clothes on your way out. I was just a rest area. Besides, you haven't used it in months."

"Regardless, she should have a key. Mallory is your girlfriend."

Jacqueline looked over at Mallory. She was dancing on the floor with Olive and Paige. "I made one for her a few weeks ago. It's been on my keychain. I couldn't figure out how to give it to her."

"You should just give it to her."

"Well, it's not that easy. I don't want to fall for her. You know? Just in case things don't work out." Jacqueline played with the key on the table.

Alex looked over her shoulder at Mallory on the dance floor. Then, she looked back at Jacqueline. She reached out and touched Jacqueline's hand. "I think you've already fallen for her. And, I think that she's fallen for you, too. There'd be no easy way out of this for either of you, now." That's exactly what Jacqueline feared most. She picked up the key and added it to her keychain.

In the middle of this haze, Shannon reappeared with a tray of drinks. Placing them on the table, she said, "Didn't I tell you that she liked you? Didn't I?"

"Yeah, you did." Jacqueline admitted.

After Shannon laid down all the glasses, she said, "I could still rock your world."

Alex laughed the drink out of her mouth. Jacqueline chuckled and placed her hand on her chest. Over her shoulder, Jacqueline said, "I never doubted it, Shannon. I never doubted it." Jacqueline took a long swig of her drink, "Well, it doesn't taste any different. Either she didn't pee in it or I can't tell. Now, come on, let's go dance with our friends." Jacqueline stood up and pushed Alex and the famous black dress onto the dance floor.

They all danced the night away. At three a.m. when the bar closed, they walked away from the bar, sweaty and tired, but no worse for the wear. Mallory said, "Did you talk to Shannon?"

"Some," Jacqueline replied.

"Any regrets?" Mallory asked. She looked fearful.

"Yea, I wish I would have had Long Islands tonight." Jacqueline replied dryly. Mallory grabbed her hand as they walked along the boardwalk on a beautiful, warm, summer night.

23

Late nights cause late mornings. However, late weeknights are an oddity for most people. Jacqueline was discovering how true that was when she was up at just after eight the next morning. Once again, she was the only person who moved from the bed to relieve the doorbell from whomever pained it. She knew that she didn't look her best, but she thought that this had to be a wrong house thing. They weren't expecting anyone. It was Wednesday. The guys were going to start coming Friday morning, but not at eight fourteen in the morning.

Jacqueline didn't even peer out the peephole. She opened the door with agitation. Her agitation was quickly dismissed when she opened the door and saw two police officers.

"Uh, good morning, officers. I'm sorry that I wasn't more prepared. How can I help you?"

"Good morning, ma'am. Are you Josephine Knight?" The taller, older officer asked.

Before Jacqueline could respond, she heard a familiar voice say, "No, sir, this is Jacqueline Emerson. Good morning, Jax."

"Hi, Elet," Jacqueline said but thought, *oh shit, oh shit, oh shit*. She couldn't see him, but she could see the outline of his tall, thin body. There were other dark outlines of male forms. She wondered if it was a SWAT Team. The officers introduced themselves, but Jacqueline did not catch their names. She had a gut-wrenching pain in her stomach as she felt the very worse about to play out in front of Elet, cops, Alex, and Elet's little sister.

The younger officer said, "Ma'am, we need to come in and speak to Mrs. Knight."

"Oh, I'm so sorry. Come in. I'll get her." Jacqueline left the door open and ran up the stairs. She ran straight into Alex's room. Shaking her, "Alex, get up. Get up. Get up, NOW. Elet is here with cops. Something's up!"

Alex rubbed her head, "What the fuck is going on?"

"I don't know, but the cops wanna talk to Jo. Go, wake her up! I'll get everyone else and get kinda dressed."

"I'm fucked." Alex began to cry.

"You're not fucked. We will work it out, but you gotta go right now. There's no time for crying." Jacqueline headed out of Alex's room. She found Elet in the hallway.

"Which one is Alex's room?" he asked.

Jacqueline was trying to gauge his emotion, but in her own frenzy, she was in no position to gauge emotions. Alex opened the door while Elet and Jacqueline were still standing there in silence. Alex walked right to him and kissed him.

"What's going on, baby?" Alex asked.

"You tell me." Elet said quickly.

"Uh, Jax says the cops want to see Jo. I gotta go get her up."

"Yeah, do that." Elet replied.

He sounded stern this time. He turned and headed back downstairs. Alex felt her entire life fall around her. Olive opened her door and looked out into the hall. She had overheard what was going on.

Jacqueline said, "Hold it together. We will work this out. Go wake up Jo and wipe your face."

In a matter of minutes, all of the women were presentable and accounted for in the living room. They were joined by the two police officers, Elet, and his brothers, Silas and Reese.

Josephine walked right to the older officer and said, "Hi, I'm Josephine Knight. Is everything okay?"

"Yes, ma'am. I am Officer Nozick and this is Office Taylor. Sorry to have bothered you. I was responding to a call placed on Monday to report a robbery. The call was placed from a cell phone owned by Jacqueline Emerson."

Jacqueline said, "Yes, that's me."

"Ms. Emerson indicated that a purse was stolen that contained cash valued at approximately one hundred fifty dollars and the military ID of Mrs. Josephine Knight, the wife of Airmen Dominic Knight. We alerted the DOD to the card's theft and that information was registered in the Defense Enrollment Eligibility Reporting System."

Alex felt like she may pass out. She was standing next to Elet listening to the officer, but none of this was registering. All she could think about was the horror she felt and the horror she was going to cause Elet and his family.

The young officer took over. He read some details from his notepad, "Ms. Emerson indicated that she believed that the robbery had occurred early on Monday morning in this home. She indicated that she thought the alleged crime was done by a Hispanic man in his late twenties to early thirties, standing nearly five foot nine inches tall weighing approximately one hundred seventy pounds. First name was Marco. Surname was not known. At nineteen hundred hours last evening, Marco Barrow attempted to enter Patrick Air Force Base in Cocoa Beach. He presented himself as Airmen Knight. However Mr. Barrow did not know that the card had been flagged as stolen. He was asked to produce further ID. Obviously, he could not produce any identification and was apprehended. He is being charged with being in possession of a stolen military ID, bearing false witness to a military police, and impersonating a member of the US armed forces. These are all federal offenses."

The older officer continued, "We were dispatched to locate you and verify that this was a robbery. Ms. Emerson did not leave a number at this residence. She left a number that was the home phone number for Ms. Alexandra Stevens."

Josephine said, "My little sister." Alex raised her hand.

"We were unable to reach her by phone, so we drove to the residence associated with the number and intercepted these gentlemen who led us here to you. We need for you, Mrs. Knight, to confirm that Mr. Barrow was in illegal possession of your military ID. That information will be supplied to the courts in review the charges brought against him."

Josephine was shaken, but she acknowledged that the card wasn't in Marco possession legally. The officer needed her to sign some documents in his car. Elet told his brother, Reese, to accompany her. The officers apologized again for waking the house and walked outside with Josephine and Reese.

Paige said, "Oh, my God. I was so scared. We didn't break any laws and I was scared. I'm so glad that's over."

Elet was angry. "I can't believe that there was a robbery and no one called me. What the fuck is going on?"

Alex said, "Relax, honey, it was no big deal."

"Uh, did you just hear about what happened? That's not something small, babe. That's a federal crime. Why didn't you tell me about this? What have you guys been doing? And, who is this guy Marco? What the hell is wrong with you guys?"

Alex began to cry under the stress. She wasn't sure what to tell Elet, but she felt like the truth was what was supposed to owed to him. She was ready to tell him when Josephine walked back in.

"Whew, that was crazy. I think I'm gonna throw up." Josephine noticed that no one was talking. As she peered around the room, she saw the stone faces. She saw her sister crying and asked, "What's going on in here?"

Elet replied, "That's what I want to know, but no one is talking."

Silas, Elet's youngest brother, said, "Calm down, man. They look shaken up. It's over. It's okay."

"I want to know what the fuck they were thinking. I want to know what happened. I got addressed by the cops like I did something wrong and I had no idea that they had even run into trouble. Someone owes me the fucking truth." Elet was seething.

Alex said, "He's right. He deserves to know. He may hate that he knows, but he deserves to know. Elet, sit down. Everyone else leave the room."

"Nope. Me and my brothers were heading over to your apartment. I've been making an appearance everyday at different times of the day, so no one would notice that you weren't there and try to break in. So, we are over there. Just hanging out for a bit when cops show up. They interrogated us. Fuck, we were in handcuffs and asked questions in separate rooms. Silas and Resse didn't know anything. Do you realize that cops don't believe you when you honestly didn't know anything? Do also realize how hard it is to prove that you are dating someone? There aren't any documents for that shit. Do you know what finally worked? There are a million pictures of me all over your apartment. So, I had to tell the cops that I knew where you were and lead them to you before they did a cavity search or some shit on me. So, no, it's been a hell of morning, but we are all staying put. Me and my brothers are all gonna hear what went down that was so horrible that we were all in handcuffs."

Silas and Reese looked like they were just along for the ride, but they appeared too fearful to argue with their brother. Elet sat down on the couch and kicked his feet up on the coffee table.

"Fine, Elet. Let's see on Sunday night, we went to the Sport's Bar. Don't you remember I told you that?"

Still pissed, Elet said, "Go on."

"That guy, Marco, was there. He and his friend, Tyler, seemed like nice guys. We played pool, played darts, watched the game. We were all having a good time. We stayed until almost the end of the night." Alex started to slow down. Her words were stuck inside her. She imagined the explosion that was about to occur.

Olive said, "Let's stop pretending. I brought a guy back to the house. I had sex with him. I barely knew him. It's not like I'm the first girl to do that. It's not like some of you, fuck, most of you haven't done that. Jesus. Fine, Elet, you wanna hate me. Fine. But, Jesus, try not to be so holier than thou."

There was silence. Elet's face sunk in. He was silent. "Well, why did they have only Alex and Jo's info?"

Jacqueline answered, "Olive was the only one who carried a purse. It had cash in it. We were at a sport bar. The only thing worthy of being reported was Jo's ID. The cash was gone. It wasn't worth reporting. We had to estimate the total amount of cash in it. And, come on, it's not like Olive was carrying some Gucci purse. You don't report a yarn purse stolen."

"But, why'd you give Alex's phone number?"

Jacqueline said, "They were all looking for the purse thinking that maybe it was just misplaced. I didn't know Jo's home number by heart. I gave Alex's number in town. This isn't our home. Hell, I don't even know this number. I never thought they'd call. I thought the dumbass would take the money, ditch the ID, Jo would get a new one, and that would be that. We weren't hurt. Our pride was hurt. We let Olive have it. We were all angry for a bit and we got over it. That's what family does. That's what we did. It wasn't something we wanted to share. We're sorry you got wrapped up in it. We aren't hurt. It was a dumb mistake that should have stayed between us."

Alex was still in tears. Elet put his arm around her and said, "I'm sorry. Babe, I was so worried and mad. I freaked out. I just didn't know what happened. I wanna kick Olive in the throat, but it sounds like you guys already took care of it."

Josephine replied, "Hell yeah. I'm sure that she's learned her damn lesson. There won't be any more shit out of her. And, I think she's found a guy she's ready to fly straight for."

Elet smiled and said, "Well, let's hope she did." Elet slipped off his boots and flipped on the TV. Alex put her head on his chest.

Reese asked Jacqueline, "Hey, how long do you have this place?"

"Uh, we check out by seven on Saturday night."

"That's awesome. Hey, Elet, are we just gonna stay here? We were coming tomorrow night anyhow. Let's not go back and work on your shack. Let's stay here in this mansion, eat, drink, and meet women."

"I'm sure the girls don't want us cramping their style. We can come back tomorrow. I'm just gonna hold her for a few and we will head back to town," Elet replied.

"Dom is already on his way. He wants to come and make sure we are okay, too." Jo said as she was texting.

"Brett will be here tomorrow morning. He took tomorrow and Friday off. He's dropping the kids off at daycare tomorrow morning and heading straight here," Paige said.

"You guys should just stay," Alex said. She was rubbing Elet's chest.

"Are you sure that you want me around? I don't want to ruin the girl's vacation."

"Nah, it'll be great to have everyone here."

Reese and Silas plopped down on the loveseat. Elet and Alex were sitting in the middle of the couch with Jo on one end. Paige was across the room in the recliner. Dee Dee, Mallory, and Paige were back upstairs.

Jacqueline crept up the stairs. First, she peeked in on Dee Dee. She was wrapped up in her comforter, sleeping like the fourteen year old she remembered. Jacqueline eased the door closed.

Next, she went to Olive's room. She could hear Olive talking. Jacqueline knocked quietly. "Come in," Olive said.

"Sorry. I didn't know you were on the phone."

"It's Drew. He's gonna come by in a bit and hang out. His friends are leaving. I told him that he could stay here with us until we left." She bit her lip.

Jacqueline wondered if she was asking more than she was telling. "That sounds great." She walked into the room, hugged Olive, and whispered, "You're an amazing friend and I love you."

"Don't say that. Mallory told me what she was gonna do to Shannon. I don't want her to plot my death, too."

Jacqueline smiled and softly left the room. She headed to her room. She opened the door. She had expected to see Mallory back in bed. She wasn't there. Closing the door behind her, she said, "Mal?"

Mallory came out of the bathroom and said, "Did you just call me 'Mal?'"

"Yea, I guess I did. That just fell out, too. Sorry."

"I think I kinda like it." Mallory smiled and hugged her. With her head resting on Jacqueline's chest, she said, "Let's try not to ever turn into them."

"We won't."

"How can you be so sure?"

"Well, you aren't stopping me from doing anything and I'm not stopping you from doing anything. We came together when we were both ready to give something a try." Jacqueline felt Mallory nod her head. "What do you want to do today?"

"Me?"

"Yes, you, silly. What do you, Mallory, want to do with me, Jacqueline, today?"

"Let's leave all eight hundred of them here tonight and get a room at the resort on the other end of the island. Before you say that you want it to be special, we have had a ton of special moments when things would've naturally happened. I'm not saying that we can't hang out with them all day or that we won't come back tomorrow. But tonight, let's be able to just be together and let things happen between us." Mallory said still wrapped in Jacqueline's arms.

"Are you sure?"

"Very." Mallory replied.

"All right. I'll call and see if there are any available rooms. Cross your fingers."

About the Author

K L Finalley wrote her first book at age thirteen when her observations about her friends evolved into an unsolicited collection of short stories. Since then, both her appreciation for friendship and her storytelling ability have progressed. After earning a bachelor's degree and pursuing her master's degree at the University of North Florida, she has worked for a Fortune 100 healthcare benefits company, been elected to local government, and serves as a notary public. But, she always returns to writing.

When she is not travelling to all the MLB baseball parks with her wife, she is creating playlists and enjoying the sunshine

Find out more at: www.facebook.com/klfinalley